The Wedding Slipper

J. Kimalie

Published by J. Kimalie, 2022.

This is a work of fiction. Similarities to real people, places, or events are entirely coincidental.

THE WEDDING SLIPPER

First edition. October 14, 2022.

Copyright © 2022 J. Kimalie.

ISBN: 979-8215603314

Written by J. Kimalie.

Chapter 1

Jacq's spirit plummeted as the Seattle-bound flight lifted off the runway. Business awaited before the chapter could be closed on what had been, by far, the worst season of Jacq's life. The gravity of the task ahead seemed oppressive. Jacq knew that, despite a depleted emotional reserve, no peace would come until Aunt Rose's estate was settled.

Jacq's thoughts were interrupted by the tall, attractive, flight attendant offering a drink and snack. No, not just offering refreshment, but to her astonishment flirting in a not too subtle way and proposing a bit more in an unspoken offer with a hitch of his left brow. Jacq's aisle mate, an older woman whose warm smile and twinkle in her eyes was the perfect look to be cast as a grandmother in a soup commercial, leaned conspiratorially toward Jacq and whispered, "Dear, he has been trying to get your attention for some time now."

Jacq glanced up at the flight attendant, considering him for the first time. He smiled and then winked before turning to serve the opposite side of the aisle. The whole exchange felt disorienting to Jacq as her thoughts were snapped back to the present.

The older woman grinned with a slightly mischievous look on her softly wrinkled face that slowly disappeared as she looked deeply into Jacq's green eyes. The woman clearly perceived not only Jacq's befuddlement at the unexpected flirting that just ensued but also the pain and fatigue that seemed deeply etched around her eyes. The old woman's amusement at the flight attendant's cheeky behavior turned instantly to grandmotherly concern. The kindly septuagenarian leaned toward Jacq and simply said, "Tell me, tell me what is burdening you." To Jacq's utter surprise, she does.

Until this moment, with a perfect stranger, Jacq had spoken very little about the horrible car accident that took both her beloved parents and her sweet Aunt Rose two years ago. Three vibrant lives snuffed out in one cursed moment. A fixed point in time that would irrevocably alter Jacq's life and would forever be emblazoned in her psyche and branded onto her heart. Likewise, Jacq had not verbally shared with anyone the crushing grief and loneliness she had felt since that fateful day when her family did not return from an orchid show they had attended together in Connecticut. At times, the shock and grief over her incalculable loss had enveloped Jacq like a suffocating blanket. On other days, she had felt almost weightless, untethered, and adrift like a kite buffeted by the wind without the anchoring of her family.

As an only child, Jacq could not turn to consoling siblings for comfort or to reminisce over shared memories. Her father, Jackson, was an only child and Helen, her mother, had just one older sister, Aunt Rose. Aunt Rose, an independent and sensitive soul, married at one point, but never had children. As a result, Jacq had no cousins, a fact that she had never given much thought until she had no family at all. Lacking family support, she soldiered on, willing herself to get out of bed, go to work, and

THE WEDDING SLIPPER   3

try her best to mimic what her life was like before – before that fateful day changed everything.

Loyal friends and colleagues had been there for Jacq as best they knew how, especially her closest friends—Beth, who she had known since college, and Christopher, the events manager at the uptown New York European-style boutique hotel that Jacq managed. Christopher had even offered to take two weeks of vacation and accompany Jacq to Seattle to help her empty out Aunt Rose's house. Jacq declined the generous offer as she felt this was a personal journey she needed to undertake on her own.

Her friends' overtures to comfort had at times been clumsy and awkward for both Jacq and for them, or at least she assumed it had been for them as it had for her. Because of that, she loved them even more for not abandoning her during the dark times when she turned inward. Jacq was aware that she had not had the energy or emotional reserve to participate in the normal give and take of a healthy friendship. Yet her friends had solidly remained there for her. Jacq resolved to do better from this point on and share with her friends just how much their unwavering love and support during this dreadful time had meant to her. But here and now, enroute to the Pacific Northwest, she found herself pouring out her story to a compassionate stranger. Until this cathartic moment, Jacq had been unable to share her feelings even with her closest friends, perhaps because her feelings were beyond words to convey.

Jacq shared with her attentive audience that her mother named her Jacqueline Rose Reed. Her first name in honor of her father, Jackson, and her middle name a tribute to her Aunt Rose. Her mother always joked that if her aunt would have named her, she would be known as Jacqueline Calypso Reed, her middle name after her aunt's favorite orchid, the Calypso Fairy Slipper. For as long as she could remember, however, she was called Jacq. Jacqueline was not a tomboy by any stretch of the imagination, but the strong, straightforward name of Jacq seemed to fit her despite her purely feminine features and thick auburn hair. As an only child, she was close to both her parents, her dad a Bioengineer and mother a Horticulturist. Jacq's love of books, particularly science fiction novels, had been nurtured by her father. She had come by her love of cooking with heirloom garden vegetables and herbs from her mother.

Jacq remained close to both parents after leaving for Cornell University, where she completed her degree in Hospitality Management. Demanding studies and long hours associated with launching her career had resulted in fewer and fewer regular opportunities to get together with her parents for dinners and weekend visits. Face-to-face time spent together gradually shifted to Facetime video calls; a reality that now she bitterly regrets.

For four hours, the saintly woman just listened with her whole being as Jacq poured out her story, her crushing grief, and her pent-up emotions. She blessed Jacq by not interrupting or even asking clarifying questions. In the end, the woman just hugged her as Jacq softly cried into her sweater. During the flight, the flirty attendant and other passengers gave the pair a wide berth sensing it would be an unwelcome intrusion to interrupt.

After collecting her luggage, Jacq exited the terminal to locate the rental car shuttle bus. Jacq inhaled the cool damp air characteristic of a Seattle winter. She noticed how sweet the air smelled compared to New York City's assortment of aromas that assaulted her every day on the crowded sidewalks. Jacq paused

THE WEDDING SLIPPER

and then after two terminally long years, she did something extraordinary—she totally and completely exhaled. Maybe it was the faint pine scent in the air that demanded a cleansing breath, but she suspected it was space created by unburdening herself to her kindly aisle mate. "Well," Jacq thought to herself, "this is a step forward." She was determined to reframe this trip from a dreaded task she must get through to an opportunity for breathing room. After all, she had taken a three month leave of absence from her job to settle her aunt's affairs.

After securing a rented Jeep and grabbing a bite to eat, Jacq plugged Aunt Rose's address into her phone. Google maps indicated she had a one hour and 19-minute drive ahead of her to reach Aunt Rose's farm which was about 74 miles from SEATAC airport. To reach the farm in Poulsbo she could either drive south to Tacoma and cross a bridge at a narrow part of Puget Sound before doubling back and turning north toward Poulsbo or take a more direct route by ferry from downtown Seattle to Bainbridge Island and head north. Given unpredictable ferry line waits, Jacq opted to drive the whole way. Even at a leisurely pace, Jacq had plenty of time to make her appointment with Nicole Richmond, the Poulsbo area real estate agent, who had been recommended and with whom Jacq had been corresponding.

Jacq idly wondered if Nicole looked like what she pictured in her head. The thought instantly triggered the question of why she had not "googled" Nicole. Having been on autopilot for much of the past two years, Jacq realized it was no great surprise as to why she had not probed more deeply. Heck, just getting out of bed and brushing her teeth everyday had been a big enough chore and on certain days she counted those tasks as a significant victory.

Through cross-country conversations, Nicole was made aware that Jacq was her Aunt's sole surviving heir. Jacq's plan was to go through Aunt Rose's personal things deciding upon what to keep, sell, give away, or toss. After that, she planned to put the farm on the market. Nicole did a drive by of the property and informed Jacq that the farm consisted of just over four acres of land upon which sat a house, large barn, and greenhouse. Nicole warned Jacq that some small repairs and general sprucing up may need to be done to get top dollar for the property.

Much of the farm's details Jacq had already known as she had been to Aunt Rose's place the summer after graduating high school. Once Jacq left for college her life had been a whirlwind of studying, summer trips with friends, finding a job and setting her career in motion. After her career was launched, Jacq was preoccupied with moving into and decorating her own very teeny-tiny place in the upper West Side, her slice of the Big Apple.

Reflecting back, Jacq confessed to being rather self-absorbed and crazy busy in her twenties, not unlike most twenty-somethings she supposed. Her frenzied decade had mostly kept her on the east coast. Her only exposure to states west of the Mississippi was visiting Aunt Rose on her farm and taking two family vacations. As a child her parents had taken her to Disneyland in California and a separate trip, years later, to the south rim of the Grand Canyon in Arizona. While the family had talked about a holiday trip to Hawaii, they always seemed to explore islands in the Caribbean rather than making the much longer trek to Polynesia. With a painful stab of regret,

THE WEDDING SLIPPER

Jacq realized that the family holiday in Hawaii would never be. So many hopes and plans lost forever, a thought that overwhelmed her for the millionth time in two years.

Unbiddenly, Jacq's thoughts wandered yet again to her past. While she had spent a significant amount of time with her aunt in the past dozen years, their time together had mostly been in New York during Aunt Rose's annual three-week visits with her family. Occasionally, the gals would select a quaint inn or bed-and-breakfast destination for a girls' getaway trip when Jacq's dad was unable to join them because of his intense workload. On those trips, the three ladies went full in on pamper mode. Afternoon tea, spa days, antiquing, wine tasting, and garden tours were often part of the itinerary. The trips always seemed to facilitate long lingering conversations where they caught up with each other to shared the joys and trials of their lives. It was usually on these languid jaunts that Aunt Rose spoke fondly about her little farm, snug home, and intense passion for hybridizing orchids in her thriving greenhouse. She always sounded perfectly content in the cozy life she had carved out for herself.

Many a time, Aunt Rose shared her love for the beauty of the Pacific Northwest and for the gift of friends whom she had made. Aunt Rose spoke of one friend more than others, a gentleman named Emmett. Aunt Rose came to know him through her friend Grace, Emmett's wife, whom they both lost several years before. It was Emmett who reached out to Jacq after the accident when Aunt Rose failed to return home as scheduled. Emmett's own unmistakable shock and grief at the news of the tragedy was palpable during the unpleasant call. Their shared anguish connecting them over the miles as if they were in the same room.

When there was nothing left to say, Emmett ended the call by offering his condolences and promising to keep an eye on the farm until affairs could be settled. Jacq never thought it would be two years before she made it out west.

Breaking into Jacq's thoughts, the familiar robotic voice indicated the destination is ahead on the left. As Jacq began to slow the Jeep, she glimpsed a woman she assumed was Nicole pacing the front porch with cell phone in hand. She looked pulled together in black slacks, grey zip up ankle boots and a fitted, fuchsia-colored polar fleece jacket. Jacq parked the car and by the time she reached the bottom step of the front porch, the energetic, young woman had stowed her phone and extended her hand out saying, "You must be Jacq."

Jacq felt an instant affinity for Nicole; although Nicole looked nothing like she had imagined. Nicole appeared younger than Jacq thought she would be given her stellar reputation. What instantly won Jacq over was Nicole's beaming smile that emitted optimism and Nicole's petite frame that seemed to barely contain the considerable energy radiating from her.

As the sun was setting, she and Nicole did a quick drive around and finished surveying the property from the front porch. They spent time discussing projects that needed to be done before putting the property on the market. Nicole captured the list of projects on her cell phone promising to send Jacq the inventory before leaving. Nicole also came armed with initial market data on comparable sales in the area that she left with Jacq to review. Nicole's easygoing style and crisp business focus created a comfortable rhythm that automatically put Jacq at ease.

Sensing Jacq's growing fatigue, Nicole said, "Oh I almost forgot, on our call last week you stated you were planning to stay

THE WEDDING SLIPPER

here in the house, so I brought you a few things. Hang on, I have a bag in the car." Nicole bounded down the front porch to her Ice Silver colored Subaru Crosstrek and returned with a huge reusable floral plastic bag that she unceremoniously handed to Jacq.

"Although Emmett has likely left a few basics in the house, I just thought you might not want to go hunting and gathering for dinner your first night, given you're on east coast time," said Nicole matter-of-factly.

Jacq was so touched by the unexpected act of kindness she almost burst into tears. Just barely, she managed to pull it together and warmly thank her. Nicole left with a wave promising to be in touch soon.

Alone in the house, Jacq sat down at the kitchen table and went through the bag of rations: a loaf of seeded whole wheat bread, a block of cheddar cheese, an apple, an orange, teriyaki beef jerky, a small pot of honey, a Theo's chocolate bar, a box of earl grey tea, sparkling water, and a refrigerator magnet advertising Nicole's real estate business complete with all of Nicole's contact information. Jacq's first ungracious thought was, "What, no coffee? I thought this was the land of coffee purveyors on every corner." After chastising herself for the uncharitable thought, Jacq stood and placed the magnet on the fridge. She opened a cupboard looking for a glass thanking God that Nicole included a bottle of sparkling water. While Jacq was starting to get hungry, she was definitely parched. As she downed the water, she was already envisioning a hot gooey grilled cheese sandwich.

Following her impromptu picnic, thanks to Nicole's practical foresight and gentle kindness, Jacq walked through

Aunt Rose's cozy house. The rest of the house, like the kitchen, was comfortable and beckoned you to sit and relax. The house boasted multiple windows framing gorgeous views not only of the lush grassy farm but of the trees and mountains beyond. Even in the dead of winter, this part of the country was shockingly green, with dozens of shades dominating the view. Towering cedar and fir trees blanketed the distant landscape in emerald and velvety bright green moss carpeted nooks, crannies and rocks. Jacq wondered just how much more beautiful the scene might be in spring or summer when bulbs and currently bare shrubs burst into life and dazzled with colors, shapes, and textures. Even now during winter's hold, the area looked simply stunning.

Jacq turned from the window and staring her in the face was not just Aunt Rose's comfortable home but the remnants of Aunt Rose's abruptly ended life. Her aunt left on a trip expecting to return in a few weeks and instead her home became a time capsule of the day she left. The thought triggered a familiar flood of depressing emotions and the urgent awareness of her growing fatigue. An early morning flight out of New York meant her day started in the middle of the night local time. Jacq headed to the guestroom, past ready to call it a day.

Chapter 2

Garrett heard the sound of a truck as he walked in through the door from the back deck where he had been tending his outdoor grill. He was expecting his three friends to join him tonight, but it seemed a bit early to be welcoming visitors.

His house was built as a log cabin, but nobody would mistake it for a small cabin in the woods. It sported high vaulted ceilings with an open layout. One of the reasons he had bought it, besides the acreage it sat on, were the windows that encompassed three sides of the house. It was almost like being in the outdoors with all of the comforts of indoor living, making it feel like double the square footage. The gathering spaces were downstairs with bedrooms on the upper level. A two-story river rock fireplace stood majestically overlooking the kitchen and dining area. Large leather and wood furniture sprawled throughout the open space creating a masculine oasis. Here and there, were nature inspired touches such as the cast iron leaves and vines climbing up the staircase creating a beautiful railing to the upper floors.

The back of the house boasted a large deck with an outdoor dining area. Beyond the deck was a creek that ran through his property. The creek was just big enough to detect the sound of water gurgling over rocks when seated on the deck. He loved his home for the peace and quiet it offered when nightmares of his time overseas became too overpowering to easily dismiss.

"Go-Go," a dust scoured voice called from the front of the house. "Where are you man?"

Boots clomped toward where Garrett was poking through his pantry looking for the snacks he had purchased earlier in the day. Go-Go was Garrett's call sign from his military days. He had joined the military to escape small town life. He and his two dogs had worked search and rescue as well as bomb detail all over the world, pulling victims out of traumatic situations that threatened their lives. It was ironic that small-town life was what he now craved.

"In the kitchen," Garrett replied. "How are you, Emmett?"

Walking through the door was a tall, lanky, gray-haired man, dressed in a simple white t-shirt, well-worn jeans, and half-laced work boots. Despite his age he had a military presence that showed in his ramrod straight posture and his precise movements. Blue eyes surrounded by laugh lines in a deeply tanned face completed the picture of a man used to commanding soldiers. Emmett, or "Crank" as the guys sometimes called him, was a Chief Navy Transport Mechanic in his younger years. Garrett had met Emmett when he purchased his property. The man was a genius when it came to fixing things and Garrett had used his services as he was establishing his small farm. The two had become fast friends, despite their age difference.

"As good as can be," Emmett answered

Reaching into the fridge, Garrett pulled out two beers, popped the tops, and handed one to Emmett. Tapping the bottle necks in a measure of male solidarity, they took long pulls from the drinks.

THE WEDDING SLIPPER

A thump and scrabbling of claws preceded the arrival of two excited canines pushing each other, competing to get in the room first. Both dogs dropped drool covered tennis balls at Emmett's feet.

"Hey dogs," Emmett looked down, "I can't be throwing balls in the house."

Two doggy grins greeted Emmett's remarks. A large black Labrador head bumped Emmett's leg, looking for an ear scratch. While the other golden lab with a graying muzzle laid down at Garrett's feet.

"Hey Nitro. What have you been up to boy?"

A wagging tail was all the answer Emmett got.

"He's been fine tuning his search and rescue skills. He's well trained in military bomb detection and wilderness search and rescue, but his urban disaster skills need some work," said Garrett.

"Sadie has been a big help," Garrett explained rubbing the toe of his boot along Sadie's back in a caress." Although she's slowed down a bit, she still can teach Nitro a thing or two."

Sadie lifted her graying muzzle off the floor and gave a small chuff in recognition of her name.

"We've been playing hide and seek with some local kids downtown, and in that setting, Nitro can't keep up with Sadie when it comes to finding his victim."

"You'll get there boy, won't you?" said Emmett, thumping Nitro's side as the dog leaned up against his legs begging for more attention.

"You keep petting him like that, he's gonna want to go home with you," teased Garrett with a smile on his face.

"He can come home with me any time," Emmett said peering down at the dog.

"Before the others arrive, I wanted you to know I had a conversation with Nicole when I was in town picking up supplies. She knows I've been taking care of Rose's farm since she passed, waiting to see what Jacq, her relative, decided to do with it. I just got word that it's likely to be sold. Nicole let me know that she has been working with Jacq to put the land on the market."

"I know that you had your eye on at least a portion of the property," Emmett continued, "wanted to give you a heads up in case you were still dreaming about expanding your acreage."

"Huh. Do you by any chance know the price they plan to put on the land?" Garrett asked. He had been eyeing Rose's place for a while now. He planned to use it to expand his budding sanctuary for neglected, abused, and forgotten horses. Garrett had always had an affinity for horses; seen how smart and big hearted the creatures could be. While he had room for a few on his property, he needed more space to provide retraining and medical facilities for the animals he planned to take in. He'd already lined up donors that were willing to invest in his venture, now he just needed the space to make his dream come true.

"I don't, but I'm sure Nicole can tell you when you see her. Rose took good care of her farm and sure loved her orchids. If I haven't said it already, thank you for pitching in to keep them alive," said Emmett.

"I was happy to do it. There are some beautiful flowers in that green house, even though, before I started to help, I probably wouldn't have recognized an orchid from any other flower. Did your wife like orchids as much as Rose?" questioned Garrett.

THE WEDDING SLIPPER   15

"Grace loved plants, but her interest ran toward herbs more than flowers. She was always making candles or soap. I still miss the smell of herb concoctions steaming on the stove. I think that is why she and Rose got along so well. They both had an affinity for green growing things," Emmett stated with a softening of his blue eyes.

"I'll take some time to get a hold of Nicole tomorrow and see if she has any other information. It would be nice to get the land secured so I can start my expansion plans."

Just as Garrett finished his thought two voices shouted, "Hey, we're here," from the front door causing the dogs to jump up and run back through the doorway in a flurry of fur and tails.

"Stop sniffing up my kilt," a disgruntled voice could be heard from the entry.

Garrett and Emmett traded grins as two men entered the kitchen. One was clearly of American Indian descent with sharp cheek bones and thick black hair. The other was of stocky build, with reddish blond hair and sported a utility kilt which Nitro was taking great delight in flipping up with his nose.

"Any more of that and I'm going to have to buy you a drink," Ian said looking down at an unrepentant Nitro.

"I thought your New Years' resolution was to give up kilt wearing at least for the winter?" chuckled Garrett.

"But what you don't know is that today is Ditch Your New Years' Resolution Day, and you know I can't pass up a holiday without bringing my kilts out of the closet," stated Ian, with a laugh in his voice.

Ian McKay and Garrett had been friends ever since basic training. The crazy Scot had made the grueling stressful hours of marching, climbing, swimming, and rappelling, if not enjoyable, at least semi-tolerable. Although the product of an English mother and a Scottish father, he took to kilt wearing at a young age. As a result, his military buddies called him "Gams" as more often than not his legs were bare to the elements, no matter the weather.

Making up the foursome was Donovan Hawk. Ian had met Donovan when he wandered into the local bar and grill and had struck up a conversation about military life with whom he thought was the bartender. Come to find out Donovan was the owner. That night he had been short-handed as his regular bartender had called in sick. Ian, no stranger to slinging drinks, had offered to help and the two had become fast friends. They were complete opposites. Ian with his red hair and boisterous personality was in direct contrast to the quiet, thoughtful restaurant owner.

Though not the classic tall, dark, and handsome type one might imagine of an Ivy League frat boy, Donovan was much more exotic in his looks. Donovan had the angular features and deep brown eyes characteristic of men in the Klallam tribe with long straight black hair, more often than not pulled back in a ponytail. Women had always found Donovan handsome but a bit of a mystery as he could have been the poster child for the strong silent type. Of the four friends, Donovan Hawk would be the least likely among them to be the proprietor of The Longhouse, the local bar and grill. Ian enjoyed holding court behind the Longhouse bar on busy summer nights and given his personality, everyone assumed he owned the place and Donovan, being Donovan, let the illusion stand.

"What can I get you to drink?" asked Garrett standing beside the refrigerator door.

THE WEDDING SLIPPER 17

"The usual," said Ian and "water," said Donovan, both piping up at the same time.

"Ian, your bottle is on the table," said Garrett, tossing a bottle of water to Donovan.

Sitting on the card table was a bottle of Oban Scotch, Ian's drink of choice. He picked up the Glencairn scotch glass Garrett saved especially for him and poured a couple fingers worth.

Sipping appreciatively, he said, "I heard Rose's land was up for sale. Scuttlebutt is a relative is finally coming to settle her affairs. Are you still interested?" Ian inquired, looking at Garrett.

Walking out to the grill, Garrett turned slightly and raising his voice said, "Yeah, I'm still interested, but we'll have to see what the owner says he wants for it."

"Emmett, have you heard anything more?" Ian enquired.

Emmett shrugged and said, "Nothing about the price."

All three of them made appreciative noises as Garrett walked back in with a platter full of perfectly grilled steaks. "Let's eat first then Donovan and I will beat the two of you at Rook."

Emmett and Ian shared an eye roll and grin as they all took their seats and prepared for their weekly evening of friendly competition.

Chapter 3

Waking up in the country is like waking up in an alternate universe if you're a New Yorker. In the city, the ambient noise alone will roll you out of bed the moment your alarm joins the cacophony of cabs being hailed, drivers laying on horns as they jockey for space, street vendors hawking their wares, even the occasional street musician busking to the early morning commuters. In the country, however, it's the distant sound of a rooster crowing, one horse whinnying to another, and the rain falling gently on the roof that nudges you awake.

Without opening her eyes, Jacq stretched every inch of her 5'6" toned and rested body beneath the bedding—the flannel sheets and down comforter on top plus the feather bed below made last night's sleep divine even though the bed was unfamiliar after all the years since she'd slept in it. Unburdening herself to the kind woman on the plane was the balm Jacq needed for a good night's sleep, her first in months, providing the boost to start tackling the emotional challenges ahead. "If only there could be a steaming hot latte on the nightstand as well," she wished when she opened her eyes.

Begrudgingly, Jacq did open her eyes and crawled out of bed. If coffee was in her future, she'd have to fend for herself. Sporting her warm, flannel PJ bottoms and a well-worn t-shirt, a giant

THE WEDDING SLIPPER

bumble bee wearing a crown on the front, she pulled on a robe and some thick, fuzzy socks, quickly pulled her long red hair into a ponytail, and rushed through her morning bathroom routine. Finally, she headed downstairs in search of that magical brew. "Please let there be coffee, please let there be coffee" she mentally chanted, "and if possible, a nice dark roast!" Hopefully, whatever Emmett may have left to get her started included coffee, but she didn't really know what to expect. The northwest was supposed to be the coffee capitol of the country right, or was that just Seattle? Well, hopefully quaint, little Poulsbo was close enough and she'd find what she really needed.

Aunt Rose's kitchen was a colorful, cozy space. Nothing had really changed much since Jacq had visited years ago, right after her high school graduation, when she spent part of the summer helping her aunt settle into her new home. Funny, she didn't think she remembered many details of what the place looked like, but now that she was back, it all looked familiar to her as though she had never forgotten.

Aunt Rose was so excited about the move and the opportunity to really pursue her passion of raising orchids and cultivating new species. The little farmhouse suited her perfectly and that summer spent helping her Aunt spruce the place up and shop for those special things that made a home so personal was the source of many of the happiest memories of Jacq's youth.

"I'm feeling lucky - let's go treasure hunting today," Aunt Rose would often say over morning coffee and off they'd go! They had rambled around the whole peninsula visiting antique stores and yard sales, funky little shops as well as some high-end gift boutiques. Her aunt had eclectic taste along with a magical way of combining things from all parts of the world, old and new, in creative ways that somehow worked. In fact, that summer was probably the time when Jacq's interest was sparked in creating unique and surprising designs that later would define her prowess as a special events planner when she first started working at the hotel. If something really memorable and different was requested by a guest, Jacq was the person who was tapped to bring it to life.

After making her mark in events, her career advanced quickly and before long she was named General Manager. That was just before disaster struck. If it wasn't for Christopher, her friend and right hand, and a devoted staff, she might not have been successful in her new role. Fortunately, the job became a refuge and the demands of managing the jewel in the hotel chain helped her set aside her grief during the workday.

The coffee mission commenced with a search of the upper cupboards and the fridge. No luck. Surely it was here somewhere. Strangely enough, no coffee maker was sitting on the countertop or tucked away in the cupboard either. I must be missing something, she thought as she proceeded to check the lower cupboards. Aunt Rose always started her day with a big heavy mug of coffee and a generous pour of heavy cream. Jacq's parents never drank coffee — they were completely into imported teas, and the smell of coffee brewing in the morning was one of the things she learned to appreciate during her stay with Aunt Rose.

She started to move on to the lower cupboards when suddenly, a loud crash interrupted the quiet morning's search, launching Jacq instantly into alert mode. The sound distinctly came from somewhere just outside the house.

THE WEDDING SLIPPER   21

Slipping on an old, oversized pair of pink rubber boots that were sitting next to the door from the kitchen to outside, she crept stealthily toward what she thought was the direction the noise came from. Picking up an old, rusted watering can for defense, she rounded the corner of the farmhouse and saw the greenhouse in person by daylight for the first time. Jacq's Aunt had told her all about the structure she'd fallen in love with and purchased from an online estate sale, importing it from England. She had sent a few digital shots when it was being put together, but yesterday's quick drive around the property with Nicole at dusk didn't give her a very good view and the photos hadn't done it justice—she hadn't pictured anything quite as lovely and special as this. It had dozens of beautiful leaded glass windows that, while in need of a good scrubbing, still refracted the morning rays. A metal trim that ran the length of the roof and gracefully supported an ornamental cupola positioned in the center, crowned the beautiful greenhouse. It looked romantic, magical even. She wanted to take it all in, but for now she focused on the source of the noise and the entry door that was partially open. She could hear someone or something moving around inside where they didn't belong. Clutching the watering can tightly, she moved slowly through the opening in the door to investigate.

A man was grumbling to himself, bent over, retrieving what appeared to be potshard and dirt that was scattered all over the floor. "Freeze and don't move a muscle!" she commanded in as stern a voice as Jacq could muster. "I'm armed, and I'm not afraid to use it." He froze in place and said nothing while she took account of the figure kneeling on one knee. He wore jeans and an open gray flannel shirt along with scuffed cowboy boots. She couldn't help but notice that the jeans were filled out quite admirably — muscular thighs, a firm butt, and what was certain to be a trim waist underneath the faded flannel. She finally adjusted her gaze up to his toned, tanned arms when he interrupted her thoughts.

"Are we going to just stay like this all day?" he enquired, "or perhaps you could tell me what you're doing trespassing here? By the way, I should warn you that I'm not alone—I have a highly trained dog that will attack on command."

A beautiful golden retriever with soft eyes made its way over to Jacq, sat down and leaned against her leg looking up at her with what looked like heartfelt affection. "Oh, this dog who seems ready to move in with me?" she asked in a sarcastic tone.

"Look, maybe I can't count on Sadie in this instance, but I should also warn you that I'm former military and am expert rated in garden instrument combat. Plus, I'm getting a little stiff kneeling down on one knee on a cold floor like this while you're checking me out."

"Wait," she replied, "why are you talking about garden tools? And I was certainly not checking you out."

The man carefully gestured toward the side window of the greenhouse where she was reflected in all of her armed, morning glory. He slowly stood up, turned around, raised his hands in surrender and looked her straight in the eye. "Now why don't you tell me what you're doing snooping around here?" he asked with a raised eyebrow.

Backing up a few steps Jacq held his gaze, staring into the bluest eyes she'd seen in years. Fringed with eyelashes she'd have to fork over $150 to an expert to rival, she hugged the watering

THE WEDDING SLIPPER   23

can to her middle and tried to find her voice. "I'm not snooping around. I happen to own this place."

"Well, you and I both know that's not true, don't we?" he countered confidently as he took a full account of the woman standing in front of him. She could feel him scan every inch of her body and yet he never seemed to break eye contact. "This house belongs to a gentleman from New York, and clearly, you're not him."

"I see," she replied, "but then from what you just said, you're obviously not the owner so do you mind telling me what you're doing here?"

He ran his hand through his thick, wavy brown hair that wasn't an inch too short or too long and took another step closer to her. "Why don't we each take a breath and sort this out?" he said slowly lowering his arms. "I'm the next-door neighbor. My name's Garrett Olsen, Emmett's friend, and I'm just helping out a little around here. This is my dog, Sadie. And she really is highly trained, but not in attacking beautiful women. Now what's your story, and why are you wandering around strange neighborhoods dressed in your royal finest?"

Jacq drew in her breath just then realizing how ridiculous she looked and used her free hand to pull her robe a little tighter. "I'm Jacq Reed, and I actually am the owner from New York. I inherited the farm from my Aunt Rose. I'm staying in the house, and I came out to investigate the noise you made. Clearly, you had a little accident?" She raised her eyebrows and nodded her head toward the mess on the floor. "I must admit that I just got up and I'm not really at my best before I've had my coffee. And for the record, I was assessing whether or not you were dangerous."

"You're Jack? I thought Jack was a guy."

"Yeah, not the first time I've heard that. It's J A C Q, short for Jacqueline."

"So, I guess an apology is in order, but in my defense, I really did think you were a guy who was arriving later in the week."

"Well, as you can see..."

"Right, well, as retribution, perhaps Sadie and I can help you find that cup of coffee?"

"That would actually be great. I haven't been able to locate any in the kitchen and I really do rely on it to start my day."

"I think I might be able to help with that. I pitch in and help Emmett around the place now and then and I know my way around a little. I take it you do know who Emmett is?" Garrett questioned with a pause.

"Yes, we've spoken, but never met," Jacq replied.

He walked past her and held the door open with an impish grin. "Now may I do the honors? I promise you won't need the watering can any longer."

She lowered the watering can onto a nearby table and with head held high, walked regally past him. She had to admit, he was as attractive from the front as he was the back and his dog Sadie was pretty damn cute. She led him back to the kitchen and said, "I'm not sure we have what we need" as he walked over and reached directly into a plain ceramic canister and pulled out a plump package of Starbuck's French Roast—her favorite! "Well, that's a relief, but I haven't been able to find a coffee maker yet either."

"No worries, your aunt adopted Emmett's love of a French press. I'll just put a kettle on, and we'll have you fixed up in no time."

THE WEDDING SLIPPER 25

"Sounds great," she replied, "and speaking of fixed up, I'm just going to duck out for a few minutes to get dressed. Since we're neighbors, I'm sure you won't mind if I change out of my royal finery, as you put it"

Garrett chuckled and teased, "Oh, I'm happy to have coffee with you in any state of dress."

She gave him a stern look, tempered by a half grin as she pivoted around to go back upstairs, hiding her blush by her quick reaction. "Why am I blushing?" she asked herself — it's not like she hadn't had strangers flirt with her before. In fact, it was almost a daily occurrence at work. "Garrett isn't even my type!" Not that dating was a regular pastime, but Jacq typically went for the posh businessmen who knew all the best restaurants in Manhattan, had connections for tickets to the latest shows, and didn't own a single pair of scuffed footwear let alone cowboy boots. Her friends would laugh if they saw her react to a guy who was literally right off the farm.

She threw on some tan denim jeans and a soft coral colored lamb's wool sweater, dragged a brush through her hair and slipped into her loafers. A five-minute "quick face" make-up job and she was done and headed downstairs. Ahhhhh, she could smell the French Roast and knew that the day was about to get better.

He met her at the bottom of the stairs with a steaming mug of coffee and an appreciative, crooked grin. "Gotta reward a woman who can get ready that fast and look that good, I hope this is how you like it." It had just the right amount of cream—not enough to dilute the rich, dark taste, but just enough to smooth it out.

"How could you possibly know how I like my coffee?" she enquired.

"Lucky guess?" he asked as he took a sip from his mug. "Okay, it's how I take mine and there was cream in the fridge. I took it as a sign."

"Good guess," she acknowledged and took a seat at the cozy little table by the window where he joined her. Outside, she could see Sadie nosing around in what looked like an old vegetable garden. She didn't remember it being there from her youth. "Sadie is beautiful," she noted. "So, what exactly is she trained to do?"

"Search and rescue. She's a natural and one of the best I ever worked with. We served together in the Middle East."

"Wow, that's impressive! How long have you both been back?"

"A few years now. I bought the place next door just about three years ago. Your aunt was a pretty wonderful neighbor to me even though we didn't know each other very well. She let my horses graze here now and then when I needed the extra pasture."

"Dogs and horses?" She asked before sipping some more of the delicious brew.

"Yep. I've got two former military dogs and the horse head count varies. Occasionally something else with four legs stays with me. I take care of rescues, but I don't have room for very many. I hope to change that one day."

"Is your other dog search and rescue too?"

"Yes, and he's also trained to sniff out explosives. He's a Black Labrador—name's "Nitro" and I helped train both of them. He's a bit of a rascal but has saved a lot of lives. He and Sadie are family to me."

"So, you've got special skills beyond garden tool combat, you've also got a way with animals."

He grinned a little mischievously and looked down at his coffee, "animals, women, and pretty much anything that is capable of breaking a heart."

She swallowed her coffee a little wrong but managed to catch herself before going into a coughing fit. "I don't think you're going to have to exercise any particular skills to get along with me for the short time I'm here. I'm just going to take care of some business and get back home to work."

"And what exactly do you do in New York City, if you don't mind my asking?"

"I manage a small, exclusive boutique hotel. We provide high level services for our guests from all over the world and host many different kinds of special events from weddings to business meetings. It's challenging, but creative work. I meet lots of different people and life is never dull."

"I don't imagine it is, if you like that big city vibe." Garrett swallowed the last of his coffee and went over to the sink and rinsed out his mug. "I prefer life outside the city, but I know many people find that to be rather boring. I've had enough excitement to last a lifetime and I still manage to find things interesting enough right here. Like meeting you today — not exactly what I expected."

Jacq got up and took her mug over to the sink as well. They each reached for the faucet handle at the same time and their hands brushed just slightly. She felt a little unexpected jolt and allowed him to take her mug and rinse it, placing it in the sink alongside of his.

"I don't mean to imply that life outside of the city is mundane, just that I enjoy what it has to offer me."

"No offense taken Ma'am," he grinned, drawing out the Ma'am in an exaggerated way. "It was nice meeting you, but Sadie and I need to get back to work. I'm sure I'll be seeing you soon, since we're neighbors for the present, at least."

"I suppose you will," she replied. "Sorry again about the mix-up this morning. "

"Next time I'll let you know if I'm working in the greenhouse."

"I'm not sure that a next time is really going to be necessary."

"Maybe not, but you never know when one of my special skills might be needed."

She grinned back and said, "Well, your search and rescue skills did locate the coffee and you didn't even need to ask Sadie for assistance. I guess that was rather helpful."

"That's how country neighbors are — helpful! In fact, I'll just clean up the mess I made in the greenhouse and be on my way."

She followed him out the door where Sadie ran up to join them. Jacq stroked her silky soft fur and let her nuzzle her hand. "That won't be necessary, I can clean it up and Sadie's welcome to come visit anytime."

"Just Sadie?" he enquired with a serious face.

"Well, Sadie's always welcome. The jury is still out on you."

"Okay, just let me know when the verdict is in." He walked away with a wave, Sadie trotting alongside.

"That guy's trouble," Jacq told herself. "Damn sexy, but definitely trouble."

Chapter 4

While finishing her second cup of divinely aromatic coffee, Jacq reflected on the unexpected start to her morning. Her attractive, flirty neighbor had the charm and good looks to be a major distraction during her stay. Jacq was determined to not let that happen. Having settled her parent's estate over the past two years, Jacq knew the three months she set aside to close her aunt's estate would fly by and she wanted to wrap things up as much as possible before returning to New York.

After calling Beth to let her know she arrived and was settling in, and texting Christopher to tell him the same, Jacq buckled down to formulate a plan to go through Aunt Rose's things. Perhaps a plan was over stating her intention, she really just needed to identify a point of attack. Jacq decided to first tackle the den for no other reason than it was the room closest to where she was standing.

Cases and cases of books was Jacq's first observation walking through the arched opening into the sunlit den. Jacq let out a big sigh knowing that she had already saved too many books from her parent's extensive library. She didn't have enough space in her tiny apartment to house the volumes she couldn't part with from her mom and dad's collections. Saving Aunt Rose's entire library was a nonstarter, only a few volumes could return with her. She would just have to find a good home for Aunt Rose's books, a local library maybe or a secondhand bookstore.

Jacq was pondering options when a familiar ring tone announced a call. Nicole was phoning to see if Jacq would like to meet her for lunch at the Poulsbo Inn, a little bistro in town, to go over business. Jacq readily accepted Nicole's welcomed invitation and they agreed on a time. In the interim Jacq was determined to focus on the library to see if there were any books she couldn't live without, having resigned herself that most must go. The cookbooks she could definitely part with as Jacq more often than not ate out with friends or dined at the restaurant of the hotel she managed. Free gourmet meals were one of the better perks of her job. Jacq took advantage of the benefit; after all she did need to ensure on-going quality control.

A cookbook on Northwest cuisine caught Jacq's eye and she took it off the shelf to peruse its contents. As she flipped through the pages something feathery fluttered to the floor. She reached down to retrieve the wafer-thin item, she noted it was a sprig of dill that had been pressed between the pages. How like Aunt Rose she mused as a smile reached her lips. Jacq smelled the flattened herb which had just the faintest hint of grass and anise notes before setting the herb aside and placing the book on the side table. The cookbook may be worth a closer inspection, as a reward Jacq thought, if she made headway into her sorting task.

While the cookbooks were grouped together, other genres seemed to be randomly placed on shelves. A book on Pacific Northwest hiking trails caught her eye and Jacq absently reached for it and plucked it off the shelf. Time permitting, Jacq would not mind doing a bit of hiking to explore the area. She couldn't help thinking it might be fun to be joined by a cute guy and

THE WEDDING SLIPPER   31

his two dogs. As she started to flip through the book, another papery thin object floated to the floor. Picking up the delicate item, Jacq deduced it was some type of fern frond. She wondered if the frond had been randomly pressed between the pages of the book or if it had been marking a special page or passage.

From here on out, Jacq decided to inspect Aunt Rose's books more carefully in case other flora was present. Jacq set the hiking book on top of the cookbook and then began to systematically pull books off the shelves one by one. To Jacq's amazement, almost every book she opened had something of various shapes and sizes pressed between pages—dainty flowers—some vibrant having retained their color, and others faded but still lovely. Some books contained herbs, leaves, or fronds.

In a poetry book, vivid blue forget-me-nots with bright yellow centers were pressed within a note. The note simply read, "You I could forget not. E." But many books contained an orchid or two, each having been lovingly and carefully sandwiched between two sheets of absorbent white paper before being pressed within the book. It was clear, Aunt Rose's favorite flowers had warranted special treatment and handling.

The next few hours became a treasure hunt resulting in a pile of beautiful botanical wonders, a small collection of enticing books that Jacq wanted to go through in more detail, and two entire cases full of books ready to find new homes. By the end of Jacq's efforts, she surmised that if the pressed flora were marking specific pages, the rhyme or reasons for the designations was lost with Rose.

Satisfied with her morning's accomplishments and gladdened beyond what she expected to be by the organic wonders and the mysterious note she had unearthed, Jacq realized she needed to wash up and head out to meet Nicole for lunch.

Chapter 5

Garrett strolled through the damp field bordering his farm, thinking about the woman he had just met. He had to admit to himself he was taken off guard, in more ways than one, by the watering-can wielding female that confronted him in Aunt Rose's greenhouse. Not only was she a beauty, but he had expected the new owner of the farm to be a man. He realized it had been a long time since he had instantly taken such an interest in a woman. Garrett tried to convince himself it was because he was only surprised in who he would be doing business with; however he knew his first encounter with the sleep tousled woman with the beautiful smile was something special. At first, he hadn't realized what she was saying to him. All he could take in was her long red hair, hastily arranged in a messy ponytail, her athletic figure, and her long, long legs that could wrap around a man and hold him close in just the right way. Her emerald, green eyes had looked at him with suspicion and just a hint of interest, but without fear. She stood before him with courage and confidence. Even in her night clothes, she had a polish about her that only came from money and exposure to fine living.

Garrett shook his head ruefully. Despite their banter, such a woman wouldn't give him a second glance, and he vowed, to himself, to keep his eye on the prize of Rose's land and off her alluring niece.

Sadie gave two quick barks and took off across the field with tail waving madly, pulling Garrett out of his musings.

From a distance, Garrett spotted Emmett's truck in his driveway. He was too far away to have his voice carry across the field, so he put two fingers in his mouth and gave a short, shrill whistle. Emmett's head swiveled in his direction and the man gave him a wave. Garrett picked up his pace, interested to see what his friend wanted. He was also curious as to why Emmett hadn't revealed Jacq was a woman.

When Garrett got within hearing distance, Emmett said, "I was at the feed store and Doug asked me if I would drop off the bags of grain you ordered."

Not acknowledging Emmett's statement, Garrett blurted, "Why didn't you tell me Jacq was a woman?"

"Met her, have you?" Emmett replied with a raised eyebrow.

"I was over there taking care of the orchids and was almost attacked by a woman, who I thought was supposed to be a man."

"Attacked?" Emmett questioned, "I don't know her well, but I've never heard of Jacqueline getting aggressive with anyone."

"Maybe attacked is a bit of an exaggeration, but you could have told me I was dealing with a woman!" Garrett exclaimed.

"Why does it matter?" Emmett replied.

"It doesn't. It just surprised me, is all."

"You're attracted to her," Emmett stated with a knowing nod, "that's what has you all in a twist. Plus, you don't have to deal with her if you don't want to. Nicole is the real estate agent. She'll be handling the sale."

THE WEDDING SLIPPER 35

"I'm not attracted to her. I was just a bit shocked. A surprise that you could have prevented if you had wanted to," replied Garrett.

"Honestly, I didn't really think about it, but your reaction to her is quite entertaining," Emmett chuckled. "Come on, I'll help you unload, and we can talk about your woman troubles."

Garrett scowled at his friend as Emmett jumped in his truck. Emmett thought he heard some softly mumbled expletives, which made him laugh all the way to the barn.

Putting on work gloves, Garrett began slinging sacks of grain into the feed room as Emmett tossed them from the truck bed. The barn was a substantial building with stalls lining the two sides, broken up by a tack and feed room at each end of the building. One stall had been walled-in to create a small, rustic office fitted with the latest technology to keep all the details of a busy, small farm in order.

Emmett heard rustling in a nearby stall and peeked his head over the stall door.

Emmett looked up and questioned, "A new addition to the stable?"

"Yeah. I've named her Angel. About a week ago, the vet in Shelton called needing to place a neglected horse. Angel was found tied to a post in an old barn that, according to animal control, hadn't been cleaned or even aired out for months. Because she has been sequestered for so long, being outside the barn makes her anxious, and she hasn't yet taken to the other horses. Even with all she's been through she is still a gentle soul. I have confidence she'll come out of her shell soon."

"She's in bad shape," Emmett stated, looking over the mare. "But it looks like she's made a friend in Nitro." The horse was lying on her side with the dog curled up at her back. Nitro picked up his head, gave a small grunt, and stretched back out in the hay. The horse never moved.

"Yeah, she is, but she's home now and we'll get her healthy again," Garrett said. "She's been sleeping most days. Her hooves are a mess, she's vitamin deficient and was practically starved. We'll see how she responds to good food and a clean place to rest. "

"Is she approachable?" Emmett asked.

"Sure, she's still a little skittish. But Nitro's presence seems to calm her down," Garrett said.

Just about that time, a black nose with a white star appeared over the stall door. Approaching her slowly, Emmett crooned to the mare as he drew near. The horse tossed her head and backed up a couple of steps.

"Here, give her this," said Garrett, handing Emmett an oatmeal cookie. "I've discovered she has a huge, sweet tooth."

Emmett slowly continued forward holding out the cookie as a peace offering. The horse stretched her long neck, reluctant to get too close to Emmett but wanting the cookie. Emmett let her nibble at the edges but backed up a step enticing the horse to come forward. The cookie proved too much of an incentive, and soon, Emmett was stroking her nose as she finished off the sweet treat.

"Angel is the last horse I'm going to be able to take on until I sell some of the others. All my stalls are full, which is why it is so important I gain more land. Unfortunately, with the way idiot people sometimes treat their animals, there always seems to be a need to protect those who are most vulnerable," stated Garrett.

THE WEDDING SLIPPER 37

Emmett nodded his head as Garrett's cell phone began to ring, startling Angel who pulled back from Emmett's gentle touch.

"This is search and rescue base station," Garrett said to Emmett after looking at the caller's number, "it looks like somebody may be in trouble."

Emmett continued to watch the mare as Garrett discussed the rescue scenario with the dispatcher on the other end of the phone.

After the short phone call, Garrett looked at Emmett and said, "I need to run. There is a missing child up at Steven's Pass. Do you mind calling Ian and seeing if he can watch the farm for a few days? Hopefully, by the time I get there, they'll have found her, but I may need some backup."

"Go," said Emmett, "we'll make sure everything is taken care of here."

Garrett let Nitro out of Angel's stall, gave Emmett a salute and ran out of the barn calling Sadie's name.

"Come on dogs, we've got work to do," called Garrett, jogging out of the barn.

Chapter 6

Jacq was pleased with herself when she found her way into town without needing to use GPS. She partially recalled the way from her time spent here so long ago, but there was also something very intuitive about the area—it just sort of felt obvious where to turn, letting the two-lane road along the bay mostly lead her into town. Nicole had sent her a text to confirm meeting for lunch at 12:30, but Jacq headed into town a little early so she could drive around a bit and get reacquainted with the quaint little village.

Visually, things hadn't changed too much from what she remembered. Poulsbo still stayed true to its Scandinavian heritage having once been a fairly active fishing village. Somehow the town leaders had managed to keep the big chain businesses away and other than the very welcome Starbucks sign, the international symbol of coffee bliss, many of the businesses sported names that identified the families that built them—Anderson's this, Olsen's that, or just a friendly first name such as Nils 'or Signe's. Thank heavens Sluys' Bakery was still there! That was a favorite stop whenever Aunt Rose drove them to town that summer long ago. Those big picture windows filled with pastries, braided loaves of fresh baked bread, and all things mouth-watering yummy never failed to tempt them. Every time

THE WEDDING SLIPPER 39

the door with its cheerful little bell opened, those smells of freshly baked goodness wafted out and encircled you like a lasso and gently drew you in. The gals that worked there wore Scandinavian-inspired uniforms and styled their hair in braids across the top of their heads. Although always busy, they were very cheerful and generous with samples. Who could forget a place like that? She'd definitely needed to stop there before heading home to make sure she was stocked up for tomorrow morning—just what she needed to go with her coffee. Perhaps she should pick up some extras, she pondered, as you never knew when a friendly neighbor might show up.

Jacq noticed the business district had altered a little, with a number of antique stores replacing some of the many tchotchke-laden gift shops that she recalled lined the main drag. Aunt Rose must have adored that change. Perhaps it would be a good idea to make the rounds and see if any might be interested in buying or consigning some of the pieces that would have to go from the house before it went on the market. The thought made her a little weepy, but she reined in the tears and tried to focus on good memories. There had been so many of them and she was going to keep them close, along with a few of the most precious treasures from the house, so that Aunt Rose always felt nearby.

Jacq found a parking place on the street not too far from the Poulsbo Inn, where she was meeting Nicole for lunch. She executed a perfect parallel park, not bad for a New Yorker who didn't drive much, and then walked over to the restaurant. It was a cheerful, modest-sized bistro inside an old, two-story brick building. The structure housed a couple other shops that she had walked by as her destination was in the back. She heard the telltale sound of espresso being made and could smell the coffee as well as soup simmering, and a delightful blend of other delicious things. Her stomach growled a little and she realized that it had not yet adjusted to the new time zone.

Although still a few minutes early, she saw Nicole already there and waving to her from a small bistro table positioned close to a cozy, lit fireplace. Nicole stood up, looking as stylish and yet comfortable as she had the day before with a long, pale pink, sweater belted over gray tights and a gorgeous hand-woven scarf that looped a couple of times around her neck and connected the whole outfit. She was clearly one of those women who just had a way of putting things together in a fashion that seemed effortless but always looked great.

They gave each other a friendly hug and sat down together. "Let's figure out what we want first, so we don't get interrupted," Nicole suggested. "We've got so much to talk about!"

"I'm all for that," Jacq replied and asked what Nicole recommended.

"Everything I've ever had here has been great. So, don't be afraid to order whatever speaks to you." Nicole kept her focus on Jacq but still managed to nod her head and wave as various people called out to her as they entered or left.

Jacq opted for the quiche of the day and a side salad as well as an extra hot, double shot latte. Nicole laughed and said, "You must have joined the conversation in my mind as the quiche is speaking to me too." With their orders in and their beverages swiftly delivered, the two women relaxed and got to know one another a little better.

"How long have you lived here?" asked Jacq. "You seem to know almost everyone."

THE WEDDING SLIPPER 41

"Most of my life, in fact," Nicole replied. "Early on, I was a navy brat as my dad was stationed at a number of places across the country and we moved around about every two years. Later, he got assigned to a management role at the Bangor sub base and my folks put down roots here when I began junior high school. Except for the four years I went to college at Western up in Bellingham, I've stayed put. I love it here! It's so close to Seattle for all things big city and yet I have so many great friendships here as well as my family. I have a big brother who commutes to Seattle but lives fairly close by and my folks still live in our family home. Dad isn't retiring anytime soon; he still works at the base and mom teaches at an elementary school. And, I have a sweetheart, Matt, who loves it here too, so I guess this is going to be home for a long time, if not forever."

"Sounds wonderful and serious," Jacq replied with a smile.

"It is. We're recently engaged," Nicole confided.

"Wow, that's really nice!" Jacq felt genuinely happy for her. Although they had just met, Nicole seemed like somebody she easily could call a friend. "I'm sure you're going to have a wonderful future."

"I think so too," she said. "But enough about me, let's figure out how to help you with everything you have on your plate. How are you doing? I hope you had a nice first night here."

"I did. I must admit, I slept really well. Thanks again for getting me all the goodies to get me started."

"My pleasure. I wanted you to have a relaxing morning so you could wake up and take your time to begin to take stock of what's ahead of you."

Jacq chuckled and said, "Well, it wasn't bad, but I wouldn't call it relaxing exactly."

Nicole looked concerned and asked, "Oh no, what happened? Is everything ok?"

"Oh yes, all is fine," Jacq reassured her. "I hadn't been up long when I heard a crash in the greenhouse and went out to investigate."

"A raccoon?" asked Nicole having had experience with the wily critters.

"Nope, a different sort of marauder altogether! It was my neighbor, Garrett. He didn't know I was there and was trying to be helpful by checking on the place, I guess, and accidentally knocked something over. We sort of surprised each other."

"Oh my, it didn't occur to me to mention to him that you were coming in earlier than I originally thought. Yes, he's been helping Emmett keep an eye on the place. Sorry about the morning surprise, but not such a bad sight first thing in the morning," she said, waggling her eyebrows.

Jacq grinned and responded, "Okay yes, he's pretty easy on the eyes not to mention a bit of a flirt."

"Garrett? A flirt? Not the Garrett I know," Nicole said with a puzzled look on her face. "I've watched half a dozen of the local ladies try to get his attention and, although he's always polite, that's about all they ever get from him. Hmm, isn't that interesting?"

Jacq shrugged and said, "Well, maybe he's more comfortable around women who don't live here. So, not a player then?"

"Nope, just a really nice guy. He moved here a few years back in the spring after he got out of the army. Hadn't been here more than a few weeks when one of our local old timers with dementia wandered off and went missing from his daughter's house and nobody could find him. It doesn't get all that cold here, but when

THE WEDDING SLIPPER   43

it cools off at night, combined with rain, the risk of hypothermia is a real threat. Garrett heard about it and showed up with his dog, Sadie. Within an hour, they found him, and he sort of became an instant hero as well as a target for some of the single girls hoping to meet someone."

"Now that's a way to make an entrance. I met Sadie too—what a sweet dog! So, what's his back story, if you don't mind telling me?"

"Not at all. He's kind of private, so I don't know all that much about his pre-Poulsbo life, but I've heard he was raised by his mom and grandparents who had orchards in Oregon. When he finished school, he helped them out for a while and then enlisted. He was in the service for a number of years and saw some action. I think he was wounded at one point but not bad enough to sideline him for very long and he chose to do another tour. He is really close to a couple of his buddies he served with and followed them out here after he finished his last tour. They are actually more like brothers and are fun to be around when they're all together. You'll meet them at some point as they all hang out at the Longhouse."

"The Longhouse?"

"Yes, it's the best local watering hole. We can go one night together if you'd like?"

"That sounds fun; I'd like that."

"Speaking of the Longhouse, I see that Lia just came in. She's my friend who works there." Nicole waved her friend over. "Hey Lia, how's the bride to be? Let me introduce you to my new friend, Jacq. She's in town for a little while to settle her aunt's estate."

"Nice to meet you Jacq; welcome to Poulsbo!" Lia was an athletic dark blond with a warm, sincere smile and windswept hair. She was dressed in smart, form-fitting athletic wear and looked like she was headed to a yoga class. "How long do you think you'll be in Poulsbo?'

"Hard to say just yet. I've just arrived and am now trying to figure out what to do with all of my aunt's things and get her property sold. It could take a while."

"I'm sorry for your loss. You couldn't ask for a better helper than Nick," she said with a nod and a nudge to her friend. "She's the best!"

"That's kind of you to say," Nicole replied, smiling and shaking her head. "Hey, have you ever settled on a location for the wedding yet? It's sort of getting down to the wire, isn't it?"

Lia sighed, "Yes and I do have a backup plan, but I haven't given up on my dream!" She turned to Jacq and explained that she'd seen a movie one time where an old barn had been transformed into an amazing wedding venue with miles and miles of gauzy white fabric, artfully draped rope, fairy lights, and a few well-placed pieces of old farm equipment. "It's been my fantasy forever, but I haven't been able to find any large barns that are empty and available for this sort of thing. Well, none that aren't falling down and rat-infested, that is."

"Hmm," Jacq pondered. "I have a big barn that I'm not using. When is your wedding?"

"Are you serious?" Lia pulled up a chair and sat down and leaned forward, hope written all over her face. "I was planning for early March, but I could still change the date if it meant finding the right place."

THE WEDDING SLIPPER 45

Jacq looked at Nicole and shrugged her shoulders. "I don't know if this would work and I don't know how much longer I'll own the place, but you can take a look and if something can be worked out soon enough, I'm happy to let you use it."

Nicole pondered the idea and added, "I think the space could work well. I'm just not so sure about the timeline. It would take some effort to get it ready, but mostly a good cleaning, a little patch work, and some fresh paint."

Lia looked optimistic and said, "I bet Donovan and the guys would pitch in. Donovan is my boss and the guys are really hard workers when they aren't playing cards and generally doing guy things."

"Those are Garrett's friends I was telling you about," Nicole explained to Jacq.

"You know Garrett?" asked Lia.

"I don't really know him, but we did get a little bit acquainted this morning," Jacq replied. "Why don't you come take a look and then think about the timeline and we can make a decision. I've had some experience with event planning, so I'd be happy to go over it with you if you need any help," she added.

"That is so sweet! I can't believe you'd do all this for me since we just met. Yes, I'd love to come take a look and I'll take all the help I can get. We're trying to do all this on a budget and that means doing most of it with the help of friends and family. So welcome to my friends and family circle Jacq!" Lia reached over and gave her a warm hug.

Jacq returned it and said, "It's my pleasure, but please don't get your hopes up too high until we see what we're working with. Every girl deserves her dream wedding if she can have it."

Their server showed up with two plates of generous slices of quiche and fresh green salads. The quiche was deep dish with a flaky crust, and it was chock full of caramelized onions, mushrooms, and other tasty ingredients. Jacq's stomach spoke up a little louder this time and they all laughed.

Lia got up and said, "I'll let you both get back to your lunch. I'm going to get right to work on this. I'll give Nick a call and we'll set up a good time to come over, okay? Thanks a million! Really, I can't believe this could be happening!" She practically floated over to the counter to order her pre-workout pressed juice.

"Well, you certainly made her day, Nicole said. "Thanks Jacq, that was incredibly generous of you."

Jacq smiled and said, "I think Aunt Rose would feel good about seeing her barn host a happy event like a wedding. I hope we can find a way to work it out before everything wraps up. So where do we start—other than here," she said taking a bite of her delicious lunch.

Nicole whipped out a folder that had a rough timeline, updated comps on the property, contacts for an inspector and some skilled contractors for any repairs she needed to do and a list of other helpful contacts. They went over them all and Jacq felt like she was taking off in the right direction. Nicole again proved herself to be resourceful, reliable, and incredibly helpful. What a find. Plus, she was feeling more and more like a friend.

Once they had finished their lunches, their business, and a refill on their coffee, Nicole paid the bill as she insisted on treating and they headed out. "Let's just be clear, the next time is on me," Jacq insisted as they walked out to the street together.

THE WEDDING SLIPPER   47

"That's fine," replied Nicole, "and I want to thank you again for being so nice to Lia. She's a real sweetheart and, in all truth, could use the help as they don't have a lot to spend on their wedding. I'll give you a call later and we'll figure out when we can stop by."

They gave each other a friendly hug goodbye and Jacq walked back to her car, via Sluys' Bakery, of course!

Chapter 7

By the time Jacq got back home, it was late in the afternoon and she was feeling a little bit lazy. Although the morning was fairly productive, there was still so much to do, so as tempting as a nap under the afghan on the couch might be, she decided to accomplish a little more before calling it a day. There was a key ring full of keys that she needed to test and label and there was no time like the present.

The key with the Subaru logo was obviously to Aunt Rose's car that she was going to have checked out later, so she removed it and set it aside. The house key was a clear match to the second one that Nicole had provided her. There were still several more that looked like they went to side doors and possibly the outbuildings and a very small one that could be to almost anything. Might as well start by checking to see which ones fit all of the house doors, she thought to herself. She quickly matched keys to the back door and the sliding door that opened to a step down to a small brick patio. The patio had white-washed Adirondack chairs, a table, and a bench that could all use a fresh coat of paint.

She walked around the house and tried another of the keys on the lock to a weathered little shed. Bingo! Inside were lawn chairs, a rather battered-looking croquet set, a slightly rusted

THE WEDDING SLIPPER   49

wheelbarrow, and assorted tools for yard maintenance. There was also the big woven hammock that Jacq remembered. Aunt Rose used to hang it up between the two large, shade trees in the back yard and it was a favorite place to sip lemonade and read mysteries while the hours passed by on a lazy summer day. Everywhere she turned she was flooded with memories that tickled her senses—she could almost feel the cool breeze tugging at the pages and the swaying of the hammock. The memory was still so vivid. She gently closed and locked the shed door.

The next stop was the greenhouse. The door had been open yesterday morning when she had walked in and taken Garrett by surprise. This time, it was shut and sure enough, it was also locked. As a general rule, one wouldn't think it needed to be, as Aunt Rose cultivated prize-winning orchids, some that were valued at over $1,000. She quickly identified the greenhouse key and fit it into the lock. The door opened easily but emitted a soft squeak and once again she stepped inside, albeit not on high alert this time. Jacq chuckled to herself as she thought back on how she looked the first time she came here, wielding a mighty watering can and marching in wearing her pajamas and oversized galoshes. Not the kind of look that one would expect to inspire a guy to flirt with you, and yet he did.

This time there was no one to distract her so she could get a better look at the poor neglected greenhouse. Along the front, there were tables set up with a variety of empty pots as well as pots with dried-up plants. But as she moved deeper into the space, she noticed that things looked decidedly different. In fact, there were signs of life all around her. Row after row of potted orchid plants. Many without blooms, but also many with. Small, medium, and even large plants stood proudly on raised table

50   **J. KIMALIE**

beds. Some had very delicate little blossoms while others shot up tall fronds bursting or about to burst with colorful blooms—deep maroon with little yellow flecks, fuchsia pink, white, and a number of other colors. How did they survive?

Jacq spotted a misting system strung overhead. It must be attached to some sort of timer, but still, they couldn't look this good without some regular attending, a heat source, and fertilizing, could they? Each plant had an identification number written on a stake as well as some sort of a code that her aunt must have used for tracking purposes. The labels didn't make much sense to her as they were all written in the formal Latin form of each plant species name.

Jacq couldn't believe how beautiful they were. She was seeing her aunt's dream fulfilled. She knew why her aunt had bought the place—to pursue her passion for growing orchids and developing new varieties. Here they were, flourishing even after she passed. The thought, while tugging at her heart, was very comforting and for the first time in a long time, Jacq began to feel a little bit of peace when she thought of her aunt. It was good to see her dreams realized and to see that her accomplishments would live on.

The squeak of the greenhouse door in the background alerted Jacq to the fact that someone else was about to join her. "Hello?" she called out, wondering a little hopefully if Garrett was going to make another appearance.

"Hello," came the response from a man who sounded a bit older than her neighbor, followed by footsteps that led him to where Jacq was standing among the orchids. He had a kind and slightly weathered face, and was wearing work boots, 501's and

THE WEDDING SLIPPER 51

a faded denim shirt. "You must be Rose's niece from New York," he said with a welcoming smile as he offered his hand in greeting.

Jacq reached out to shake his hand and he clasped it firmly between both of his. His hands were a little rough as if from plenty of hard work, but warm and oddly grounding. "Yes, I'm Jacq Reed and you must be Emmett!" she responded. "We've spoken on the phone, of course, but I've been looking forward to meeting you in person and thanking you for all the help you've provided. I appreciated the kitchen provisions too—especially the coffee and cream. I don't know how I can repay you for your kindness."

"Yes ma'am, it's nice to meet you. I'm Emmett Foster and you don't owe me anything. It's been my pleasure to keep an eye on the place. Rose was a very dear friend to both me and my wife almost from the day she moved here. When my Grace passed some years back, Rose sort of helped me get through it and carry on. There's nothing I wouldn't do for her or her niece."

Emmett had the most arresting eyes—a little sad, wise, and yet twinkly at the same time. He seemed to look right into you and made it feel like he had taken your full measure with approval, even though you were meeting for the first time. It wasn't off-putting at all; rather, it felt like he could cut through all the opening chapters and get right into the business of knowing you.

"Yes, Aunt Rose was so special," Jacq agreed. "She talked about you frequently and I know that she felt just as close to you, so it's a treat to finally meet you in person. Of course, I always thought she'd be making our introductions," Jacq said with a slight note of melancholy in her voice.

52

J. KIMALIE

Emmett pointed to two bar-height stools that were tucked under a potting table behind them. "Shall we sit for a minute?" He walked over and pulled them both out and waited for Jacq to sit down first. "You know, you look a little bit like your aunt. Do you have her green thumb too?"

"Oh gosh no, I'm afraid I'm sort of the throwback in my family. I'm the only one who struggles to keep my few plants alive, and they have to be pretty hearty to begin with. Hard to believe given the family I come from." She smiled and gestured toward all the orchids. "I know enough though to suspect that these could never have survived all this time on their own, so I'm guessing you had something to do with it?"

He shrugged and looked down rather humbly for a second and then looked at her again. "I may have put in a little time now and then. They meant a lot to your aunt and I wouldn't want anything to happen to them. I pitched in and helped build the beds and string the misters and your aunt taught me enough along the way to at least keep them alive."

"Well, you did more than keep them alive Emmett; they seem to be thriving!" Jacq exclaimed. "Just look at all of them. There are more here than I would have guessed."

"They're awfully pretty, aren't they?" Emmett got up and walked over to one of the raised beds and retrieved a potted plant and set it reverently in front of Jacq. "This one was her pride and joy," he said. "It's the orchid she created that won the grand prize at the last show," his voice catching just a bit at the end.

It was a medium-sized orchid with a subtle beauty. A somewhat narrow blossom that had a heart-shaped center petal that was pure, velvety white with two descending petals of a very

THE WEDDING SLIPPER 53

pale blush color, tinged with white. There were pale, faint green striation lines on the throat of the blossom and it resembled a Victorian shoe. It was simply exquisite. It too, was staked with a code and the label "*Nuptialem Cypripedium Parviflorum.*"

"It's gorgeous," Jacq said softly. "I wonder what she called it.."

"I can tell you," Emmett said wistfully. "She named it the 'Wedding Slipper' and if I'm not mistaken, she dedicated it to you."

Jacq's hand rose on its own to her heart as she took in the information. She could feel her eyes start to blur once again. Just when she thought she was getting a handle on her emotions, something caught her by surprise and took her back to the place where the tears took over. When two firm arms encircled her, she let herself lean into the embrace and she laid her head on Emmett's shoulder, absorbing his comfort. He smelled like hay and sunshine with a faint hint of gasoline—not altogether unpleasant, and he patted her back making her feel safe. After a few moments, she straightened back up and accepted the folded red bandana handkerchief he'd produced like a vintage romance hero.

"Thanks Emmett, I thought I had just about emptied the well by now.'

"Ah sweetheart, when you are lucky enough to have someone like Rose in your life, the well runs pretty darn deep," he replied. "She was one in a million."

Jacq wiped her eyes again and held the handkerchief up. "I'll give this back to you after I've washed it. I really can't thank you enough for keeping Aunt Rose's legacy alive," she said. "Do you think you might be able to teach me how to take care of all this?" she asked, gesturing to the orchids. "It'd be a shame if something happened to them, before I can sell or find them good homes, because they inherited me as a caretaker."

"Of course, I can," he replied, "and Garrett can lend a hand too. He's been pitching in just as much as I have and seems to be pretty good at it. I heard you two met already."

"Yes, we did. I didn't realize he'd been helping to take care of the orchids, so that explains why I caught him in the greenhouse."

"You caught him?" Emmett asked with an amused look on his tanned face.

"Well, 'surprised him' is probably a better way to say it," she chuckled, "although I think we were equally surprised by each other. I didn't realize anyone would be coming over and rattling about out here, so we met under unusual circumstances. In fact, when I heard the door open just now, I thought you might have been him."

Emmett returned the special orchid back to its proper place and explained, "Garrett has been great about helping me look after things around here. We've been buddies for a long time and he's a good worker. Now it's one of my turns to help him. He's away for a couple of days on a job so I'm checking on his place and feeding the horses. Speaking of which, I'd best get over there and get that done as horses get a little anxious if they don't get their dinner on time."

"Of course, but before you go—I really would like to do something to thank you both for lending a hand. Please, will you let me know what I might do?" she asked sincerely.

"Like I said, you don't need to do anything," he reassured her, "but if you really want to do something to feel better about it, well, I'd suggest taking some homemade oatmeal cookies over

THE WEDDING SLIPPER 55

to Garrett. He'll know what to do with them for sure." Emmett winked at her and smiled even bigger when he said it.

"Well, that's easy enough. I'll be sure to take him some of his favorite cookies. And what about you? Surely there is something that I could do for you?" she asked again.

He thought about the question for a minute and then looked directly at her in that piercing way of his. "Okay, there is one thing. I'd appreciate having one of your aunt's books to remember her by."

"Just a book? Of course, you can have as many books as you'd like," Jacq responded. "Is there any particular title or subject you'd prefer? Or do you want to go through them? She had so many and I've just started to take stock of what's there."

"I think you'll know the right one when you come across it," he said with a slightly sheepish look on his face.

He patted Jacq on the shoulder and then turned and walked away. "I'll see you soon," he called back to her and with a wave, headed across the pasture toward Garrett's barn.

Jacq sat back down on the stool in the greenhouse and reflected on their conversation awhile longer. She couldn't imagine how she would know which book Emmett might want, but she decided to see which one spoke to her as he suggested would happen. It seemed like with each passing day, she looked forward even more to the time she was spending here. What she had anticipated to be a solitary journey was turning out to be anything but. Tonight, she was going to call Christopher and Beth to debrief all that had happened so far.

She walked over and looked at the Wedding Slipper orchid again. The fact that her aunt had dedicated it to her touched her heart and reinforced the bond that they had built over the years.

In many ways, her aunt had known her even better than her parents. Aunt Rose was her confidante when she first decided to move to New York away from her folks. She was the person Jacq turned to over the years for comfort with each broken heart, to celebrate some of her big successes or to just confide in when she needed the voice of experience.

While it wasn't surprising that her aunt would dedicate a romance-themed orchid to a beloved niece, Jacq had at times thought that her aunt was hovering on the verge of confiding to her—that perhaps there was someone very special in her life. Whenever she probed, her aunt had deftly changed the direction of the conversation or said they'd talk about it later. Well, she'd never know now, but she liked to think that her aunt had enjoyed at least one more good romance in her life. Could that be why she named the orchid the Wedding Slipper?

Chapter 8

Jacq parked her car in front of the grey weathered barn. She had seen Garrett out in the pasture as she drove up and figured she would find him near the animals. Emmett had let it slip that when Garrett came back from a search and rescue assignment he often liked to unwind with the animals. They helped bring him down off the adrenaline rush or provided the solace that he needed depending on the rescue outcome. Luckily, according to Emmett, the rescue was a success and the little girl was unharmed and happily reunited with her parents.

Jacq sat in her car and absorbed the peacefulness of the northwest scene. The barn set off to the side of the parking area with a fairly new truck and what looked like a small tractor parked beside it. Looking past the barn was a

tangle of evergreens and deciduous trees running together to create a small forest. Although the barn looked like it had survived many storms, its grey patina was offset by cheerful white trim that showed signs of recent painting. Fences lined either side demarking the pastureland from the barn. The barn door was wide open, but the specifics of the interior were hard to make out from the angle of her car window.

Jacq slid out of the car and went to the trunk to fetch the oatmeal cookies she had made. Emmett had said something about Garrett having a thing for oatmeal cookies. In fact, the way he said it sounded like oatmeal cookies were Garrett's favorite treat. She figured as a thank you went, making a man his favorite cookie was a good way to show gratitude. She still couldn't believe that between the duo of Garrett and Emmett they had kept Aunt Rose's orchids, not only alive, but thriving. She had found herself spending more and more time in the greenhouse admiring the orchids which seemed to be imbued with Aunt Rose's spirit. They never failed to bring back good memories and, although at times painful to recall, filled her with love and comfort.

Jacq had spotted Garrett on the far side of the barn. Armed with the tub of cookies, Jacq made her way across the pasture where Garrett stood grooming a beautiful, but painfully thin, mare who seemed to be standing so still she appeared to be telegraphing that she didn't want the man who was running his hands over her body, to ever stop. Jacq had a brief fantasy of Garrett running his gentle hands over her body with his deep voice rumbling in her ear about all the seductive things he was going to do to her. A shiver ran down her spine from sheer longing until she realized Garrett was trying to get her attention. She could feel the embarrassment start at the base of her neck and make its way to the tips of her ears when she realized both the man and horse were waiting for her to answer a question that she had totally missed while she was standing there fantasizing.

Rapidly walking forward, Jacq shoved the white tub of cookies into Garrett's chest and said, "Here these are for you."

Garrett took a half step back as he tried to keep from dropping whatever Jacq had just shoved at him. He was hoping it wasn't breakable as he began to juggle it when she quickly

THE WEDDING SLIPPER   59

retracted her hands. Seeing that Garrett was fumbling the hand-off, Jacq jumped in to rescue the cookies and ended up elbowing him in the gut and startling the mare, who, until that time had been watching with, what Jacq was sure, was amusement.

"Oomph," Garret hissed and stumbled back, thankfully still holding onto the container.

"Damn," Jacq whispered under her breath as she felt her face once again blossom with embarrassment. She was a professional. Not many things unnerved her, but apparently, being around Garrett was one of those things. She noticed the horse had backed up several steps and was eyeing her with suspicion.

"Thank you...I think," said Garrett, rubbing his stomach, not sure what just happened. Jacq stood before him, eyes down, hands in her back pockets, looking like she wanted to be anywhere but right where she was. "Hi Jacq," Garrett said, grinning.

Jacq looked up, with cheeks still tinged with pink. "Hi. Your horse is really skinny." *Your horse is really skinny!* Jacq thought to herself. God, what was wrong with her. When did she revert to an awkward teenager?

Garrett looked behind him where the little black mare was standing continuing to stare at them. "Yeah, Angel's been ill, but she'll be okay. What's in the container?" asked Garrett holding up the tub of cookies.

"That's just a thank you for taking care of Aunt Rose's orchids. Emmett told me that you and he took turns making sure the orchids survived. Emmett mentioned you went through a lot of oatmeal cookies."

Curious, Garrett opened up the container and took out a cookie. He turned around and offered it to Angel. The horse snorted and slowly made her way to Garrett's side, gently taking the cookie from his hand.

"What are you doing?" asked Jacq, incredulous that Garrett had given one of her homemade cookies to a horse that was now munching away contentedly.

"Angel loves oatmeal cookies and she needs to fatten up a bit."

"Those were for you," said Jacq continuing to watch the mare. "Although she does appear to be enjoying it."

"I'm sure they're great. How did you know Angel loves oatmeal cookies?" asked Garrett, turning back to Jacq with a questioning look on his face.

"I didn't. I thought when Emmett said you would appreciate oatmeal cookies, that they were your favorite," Jacq said.

Garrett began to chuckle, then couldn't help it and started to laugh.

Jacq was mesmerized by his laugh. It was so rich and full of joy. It was impossible not to laugh right along with him.

"I'm sorry," Garrett said with a huge smile on his face, his eyes twinkling with merriment, "Oatmeal cookies aren't one of my favorites, but it was a nice gesture and Angel will be your friend forever."

Jacq continued to giggle, "Well, thank you anyway. Keeping a part of Aunt Rose's legacy alive means a lot to me."

Jacq watched the mare nudge Garrett's arm for attention. "You're welcome," said Garrett as he ran his hand lovingly under the mare's white-stared forelock.

"You mentioned Angel's been ill," Jacq commented.

THE WEDDING SLIPPER   61

"More like neglected and abused," mused Garrett. "She's my newest guest at the farm. She was found up in Shelton in a bad situation. The rescue facility up there had run out of room, so they called me."

"You save neglected animals," stated Jacq looking around and nodding her head like it all made sense now.

Garrett glanced at her. "Yeah, this farm is a rescue facility. I have about six horses and various animals roaming around. Goats, ducks, and a one-eyed ewe named Pirate."

"You're kidding. Pirate?" questioned Jacq.

"Yes, she's a strong woman figure and rocks her peg leg," the corners of Garrett's eyes crinkled as he grinned.

"You're kidding?" Jacq restated.

"I am. She's missing an eye, not a leg. But she does like her red bandana," Garrett said. Turning away from her, Garret commented, "I need to take Angel to the barn. Would you like to see the rest of the farm and then maybe head up to the house for something to drink?"

Jacq nodded and followed Garrett as he led Angel to the barn. On the way Garrett pointed out the barn, a large shed that held farm implements and the house in the distance. It was beautiful property surrounded by a wealth of greenery and she spotted several more horses out grazing in a distant pasture. He led Angel into her stall, unbuckled her halter, checked her feed, and walked out latching the stall door behind him. Angel whickered as they started to walk out. Garrett turned around, grabbed a second cookie out of the tub and fed it to Angel. He turned back to Jacq with yet another cookie in his hand.

"I thought you didn't like oatmeal cookies," Jacq questioned with a raised eyebrow.

"I didn't say I didn't like them, just that they weren't my favorite. But how could I turn down a gift from a beautiful woman?"

Jacq smirked and watched him munch on the cookie. "I don't know how I should take a compliment from a man who doesn't like my cookies," she said.

Garrett just grinned and walked out of the barn assuming she would follow. "After I got out of the service, my dream was to find a place that was simple, peaceful and where I could house animals that had been neglected and abused. I've always liked being around animals. I can't tell you the number of strays I picked up as a kid. Mom acted as nurse and helped me splint legs, de-lice and generally clean up the animals I found. I didn't get to keep all of them, but we found good people that would take them in. Horses have been a part of my life as well, and of course, dogs. I was lucky to combine my love for animals with my military career. As you know, I am still on call for search and rescue incidents, so the dogs pay for their upkeep," he said proudly. "However, now I need to expand this place. I've run out of stable space for the horses and another few acres of pasture would come in handy as well."

Jacq looked over his land and nodded her head. "I think it's beautiful and your animals seem very content here."

"Come on, let me introduce you to Pirate."

Jacq and Garrett made their way to a large fenced-in area where a medium-sized ewe stood munching on some grass.

"This is Pirate," said Garrett, opening up the gate and walking toward the sheep. Hearing a familiar voice, the animal turned its head toward Garrett and began walking toward him. The sheep had a completely black face followed by a white

THE WEDDING SLIPPER 63

wool-covered body with black socks. Pirate didn't stop when she reached Garrett but kept right on going until she butted her head against his leg.

"Hey Pirate, I've got somebody here I want you to meet." Pirate let out a bleat which Jacq assumed was a hello.

Jacq held out her hand and said, "Hello Pirate," to the animal that was now leaning against Garrett and rubbing her head against Garrett's leg. One eye was sewn shut while the other looked wary, but curious. She seemed to be wondering if Jacq had anything tasty in her hand as an offering.

"Does she like oatmeal cookies too," asked Jacq.

"No, she pretty much sticks to her own food. Here give her this," Jacq said as he handed her a couple of stalks of hay.

Jacq took the offering and held it out to the reluctant animal. The food proved too much of an incentive to Pirate and she slowly approached Jacq. Taking the food gently from her hand, Pirate allowed Jacq to scratch behind her ears. Jacq noticed that Pirate did sport a red bandana tied around her neck looking like she was the farmer instead of the livestock.

"Nicole let me know that you were thinking of selling Rose's land," said Garrett, gesturing toward Aunt Rose's farm. "I'd like to get a chance to discuss it with you or, if you would prefer, I can speak with Nicole."

"Nicole would know the most about the sale. She is working on coming up with a fair value for the farm. Are you interested in the whole thing or just a piece?"

"I'm not sure I can afford the whole thing, but would be interested in negotiating," said Garrett.

"Why don't we talk after Nicole goes over all the comps for the property with me and I have a better idea what to expect. I do have to tell you, I promised Lia that she could use the barn for her wedding before I sell. I'm also, obviously, cleaning up the place and going through Aunt Rose's possessions. I'm not sure how long that will take me, but maybe we can make a deal," commented Jacq, still stroking Pirate's ears.

"That's good enough for me. Isn't Lia's wedding in a few months? Do you need a clean-up crew?" asked Garrett.

A smile bloomed on Jacq's face. "I was hoping you would ask. I was going to invite you to the Longhouse for a drink to discuss some help. Do you have a clean-up crew you can call on and could they meet us at the Longhouse on Thursday?" asked Jacq.

"Let me make a few calls and I'll let you know," stated Garrett.

Pirate was leaning up against Jacq's leg, rubbing her head begging for further attention.

"I don't think she is going to let you leave," said Garret. "Would you like to hang around for a bit longer? We could always go over to the house for something to drink before you head out?"

Jacq looked up at Garret through her lashes as she stroked the ewe wondering if it was safe to be alone in Garrett's house on her own. Not that she was afraid of him but was hesitant due to her body's reaction to his presence. *You only get one chance to live life to the fullest,* her Aunt Rose would have told her. Taking her aunt's advice, Jacq glanced back up and said, "I'd like that."

Jacq straightened from petting Pirate just as Garrett reached for her hand. As he led her toward his house, she thought back to the last time she'd held hands with a man and couldn't remember. Needless to say, it had been a long time. She had

THE WEDDING SLIPPER 65

to admit the slight scrape of his calluses against her palm as their hands moved together, felt safe and comfortable. As they reached the back porch, Garrett opened the door and stood aside for Jacq to enter first. Jacq felt the soft touch of his hand on her lower back as he guided her into the kitchen.

"What can I get you to drink?" Garrett asked, "I have iced tea, beer, and water. I also keep harder stuff if you would like an afternoon cocktail."

Jacq smiled, "Just water with a little ice would be fine."

As Garrett busied himself fixing her drink and grabbing a beer out of the fridge, Jacq looked around at the decidedly masculine but non-bachelor-padish home. She was peering at some landscape art when Garrett appeared at her side and handed her iced water. She carried it to the opposite end of the couch where Garrett had planted himself.

He took a pull of his beer and asked, "What's your favorite color?"

Jacq looked at him confused, "um....fuchsia." When she remained quiet, he raised an eyebrow.

"What kind of music do you like?" asked Garrett with an amused light in his eyes.

"What is this? Twenty questions?" Jacq said.

"Isn't this what people do when they are trying to get to know each other? Ask all the easy questions."

Jacq chuckled, playing along, "My favorite color is fuchsia, my middle name is Rose, I like sugar in my tea, cream in my coffee, my meat well-done, my wine red, my movies full of romance, my books sci-fi, and I like boy bands as well as music from the 80's." She finished in a rush.

66 **J. KIMALIE**

Garrett didn't catch part of her laundry list, but it had sounded like she had said she liked boy bands. "Was that boy bands?" he asked.

"Yes, and songs from the 80's, but don't laugh," she declared, crossing her arms over her chest defensively.

"Far be it for me to criticize your choice in music," he said, trying not to laugh, "I like the type of music where "my woman left me, took my dog and I was flushed from the bathroom of her life" country music."

Jacq burst out laughing, "That is so down-home of you."

"Well, I did steal that line from the Man in Black," Garrett said, laughing right along with her.

She liked his laugh. It was a little bit husky, like it came from deep down in his chest.

"Tell me what a typical day looks like back home in New York? You've already seen what fills most of my days."

"Well, up by five to spend some time on the yoga mat, then showered and dressed and into the office by 7:30. Then it's a day of hotel happenings, housekeeping, difficult customers, event details and temperamental chefs. Some evenings are spent overseeing a hotel event or, if I'm lucky, enjoying a drink and dinner with my friends," Jacq explained.

"You love it. I can hear it in your voice."

Jacq nodded, "I do love it, but there are days when being in the hospitality business can be filled with unhappy customers or discourteous people. Those are the days when I want to do something else, something on my own terms."

"Like what?" asked Garrett.

THE WEDDING SLIPPER   67

"I don't know. But for right now, I am content with my life," Jacq sighed, "and I will be really happy when I've made my way through Aunt Rose's things and can wrap up her estate."

Her comments brought Garrett back to the fact that she would be leaving. She didn't think she belonged here and maybe she didn't, but he had an impulse to convince her to take a look around and see if she could consider staying. She seemed like a woman he would like to get to know better. He mentally shook himself out of the fantasy he had fallen into and brought his attention back to what she was saying.

"I do like it here, the quiet, the open spaces, the way everything is one shade or another of green. So different from where I live," Jacq sighed.

And Garrett liked seeing her here in his space. He liked the way her face pinkened when she was embarrassed. He liked her almost southern manners, bringing a gift to commemorate a good deed done by a neighbor. He liked her gentleness with the animals and the way she listened to him like he was the most important person in the world. He liked her smile, her laugh, and even the way she walked. He just liked her and that hadn't happened in quite a while.

Chapter 9

Nicole's silver Subaru pulled up to the house right on time; another one of Nicole's traits that Jacq appreciated. Lia sprung from the passenger seat and greeted Jacq with an exuberant hug. Nicole walked around the car and Jacq welcomed her warmly. Lia was looking across the pasture toward the barn and suddenly blurted, "It's perfect, it's absolutely perfect."

Jacq chuckled and replied, "You may want to withhold judgment until you look inside as it's not exactly wedding ready."

The gals strolled toward the weathered barn, Lia practically skipping two steps ahead unable to contain her growing excitement. The large barn was situated parallel to the street but set way back, at least 300 yards, from the road and house. The cupola-topped barn was a solid, good-looking, structure with a gambrel roof providing more storage space on the top loft while creating a classic exterior appearance. The cupola was capped with a sleepy moon weathervane with a tiny star dangling down from the top of the moon. Rather than an arrow pointing out wind direction, the ends of the rotating rod had a sun on one side and a larger star on the other.

As Jacq was thinking the barn could use a fresh coat of paint, Lia said, "The patina of the barn wood is lovely; I'm going for a rustic, casual look for the wedding. My medi-length wedding

THE WEDDING SLIPPER 69

dress is made of champagne-colored lace, just the right length to show off my dress cowboy boots. My prized boots are the first gift Brett ever gave me."

As Jacq tugged back the heavy barn door, sunlight cut an angle into the barn spotlighting dust particles floating in the air. Jacq walked across the width of the barn and slid open matching doors directly across from the doors they had just entered. More natural light poured into the center of the impressive structure. The barn smelled of hay, leather, and scents that Jacq could not place but were not entirely unpleasant. Clearly, the barn had not housed animals in recent years. In fact, Aunt Rose had only spoken of trees, plants, and flowers when discussing the farm.

"The beams and rafters are lovely," Nicole announced as she ran her appraising eyes along the length of the roof. "If you're planning to drape tulle from the rafters you are going to need bolts and bolts of it," she added with a dubious expression.

Lia affirmed Nicole's observation stating, "I discovered a discount fabric warehouse in Seattle that has extra wide bolts of ivory tulle and they are holding them for me. I knew no matter where we chose to get married, I wanted the romance and magic touch that tulle adds to almost any setting. It's my one and only splurge for what will be a budget-conscious affair. While I'd love to string party lights all over the barn, I'll make do with tea lights in mason jars on the table and we'll get married in the afternoon so lighting and heating will not be as important."

While Lia continued to share details of her wedding plans, Jacq was wishing Lia had even a tenth of the budget her New York clients routinely spent on wedding decorations and event lighting at the hotel. If so, she could help Lia create a wedding fantasy beyond what she had ever imagined. Jacq had a dozen or more ideas ricocheting around in her mind on how the space could transform into a jaw-dropping wedding venue, but she kept them to herself knowing that Lia simply did not have the budget to finance more than what she already had planned.

Jacq decided to try and be helpful and focus Lia on the practical considerations of an event. "How many people will be at the wedding?" she inquired.

"No more than 50, just family and close friends," Lia added.

"Luckily, there are not too many items in the barn that need to be cleared out, but it will still take some work to move all the old hay into a corner and a good sweeping all around will be needed," Jacq observed. "I can help of course, but I don't have a lot of time to spend on clearing and cleaning," she added.

"Oh, don't worry about that," Lia quickly added, "I don't expect you to do any of the work, you've already done enough just lending me the barn. I have already recruited my family and my boss to pitch in. Donovan already said he'd be happy to help, and he'll recruit his friends; you'd like the notorious bunch. In fact, one of the guys you've met, your neighbor Garrett."

Garrett's graceful masculine form unbiddenly materialized in Jacq's mind. "What is it about him that I find so appealing?" Jacq pondered. Garrett, while good-looking, was not the most handsome man Jacq had ever laid eyes on, but he had an elusive quality that she was drawn to on several levels. Perhaps it was his mix of both strength and gentleness that was so alluring. Or maybe it was just a primitive carnal desire that, like a magnet, pulled her toward him. Just as Jacq's thoughts were turning in a lascivious direction related to Garrett's attributes, Lia asked a question pulling her thoughts back to the task at hand.

THE WEDDING SLIPPER 71

Lia soon discovered Jacq's wealth of knowledge related to event planning. In less than an hour they covered a multitude of considerations from the utilitarian: table and chair rentals; parking locations for guests; porta potty placement; contingencies in case of rain; to the sublime: the location where the ceremony would take place; a focal point to frame the wedding party for the ceremony; how the bride would arrive; and the type of music to set the mood for the event. Lia's building excitement of her dream wedding being within reach was tempered by how much she needed to get done in the next month. Now that the location was locked in, she needed to get the invitations out by the end of the week. She and her fiancé, Brett, had thankfully sent out save-the-date cards two months ago but even so, she was cutting things a little close.

Jacq encouraged Lia to come and go as she pleased to ready the barn for the happy event and to use it to store wedding supplies. "The more you can get done prior to the week of the wedding the better," Jacq urged. On that note, Lia was anxious to start checking off her to-do list, Nicole had a house showing with a client, and Jacq needed to get back to her "sort and export" house clearing chore as she had come to think of it.

As Jacq climbed the stairs to the front porch, she glanced left toward her neighbor's house and her mind drifted to lustful thoughts that she knew she had no business thinking. "What's wrong with me?" she wondered. She wasn't some young sorority freshman infatuated with a college upperclassman; yet she couldn't quite convince her humming body of that fact whenever she thought of Garrett. "Best to keep my distance," she concluded as she determinedly walked into the house and firmly closed the front door behind her.

Chapter 10

Slowly but surely, Jacq was making headway going through all of her aunt's belongings. She'd had to be both a good organizer and strategist in her work at the hotel and those skills came in handy. Her emotions were fairly well corralled and so had gotten underway with the business at hand. She had organized two of the bedrooms into staging space for items to donate and items to sell. Items that could be disposed of were bagged and relegated to the garage where she would load the jeep and haul them away each time it looked like she had a full load. The downstairs closet was the space she granted herself to store any personal items she wanted to keep and ship home. Instituting a finite space limitation would help keep her faithful to the limit she set for herself as her apartment back in New York was already pretty full. She'd figure out how to integrate Aunt Rose's things with her own once she got back home.

Jacq had already gone through Aunt Rose's laundry room. The kitchen and most of the furniture would be dealt with last as it was needed for her own use during her stay. Today she was ready to tackle many of the items that were purely her aunt's finds and treasures, placed here and there to add even more cheer to the little farmhouse and serve as reminders from her travels. Many of these had been discovered in the company of "the girls"

THE WEDDING SLIPPER 73

that brought back shared memories. Jacq kept her cell phone handy so she could photograph and research any of the items that might be of some worth. Her aunt had acquired a broad variety of treasures that caught her fancy and didn't particularly care if the rest of the world valued them or not.

With the radio tuned to good vintage rock and the volume turned up louder than she would have allowed in her apartment back home, Jacq dove in starting with the large armoire in the dining room. It was filled with beautiful tableware for entertaining—at least two dozen bone china teacups with matching saucers. The floral designs would have appealed to her aunt, particularly those that were hand painted on both the outside and inside of the delicate cups. These would need to be wrapped carefully but would surely be welcomed by one of the local antique dealers. She set them on the dining room table and continued to explore. There was a collection of glass and pottery vases, a couple that she remembered her aunt finding during one of their jaunts. As a girl, she loved to help her aunt arrange freshly cut flowers in them and there was always a bouquet on the nightstand in her room. One of these would need to be chosen and boxed for the "keeper" closet.

A beautiful silver tea service was in need of a good polish but would also be easy to sell. A stack of linens was neatly folded and layered on the bottom shelf—tablecloths, tea towels and napkins. These could be donated, along with a cheerful ceramic teapot that had a miniscule chip in the spout. Her aunt was never bothered by a flaw if it wasn't too big and didn't interfere with an items function. In fact, she often commented that small, manageable signs of wear and tear were what made some of her treasures, and most of her friends, more interesting and dearer to her!

She found the beautiful Portuguese pottery platter that her aunt always piled high with food when it was warm enough to take dinner outside, that summer she had visited. There was also a dozen vintage, cut crystal wine glasses. Jacq sighed as she wished she could keep them but had to make some hard choices and decided to let them go.

In the back of the cabinet, she found a small collection of Murano style glass paperweights with colored swirls and pressed flowers embedded within. Jacq snapped photos to research before making the sell or donate decision.

Jacq sat on the floor and continued to work her way digging through the cabinet's lower shelves, sorting out, singing softly along with the music as she went. When Linda Ronstadt's hit *When Will I Be Loved* came on, she couldn't help herself belting it out right along with her. Though she didn't have a very good singing voice, she always enjoyed letting go when the song moved her. As she pulled out a china serving bowl and turned to find some bubble wrap for it, she was rounding the bend on the chorus when she encountered a pair of denim covered legs standing right behind the pile of wrapping. She stopped singing abruptly as the bowl slipped from her hands. "I'm sorry I startled you," Garrett said loudly over the music while bending down to retrieve the bowl that he hoped wasn't broken. Miraculously it was not. He had knocked but knew there was no way Jacq could have heard him over the music. He let himself in and found her singing at the top of her lungs. He couldn't help but admire the woman before him, the delicate arc of her neck, her straight back and curvy waist as she swayed to the music and wrapped

THE WEDDING SLIPPER   75

up dishes. Her ponytail bounced in a way that tempted him to wrap his hand around it, drawing her in to capture a passionate kiss. He mentally shook himself as he semi shouted, "I did knock but..." as he gestured toward the radio.

Jacq got up and tried to laugh off her embarrassment as she went to turn down the volume. "Hi Garrett," she said, "What brings you over?"

"Emmett mentioned you'd asked for some help learning how to take care of the orchids so I thought this might be a good time for a lesson," he replied. His smile clearly gave away his amusement at catching her in the act of singing. "One of your favorites, or just putting the question out to the universe?" he enquired.

"Excuse me?" she asked, still a little pink.

"When will I be loved?" He sang in a soft voice with perfect pitch. While he had to admit to himself, he enjoyed catching her at an embarrassing moment, he couldn't help but feel a little bad that he'd made her uncomfortable. And yet, it was worth it as he also noticed how beautiful she looked when she was a little flushed. Heck, she was beautiful anyway, but at this moment it was like she was lit from within. He always did have a soft spot for red heads, but Jacq's beauty went well beyond her long, burnished locks. Her green eyes had specks of gold that looked a little like sparks when she got defensive. Her skin was exactly what poets meant when they referred to "creamy" with a hint of blush in it, and he could only imagine how far down the blush traveled. It would be so easy to reach out and gently adjust her loose top. It looked like it could be caressed off her shoulders or easily pulled down a bit in the front—just enough to see how low that delightful pink flush covered. Just thinking about it was starting to have an effect on him—suddenly, he began to feel a blush himself coming on as his jeans began to feel a little tight in the front. What the hell? He wasn't an inexperienced teenager and yet he instantly remembered what it was like to have his body take over command central. "Get yourself under control GoGo," he mentally admonished himself, as he turned slightly away to look at some undefined focal point in the room behind him—anywhere but directly at her.

Jacq automatically adjusted the bottom of her shirt as she'd noticed him looking at it and tried to change the subject. "I was about ready for a coffee break—would you care to join me? I might even still have a few oatmeal cookies to go with them."

Garrett nodded, "I'll pass on the cookies, thank you, but coffee sounds great."

Jacq laughed, "Just kidding. I haven't made any more of them. Sit tight and I'll get the coffee going." She escaped to the kitchen and took the opportunity to compose herself. Jacq had a funny feeling, however, that she wasn't the only one who needed to get composed. She could have sworn that Garrett looked a little flushed himself, although she wasn't sure why. He'd seemed so amused to catch her singing at the top of her lungs like an idiot.

Garrett watched her walk away to the kitchen and noticed how perfectly proportioned her curves were. Why did he have to look? Of Course, how could he not? Garrett was happy to take a seat and let the party in his pants calm down before it got too far out of control. He'd certainly enjoyed female companionship over the years, but the attraction he was feeling for Jacq was more powerful than he'd experienced in a very long time. He didn't need this. For one thing, she wasn't going to be here much

THE WEDDING SLIPPER   77

longer. For another, he hoped to be negotiating a property deal before she left, not an awkward goodbye. In fact, he'd hoped that after talking about orchid care the right opportunity might come up for him to again broach the subject of a sale. He needed the room to expand, but he also needed a great price as he was stretched pretty far after the most recent renovations he'd made to his cabin and barn.

Jacq returned with two steaming mugs of coffee and handed him one that was exactly the way he liked it. She had obviously taken note and remembered from the time before. "So where do we start?" she asked, her blush absent.

"Start?" he asked, still thinking about what he really had imagined starting.

"Orchid care 101," she reminded him.

"Right." He pulled his attention away from his fantasies, "Well, it's really not as hard as you might think," he said. "First, you only need to water them once a week. The misting system is set up and regulated to maintain an optimum environment. They are heartier than they look and it's just a matter of being faithful to the feeding and watering schedule." Explaining about the orchids was just what he needed to get his thoughts under control.

"Okay, that sounds easy enough," she said, a little puzzled by how formal the conversation had turned, "but don't they need special fertilizer and trimming and stuff?"

"They need orchid food each week, but you just mix it into the water. You've got a good supply of it out there and I'll show you how much to mix in. They don't really need to be trimmed so much as repotted after they are finished blooming," Garrett explained as they made their way inside the green house. "There's a special soil mix you put them in when you do that, but it's really only once a year. They grow very slowly. Most of the plants bloom in the fall, but there are some that are on different schedules. Your aunt had them all positioned so the different species got the right kind of light that they needed, so as long as you don't move them around, you should be good to go."

"Well, I think I can handle that," she said. "It actually sounds easier than taking care of most house plants. The big challenge will be figuring out what to do with them all. I thought possibly one of the local nurseries might have an interest in buying them. Any ideas?"

Garrett rubbed his face with one of his big, tanned hands and scrunched up his brow as he thought about it. "Maybe. Let me think about it. I'm trying to think if any of the garden stores or nurseries around here handle anything more than the basic little gift style orchids that you see in the grocery stores. I've been babying these plants along with Emmett for so long now that I care about where they go too," he said smiling looking at the array of flowers in front of him. "I'm sure we'll figure something out."

"I hope so," she sighed. "They were like children to Aunt Rose. I want to make sure I treat them with the reverence they deserve." She gestured toward the table of pots, gloves, and planting materials she'd been sorting through. "There's so much to still go through. I'm making some good headway, but it's probably going to take me longer than I thought. I'd hoped to only be gone from work for a few months."

"Are you going to stay longer or make a second trip back?" he asked.

THE WEDDING SLIPPER   79

"I'm not sure yet. I guess it depends on whether or not I pick up speed along the way. Either way, it's okay. I had hoped to have everything dealt with in a couple of months, but it's just a goal. I can adjust the timeline if need be as I took a three month leave of absence," she stated.

"When do you plan on putting the farm on the market?" he inquired.

"Well, I had originally thought about next week, but I'm realizing now that it's way too soon. This isn't necessarily a bad thing as it will give us more time to wrap up after Lia's wedding. It's nice to not have to rush to break everything down after an event like that," she said with resolve. "A little more time will actually be good for me too. I'm finding it harder than I thought to let go of things and the farm is going to be the hardest of all to say good-bye to."

Garrett decided it wasn't quite the right time to push the subject of selling the farm. "I understand. I'd struggle with it too. If you do go back to New York for a while, I'm happy to still help look after the orchids. Emmett and I have the routine down pat now and it doesn't take very long."

"That's really nice of you. I appreciate everything you've done for me. Can I get you a warmup on your coffee?" she asked.

"No, but thanks. I didn't mean to interrupt you for so long anyway, but I wanted to make sure you knew what to do with the orchids. I should head back now to get my chores done. I'm meeting all the guys at the Longhouse tonight and if I'm not there in time to keep an eye on them, no tellin' what could happen," he declared handing her back her mug.

"Well, I'll be seeing you later then," she replied. "Nicole is picking me up and introducing me to the place tonight, so I guess it's a good thing you'll be there to keep us all out of trouble!"

Garrett smiled warmly and got up to go. "Sounds good. I'll see you there then." He walked away, heading out the back door. He found himself whistling as he was crossing the field home. The thought of beers with the boys seemed a lot more enticing than it had just 10 minutes earlier.

Jacq made her way back inside the house and sat down on the couch. She should probably do a little more sorting and packing, but the temptation to curl up on the couch for a short nap was greater than her resolve and she wanted to think more about why Garrett could fluster her so easily. She tucked her legs under the afghan and sipped the last dregs of her coffee, then set the cup down. He was cute, no doubt about it, but not any more attractive than many of the men she had dated. So, it wasn't his looks that constantly made her feel so vulnerable. It was something else, sort of a combination of things. She yawned and closed her eyes to ponder it further. Could it be that combo of military tough guy with animal/orchid loving tenderness that was throwing her for a loop? He did like to tease her and while that didn't usually unsettle her much, with him it sort of did. Was that it? She thought about how surprisingly lovely his voice was when he sang as she drifted off to sleep.

Aunt Rose handed her a towel and said, "I'll wash and you dry?"

"Sure," Jacq responded and began drying the drops off of a big tumbler that she'd sipped iced tea from earlier that day.

"So!" Aunt Rose remarked. "You like him."

THE WEDDING SLIPPER 81

"Of course, I like him," Jacq responded. "He seems like a pretty nice guy."

"You know what I mean. You LIKE him like him," Aunt Rose replied.

"I might." Jacq mused. "I'm trying to figure out exactly how I feel about him."

Aunt Rose filled the dish drainer with the remaining assortment of mugs and glasses from the morning, all washed and sparkling.

"You know Jacq, you don't have to always try to figure things out. It's okay to just let things happen now and then because they need to happen. Sometimes, love just happens. You can either let it take root, nurture it a little, and enjoy the bloom, or you can miss out if you waste too much time trying to understand it before it even gets underway. It's not hard to find attraction in life. Finding an attraction that endures and lasts long enough to achieve a rare bloom, now that's an event!"

"You make it sound so easy and yet mysterious. Are you talking about your own experience or what exactly?" Jacq asked, a little confused. "You're not suggesting that I jump into something with someone I don't know who lives 3000 miles away, are you?"

Her aunt looked up from rinsing the last of the dish soap bubbles out of the sink and turned to her with a serious look on her face. She opened her mouth to speak, but all Jacq could hear was Beethoven's "Ode to Joy" coming from out of her mouth like a singer on a stage. Jacq woke up fuzzy and confused and then realized her cell phone was ringing.

Christopher Park, her friend, and events manager at the hotel, had set up her cell phone and assigned unique tones so

82

J. KIMALIE

that she would always answer knowing who was calling and if it was important. Ode to Joy was his choice for himself.

"Chris is everything okay?" she asked.

"Well, hello Chris; so wonderful to hear from you!" Christopher teased in response. "You sound a little groggy. Are YOU okay is the question?" he shot back.

"Yes, I just nodded off for a few minutes and the phone woke me up. I must still be adjusting to the time change. So really, is everything okay?" she repeated.

"Everything's fine," he assured her. "I'm just checking in to see how it's going and to let you know you're missed. Are you getting lonely out there all by yourself? I'm still willing to take some time off to come help you, you know."

"I appreciate it," she responded with a small yawn, "but this is mostly stuff I have to take care of myself. I've met some nice people out here and so I'm not lonely at all and I'm sleeping like a baby. Besides, if I didn't have you there to take care of things in New York, who knows what I'd be returning to!"

"Well, I can see how that might be true, but then again, you know that I have everything so well organized that it could practically run without me for at least a week or two," he reminded her. "So, doing anything fun with these new best friends of yours?"

"Ha ha! You and Beth are my besties and you both know it! Actually, I'm going out tonight to meet a few of the other locals and enjoy a couple of drinks and a night off."

"What are you going to wear?" he asked curiously.

"Seriously? This isn't the city. You don't have to worry about how I look," Jacq replied, although she'd been already thinking

THE WEDDING SLIPPER   83

about what she could wear since she knew she'd be running into Garrett.

"Jacq, you have a responsibility to do your home team proud," Christopher teased, "show those northwest mountain men what they are missing out on. I'd recommend tastefully tight, and a little bit risqué. Think, sophisticated sex kitten goes hiking in the woods. "

Jacq laughed heartily, "I don't know what that would even look like and I can't imagine that if I did, it could possibly be achieved by anything out of my one suitcase. The home team will just have to make do with what I have, but because you care so much, I'll take a little extra time with my hair and make-up," she promised.

"Who is he?" he asked.

"What, who?" she asked back.

"The guy Darlin', I know you. You take great pains with your clothes and hair, but you only do make-up for someone you're attracted to. So, who's the guy?" Christopher nailed her with his observation.

"Okay, it's nothing really, but I do have a neighbor who has been flirting with me a little. Just having some fun, so don't think there's any big romance brewing here."

"Hmmm, me thinks she doth protest too much."

"Really Chris, it's not a big deal. Just passing the time and distracting myself from all the family reminders here that I'm constantly pulling myself together over. I promise, all is fine," she said with finality.

"Okay, I understand. It's got to be really tough. Like I said, I can be there in a heartbeat."

"I know, and I appreciate it. Just take care of things there and I'll check back in later in the week. But call if anything happens," she insisted.

"I will if you will," he joked. "Okay, later!"

"Bye Chris, I'm glad you called."

She hung up and saw that it was time to start getting ready for her night out. She'd slept longer than she had intended. It was a weird dream she had about doing dishes with her aunt. It was as if Aunt Rose was talking about her own love life and they'd never had a conversation like that before. As far as she knew, her aunt had never even dated since her husband had died when Jacq was too young to remember, but then again, she'd never thought much about that side of her aunt's life. Perhaps there was much more to her aunt than she'd even realized.

Chapter 11

Will Smith's *Gettin Jiggy Wit It* was spilling out of the heavy oak doors of the Longhouse as Garrett walked into the bar. He wondered if it was 90's hit night and somebody had forgotten to tell him. He also wondered if that would encourage Ian to wear a special kilt to commemorate the anniversary of the utility kilt creation in the late 90's. He only knew the history due to Ian's obsession with that particular piece of clothing.

Thursday night wasn't usually a busy night for the bar, however, it looked like the town was getting ready for the weekend. The dark wood chairs were filled with mostly locals and he took the time to shake hands and smile at acquaintances as he made his way to the bar.

The bar was a beautiful hand carved creation of deep mahogany. Donavan said it had been imported from a pub in Ireland in the 60's and had slowly made its way to Poulsbo on a circuitous route from a bankrupt millionaire's mansion to a pub in Seattle before it found a permanent home at the Longhouse. It was a whimsical piece of furniture carved with mystical creatures of the British Isles. Each corner was weighed down by reliefs of Kelpies in the shape of winged horses, with mermaids floating along wooden waves at the bottom. The rolled top of the bar

86   J. KIMALIE

sported miniature ferns leaves and cat tails. If you looked closely enough at the carving you might see little leprechaun faces peeking out amongst the foliage.

"I reserved the back room for the group," Donovan said without looking up from the drink he was mixing.

"Are you going to be able to join us or would you like me to volunteer you as part of the clean-up crew in your absence?" asked Garrett, smiling a greeting at his friend.

"I'll be there in a bit as soon as I get some relief here," said Donovan as he set a group of drinks on a tray to be swept away by a waiter.

"Roger that," Garrett said as he made his way to the back of the building.

As Garrett walked in the back room, he was welcomed by a burst of laughter from the group lounging around a scarred wooden table. Everybody looked up smiling as he entered. Ian hooked a boot clad foot around a vacant chair and pulled it out for Garrett as he approached.

"What's the joke?" Garrett asked as he took a seat between Ian and Emmett. Nicole and her fiancé Matt sat across from him with Jacq sitting next to Nicole. Lia and her fiancé Brett were sitting close together at the end of the table.

"Ian was telling stories of all the crazy bets you guys made to pass the time while camped in the desert," said Nicole. She was sitting with Matt's arm draped around her shoulders. "I can't believe you used to bet on beetle races."

Garrett chuckled, "Beetle races were the best. Of course, you had to capture the little buggers first, but it was well worth the entertainment. The prize was usually a clean pair of socks. They

THE WEDDING SLIPPER

were at a premium in the desert and Ian was allergic to doing laundry, so he was always trying to win my socks."

"What other bets did you make with each other?" inquired Jacq looking curiously between Ian and Garrett.

The guys shared a conspiratorial look. "We used to have a sergeant who owned exactly seven team t-shirts. His favorite was the Dallas Cowboys, but he had the Toronto Maple Leaf as well as the University of Southern California Trojans. There were a few others, but we would make bets which t-shirt he would wear on any given day. We would sit at morning mess with our coffee and wait for him to come through the door. It was like playing 'name that tune' except it was name that t-shirt," explained Ian, "and six times out of seven, I won!"

"That is such bullshit Gams. The man wore Dallas Cowboys every Wednesday and USC every Friday. It was some kind of ritual. I at least won on those days," laughed Garrett. "The Sarge and I used to bet on the kilts Ian would wear on his days off."

"You did not! That is not cool dude," exclaimed Ian as he tried to shove Garrett out of his chair.

The group laughed at the antics of the two friends.

Donovan quietly walked into the room with a pitcher of beer and sangria with enough clean glasses for the table. "I thought you could use some refreshments," he said in his deep voice.

"Thanks Donovan, please keep track and let me know what I owe you. Tonight, the drinks are on me because I need a big favor from all of you," said Lia looking around the table. "You all know we are getting married in just six weeks," Lia said as she locked eyes on her fiancé. "And you know I've been having a hard time finding the perfect place to have the wedding until Jacq offered up her most excellent barn, without all the dirt and cobwebs, of course. I need a clean-up and small renovation crew to get the barn looking like its habitable and fit for a wedding. My family has already volunteered, but I was wondering if you all would join the work party?"

The guys all looked at each other with various glances of "here we go" and "I knew we were in for something when we were invited tonight."

"I'm going to need something stronger than beer for this," Ian said. "I should have known not to wear a kilt in commemoration of National Wedding Month." The group chuckled already knowing the guys would help in any way they could.

"I'll have some tequila brought in," Donovan said as he walked toward the door.

"Don't forget the lime and salt," called Garrett. Donovan acknowledged the request with a backward wave of his hand. "If you are going to stage a wedding in Jacq's barn it's going to need a lot more than just a clean-up. Although the barn is sound, the paint is peeling, I'm sure there are mice and birds making the place their home and you may even have a little dry rot here and there. Are you sure that is where you want to hold your wedding?" questioned Garrett with a dubious look on his face.

"Yes," Lia said clapping her hands once with enthusiasm. "So, will you help?"

The guys all looked at each other waiting for someone to commit first.

"Hell, why not?" Donovan said as he came back into the room with a bottle of Patron and all the fixings. The others rolled their eyes.

THE WEDDING SLIPPER   89

"You didn't have to be such a push over," exclaimed Emmett. "You could have held out for something, like a week of home cooked meals or a pie a month. You are such a soft touch."

The crowd laughed, knowing full well that nobody could push Donovan anywhere unless it was a place he wanted to go.

Looking at the group, Emmett stated, "We'll need to make a list of everything that needs to be done. Jacq, do you mind if I come over tomorrow morning to take a look? At least I can outline a supply list and make sure there is nothing wrong with the barn that would prevent the wedding from happening. We wouldn't want the roof to cave in on your guests."

"Do you think it's that bad?" asked Jacq turning a worried gaze on Lia.

"It's perfectly sound," Nicole piped up. "When Jacq said she was looking to sell, I had all the buildings inspected. However, Garrett is right, it is a dusty and dirty mess."

"I'll pass out the assignments at our next Rook game. Is everybody in?" asked Emmett as he looked around at all his friends. "I'm in" chimed a variety of voices and raised hands indicating everybody would do their part to get the barn ready.

"Not you Jacq," said Lia, "you are donating your barn, you don't need to be a part of all the work. I know you already have a lot of cleaning to do in Rose's house, so you are off the hook."

"That's not necessary. I'm willing to do my part," said Jacq.

"If you don't mind, how about you take on the job of providing something to drink at the clean-up party. Nothing alcoholic, as we'll have to keep the guys working," smiled Lia looking at all the faces turned toward her.

"Okay, now that's settled. Who's up for a friendly game of darts?" asked Garrett slapping his hands on his jean-clad thighs.

"I'll play," said Jacq, much to Garrett's surprise. Given his dubious look, Jacq said defensively, "What, you don't think I can beat you at darts?"

Garrett watched in fascination as Jacq walked toward him with a swagger and an arrogant wink. "I won't have any problems beating a country boy."

As Jacq and Garrett moved toward the dart board, Garrett questioned, "What are we playing for city girl?" Jacq narrowed her eyes and looked around. Spotting the Patron on the table, she gave Garrett a devilish grin.

Garrett wondered what he'd gotten himself into. That grin looked like nothing good was going to come his way.

"We'll play for my brand of tequila shots," said Jacq with a raised eyebrow, taunting Garrett to take her up on it.

"I don't know what that is but you're on," whispered Garrett in her ear. "Let's play noughts and crosses or x's and o's, three rounds, three darts per person each round. The person with the highest score wins."

"Okay," Jacq said. All her bravado had fled as she was still trying to recover from the shiver that moved through her frame when she had felt Garrett's breath in her ear. Sheesh, if she could be turned on by just a little whisper, she wondered what his kiss would do to her. Why was she thinking about his kisses when she should be thinking about winning the dart game?

The group was chatting about everything that needed to be done to the barn as Jacq and Garrett squared up in front of the dart board. Picking up the blue feathered darts, round one went to Garrett and round two to Jacq. They were pretty evenly matched. As the last round drew to a close, the winner whooped out a victory yell and the crowd cheered.

Chapter 12

The soft slap of cards being thrown in the center of table could be heard as the men concentrated on counting cards. Groans and mutters emanated from Ian and Emmett as the last card was thrown on the table and Donovan scooped them up in triumph.

"Loser has to serve," crowed Garrett as Donovan counted the points, they had won in the last hand which handily put them over the five hundred points they needed to be victorious.

"I think two fingers of Ian's scotch would go down smooth right about now," smirked Donovan as Ian clutched his bottle of Oban to his chest.

"I hate when we lose," Ian complained as he reluctantly got up to grab a glass for Donovan. "I suppose you want a taste of this nectar of the gods too?" he shot over his shoulder at Garrett on his way to kitchen.

"No, I'll take the Guinness that's in the fridge," said Garrett.

"That's probably the last Guinness," grumbled Emmett as he followed Ian out of the room.

The two friends grinned at each other across the table. "I love beating their asses," said Donovan, "It makes putting up with Ian's abysmal lack of fashion sense worth it."

"I heard that," shouted Ian from the kitchen. Ian was sporting a strawberry red utility kilt with black straps and silver buckles. He had paired it with a bright yellow t-shirt with a winking happy face emblazoned on the front and his usual black army boots were on his feet.

Garrett and Donovan laughed and bumped fists. "Have you heard from Jacq about the farm?" asked Donovan.

"No, last time we discussed it she said Nicole was working on a sale price," Garrett replied. "I'll give Nicole a few days and give her a call."

"You do know the quicker the sale goes through, the quicker she leaves," said Donovan.

Garrett looked at Donovan with a question in his blue eyes. "What do you mean?" asked Garrett. "She was always going to leave."

Donovan casually shuffled the deck of cards. "I got the impression the other night at the bar that her leaving was the last thing on your mind."

Garrett didn't want to go there with his friend. He couldn't afford to let his feelings get tangled up in Jacq, no matter how much he wanted to see where their flirting might take them. Every night this week he had gone to sleep with her on his mind and she was still there when he woke up in the morning. He remembered playing darts, her competitive spirit, and her beaming smile when she won the bet. It seemed his feelings were already a little bit out of control.

"I'm out a bottle of tequila from that dart game. I was told to bring the good stuff," said Garrett changing the subject, thinking about the New York style of tequila shots Jacq had hinted at. Garrett had been wondering about those shots since he had said

THE WEDDING SLIPPER 93

goodbye to her in front of the Longhouse. He needed to work a visit to the liquor store into his already packed schedule before his curiosity killed him.

Donovan let Garrett off the hook and didn't follow up on his comments about Garrett's interest in Jacq. "I don't know Jacq well, but there seems to be a mischievous spirit hidden under those expensive city clothes, so it could be just about anything. Maybe a New York tequila shot is delivered with a raised pinky, or something else specific to those that live in the Big Apple," said Donovan.

"Yeah, maybe," Garrett muttered as Ian and Emmett strolled back into the card room with drinks and snacks.

The card room was Garrett's favorite room in his house. It was just this side of too classy to be a man-cave. Sort of a cross between a gentlemen's smoking parlor, a beer joint, and a library. Built in bookcases lined two walls filled with biographies, war novels, history, and animal husbandry books. He knew that people mostly read books online now, but there was something comforting about sitting among your favorite stories that made you feel a part of something bigger. One wall sported a tribute to those who died in the Vietnam War in a print of Lee Teter's work "Reflections". The last wall had pictures of all shapes and sizes making up a collage of all the animals that had come to convalesce with Garrett. All those healthy animal faces reminded him of Phoenix rising from the ashes.

"So, what do you think about our new friend Jacq?" asked Ian, reluctantly handing a glass of scotch to Donovan. Donovan lips twitched as he looked at Garrett with one eyebrow raised.

"Why is everyone so interested in Jacq all of the sudden?" asked Garrett gruffly.

"Is the topic of Jacq off limits?" asked Ian widening his eyes, trying to look innocent. "It seemed to me you two were pretty chummy the other night. Do you have your heart set on the city girl? Are you going to make an honest woman out of her?"

Garrett's lips thinned as he looked at his friend with irritation. "We just made a friendly bet over a game of darts. Can't a guy have fun with a beautiful woman once in a while?"

"Of course," Ian nodded sagely. "Of course, you can, but you don't usually and that is what makes this all so intriguing." Ian had his elbows up on the table tapping his fingertips together like he was a detective interrogating an unwitting suspect.

"Our relationship is off limits," said Garrett quietly.

"Oh ho, now it's a relationship!" exclaimed Ian, "this just gets more and more interesting."

Seeing Garrett's shoulders tense, Donovan intervened between the two friends. "Ian, what's with the big yellow happy face?"

Graciously Ian allowed the change of subject. "It's National Retro Day. What could be more retro than a happy face, plus I want to spread positive thinking and cheer wherever I go," said Ian with a big cheesy smile.

"How's that working out for you?" asked Emmett with a frown on his face.

The friends burst into laughter, smoothing over any tension left in the room.

Garrett knew his friends meant well, but his feelings for Jacq were complicated. One minute he wanted to live in the moment with her and enjoy the flirting and easy camaraderie. The next minute he wanted to ask her out on a real date where they could talk and really get to know each other and see if they could build

THE WEDDING SLIPPER   95

something for the future. His mind tried to shut down when looking further ahead. He didn't want to fall for a woman who was set on living in a huge city across the country. He didn't want to put his heart out there and have it rejected. He had already had a lot of pain in his life. He was honored to serve his country, but it came with the price of lingering sorrow of having to say goodbye to friends and comrades either permanently through death or temporarily through constant deployment. He just didn't know if he had the strength to go there again.

Chapter 13

Lia phoned Jacq letting her know that the work party would be gathering late Sunday morning to clean out the barn for the wedding. Graciously, Lia reminded Jacq she was off the hook for the menial labor but invited her to join the work crew at the Longhouse for a late lunch or an early dinner, whatever the case may be, when the work was complete. Lia also wanted the opportunity to introduce Jacq to her family.

"My mom especially wants to meet you and personally thank you for the generous use of your place," Lia gushed. "I had her so concerned that a little more than a month before the wedding I still had not landed on a venue. She was convinced that she would be hosting a standing room only ceremony in her tiny backyard or, in case of rain, cramming everyone into her family room which would have been even more crowded. I can't tell you how relieved she is," Lia continued, "and so am I for that matter, I really can't thank you enough."

Jacq asked when she needed to let Lia know if she would be joining them at the Longhouse as Jacq was making decent headway on her "sort and export" project and did not want to lose momentum. Lia assured Jacq she could decide on Sunday at the last minute as the gathering would be extremely informal

THE WEDDING SLIPPER   97

with most people heading straight to the bar from the barn cleaning.

Sunday morning rolled around drizzly and cool. Jacq lingered in bed with a cup of steaming coffee and was thumbing through the hiking trail book she had found in Aunt Rose's collection when Beth telephoned. The friends spent some enjoyable time catching each other up on what was happening in their two worlds. Jacq reflected upon New York and Poulsbo being polar opposites in so many ways. Jacq had been at Aunt Rose's for less than two weeks and she was already meeting people and was somewhere on the scale of moving from having acquaintances to friends; something almost impossible to do in New York given the same period of time. She had been told that people were more friendly on the west coast and she always wrote off those comments to regional rivalries. Maybe there was something to it after all or maybe it was just the difference between a big city and a small rural town. Either way, Jacq had expected to long to return to New York the minute she set foot off the plane in Seattle and instead she found herself enjoying the respite from the hustle and bustle of her very scheduled life in New York.

During the call Beth had picked up on the change in Jacq's demeanor from even a month ago and hoped she was coming out of her completely understandable state of depression. It had been so hard for Beth and Jacq's other friends to watch Jacq bury her parents and aunt, sort out her parent's estate, and to witness her folding in on herself as a survival mechanism. Beth had been concerned when Jacq declined company to work on her aunt's place, but Beth sensed that day by day Jacq was becoming more like her pre-tragedy self. Beth desperately hoped so as she wanted her old friend back, even though she knew Jacq was forever changed. How could one not change given the grief Jacq had endured and the fallout she was still sorting through? The two friends rang off promising to talk again soon.

Even though Jacq knew it was time to get out of bed, she stayed put a bit longer feeling grateful Lia had given her a graceful way out of the dirt and grime awaiting the work party. Although, if she pitched in to help, she might just get a chance to visit with Garrett and with any luck he would be filling out the same jeans she had first seen him in. Laying in a clean warm bed, the price of dirty work on a cold day seemed too high a price to pay to cavort with Garrett when he would probably be too busy to pay her any mind. Perhaps she would accept Lia's invitation to join them all at the Longhouse later in the day. Reality came crashing back to Jacq. "What was she thinking anyway?" She was returning to New York in two months or sooner if she could close out Aunt Rose's estate earlier than planned. She just needed to get Garrett out of her mind, but darn, if those mental images of him liked to linger in her psyche.

Around eleven, Jacq noticed cars, a pick-up truck or two, and what must be a deranged, kilt wearing, Ian on a motorcycle, pulling up to the barn. Really now, was that a utility kilt he was wearing again on such a drippy cool day? Oh god, she hoped the wild looking Scot hadn't caught her looking out the window as he dismounted his motorcycle and gave her a most unexpected view of what most certainly should have stayed covered. She thankfully realized that he was probably too far away for him to spot her peering out the window. Out of Jacq's peripheral vision she saw Garrett coming out of his back door, and wouldn't you know it, Jacq thought, he had on what looked to be *those* jeans

THE WEDDING SLIPPER 99

that he filled out so well. Jacq was still taking in the fit of his jeans when she realized he was headed her way and not toward the barn. Jacq hurriedly backed away from the window not wanting to be caught spying. She raced into the kitchen quickly piling some dirty dishes into the sink. A minute later she heard three quick raps at the door.

She opened the door to see Garrett standing there with a push broom in his hand broom part up. Jacq grinned as Garrett's stance reminded her of the man holding the pitchfork in the famous American Gothic painting. Had Garrett walked out of his house with the broom she wondered? Apparently, she had been focused on other parts of him to know for sure.

"Good morning," Jacq said, "come on in out of the cold if you'd like."

"No, I better not," Garrett said, "I have to get over to the barn. I was just wondering if I could borrow your push broom from the greenhouse?"

"If I have a push broom, you are welcome to it," Jacq replied.

"You do," Garrett assured her, "and I'll put it back when we're done. What smells so good?" Garrett pondered aloud.

"I'm baking cookies to bring over to the work crew in a couple hours. I thought some freshly baked cookies and hot coffee might be cause for a welcome respite for the troops," Jacq offered.

As if on cue the timer went off and Jacq turned toward the oven reaching for the hot pad on the counter as she passed by. As she nimbly took the cookie sheet out of the oven, Garrett having followed her into the kitchen asked, "They're not oatmeal, are they?"

Jacq raised an eyebrow and said, "You'll have to make do with snickerdoodles today."

"Any chance a do-gooder could snag one hot out of the oven?" Garrett inquired in a pleading, almost boyish, tone.

"For you or for Angel?" Jacq taunted.

"Oh, definitely for me," Garrett replied, as he took a tentative step toward Jacq and said in a seductive tone, "I adore sugar and spice."

Jacq could not help herself, her thoughts flitted back to how flabbergasted she had been when Garrett began feeding her lovingly baked cookies to the emaciated horse, and she started snickering at the recollection. Garrett shot her a puzzled look given he had just flirted a little with her, that prompted the snickers to advance to laughter that escalated close to the point of convulsions.

She got herself under control and exclaimed, "Unless it has raisins or oatmeal in it." The alluring spell Garrett was attempting to weave was broken as he too began chuckling.

"Not one of my better moves to show appreciation," he acknowledged with good humor. "But I assure you, the cookies you gave me were just what the vet would have ordered to give Angel a reason to live. I've been breaking them up and mixing them in with her feed. She can't resist them, and I can't resist one of these," he declared, as he reached across the counter and picked up a hot cookie which broke apart in his hand.

"Hot, hot, hot," Garrett cried, as he juggled the large pieces of the crumbling cookie. By the time the pillowy cookie chunks hit the counter, Jacq had fetched a tea towel and, in an automatic motherly gesture like Jacq's mother had done for her on more than one occasion, she quickly wiped off the hot buttery residue

THE WEDDING SLIPPER 101

from Garrett's fingers and kissed each fingertip pronouncing them, "all better!" When her gaze lifted to meet Garrett's, she instantly realized that Garrett had not at all taken her gesture in a motherly way. He was looking at her with an intensity and hunger that was undeniable. It looked as though he had forgotten all about the cookie and was about to devour her.

Her heart began to race as Garrett slowly moved toward her and then it skipped a beat when one thunderous knock at the door broke the spell between them.

A booming voice, matching the resounding knock, on the other side of the door loudly proclaimed, "Send out the deserter and no one will get hurt."

Jacq watched Garrett shoulders deflate and his eyes close as he loudly exhaled. Garrett was fervently wishing for the interloper to magically disappear. Garrett wanted to throttle Ian and his blasted timing. Instead, Garrett walked to the door and opened it with a sweeping gesture of his arm and the larger than life, kilt wearing, Ian entered Jacq's kitchen. The warm smile and twinkle in the eyes of the barrel shaped man gave away he was more teddy bear than madman. Jacq was instantly at ease in his presence until she uncomfortably remembered the flash of flesh from under his kilt.

"Jacq, you remember Ian, or Gams as we often refer to him on days when he wears his kilt, which seems to be happening more and more often," Garrett announced "Gams, you already know Jacq, Rose's niece."

"Nice to see you again," Ian said with a slight bow of his head. Looking around the kitchen and taking in the scene and the perturbed look on Garrett's face, he added with a questioning expression, "I hope I didn't interrupt a game of patty cakes or anything."

"I came to fetch a broom," stated Garret somewhat defensively and clearly annoyed.

"It looks like you already have a fetching broom," Ian retorted feeling quite clever as he pointed to the broom in the corner of the kitchen where Garrett had left it just moments ago. "I came to fetch another broom, so you'd have something to do," Garrett snapped.

"Then lead on captain oh my captain," Ian wisecracked dramatically as he winked at Jacq, "the groom awaits his 'broomsmen.'"

Jacq watched the two buddies enter the greenhouse and each one exited armed with a push broom as they headed in the direction of their awaiting chores. She was both amused by and slightly irritated with Ian, really it was just his timing that irritated her. She had been relishing the kiss that she was sure had been coming before Ian swept on the scene. She groaned at the pun her thoughts had conjured describing Ian's arrival and then giggled at both Ian's flare for the dramatic and Garrett's obvious disappointment at the untimely interruption. How good it felt to giggle again! It had been so long since she was cheered by silliness and even longer since her body was awakened by the attention of an attractive man. Decision made, she would be going to the dinner this evening and maybe, just maybe, they could pick up where she and Garrett left off.

A couple hours later, Jacq was picking her way across the wet field, carefully avoiding tripping hazards. She was balancing a heavy tray loaded with a large Tupperware container full of cookies along with a gigantic thermos of coffee and colorful

THE WEDDING SLIPPER 103

floral paper napkins and cups seemingly at odds with the gray day. Approximately a third of the way to the barn, two streaks raced toward her at alarming speed. Jacq braced herself for a raucous greeting and what she hoped would not be a disastrous impact as Nitro and Sadie quickly closed the ground between them and her. From somewhere in the direction of the barn a high-pitched whistle stopped the dogs in their tracks. Both dogs, almost in unison, turned around trotting back toward the barn, each looking over their shoulders back at Jacq, with what looked like expressions of resignation, before heading directly toward their master.

Garrett's handsome form emerged from the side of the barn and pointed to his house, gave the dogs a command that Jacq was not able to make out from her distance, and the dogs obediently loped back to Garrett's place. With easy athletic strides a smiling Garrett was soon standing in front of Jacq offering to take the heavily laden tray.

"Thanks for the canine rescue," Jacq voiced, "I imagined me and everything on the tray ending up in the muddy grass."

"I have them better trained than that," Garrett assured her, "but they did seem happy to see you as will everyone else. Your timing is impeccable. We were all just stopping for a break." Garrett and Jacq walked companionably the rest of the way to the group scattered around the gaping doors. At the site of Jacq entering the barn, which by this point was much cleaner and more organized than when Jacq had last seen it, Lia jumped up from where she was resting and introduced Jacq to her family and friends.

The next half hour went by in a blur of lively introductions and genuine thanks being poured out to Jacq for her openhandedness and largesse in offering the barn for the wedding and her thoughtfulness in supplying coffee and cookies for the work party. Normally Jacq could feel quite awkward in situations in which she was the only odd person out of a group that was well acquainted with one another. But Lia's mother and her entire family had a way of embracing a stranger as part of their own clan. Lia's friends were equally engaging and welcoming and Ian had not wasted an opportunity to amuse Jacq with some witty banter entertaining both her and Donovan, his more circumspect friend. By the time the cookies were devoured, the thermos emptied, and the break deemed over, Jacq felt like an honorary member of the family. Somehow, in less than thirty minutes, Lia's folks had managed to secure Jacq's commitment to attend the wedding and meet the group at the Longhouse later in the day without Jacq feeling pressured or trapped into accepting their sweet invitations.

Coffee break concluded; Jacq swiveled her head in search of the tray to carry back to the house. Her eyes landed on Garrett's muscular form casually leaning against the barn door with the tray dangling from one hand, the coffee thermos in the other hand, and the empty plastic container on the ground beside him. Walking toward Garrett to collect the serving gear Jacq noticed that he didn't budge, his alert, azure blue eyes not leaving hers.

When Jacq was within range for Garrett to hand over the implements, he still didn't move which forced Jacq to step in closer to him in order to retrieve the items. Just at that moment Garrett pushed away from the barn door to stand completely upright and their bodies ended up lightly brushing up against each other's, close enough to feel the heat emanating from each of them. Before Jacq had a chance to back up a bit, Garrett

THE WEDDING SLIPPER 105

leaned in and kissed her on the cheek and whispered in her ear, "Thank you for the mighty fine cookies, they beat the heck out of the oatmeal ones."

Neither one moved, both rooted in place, Jacq in surprise and Garrett in anticipation of how Jacq might react. Jacq felt her cheek burning hot where Garrett's soft, yet firm, lips had pressed into her skin. Rather than back up, Jacq stood firm taking in Garrett's scent which smelled of cedar with a slight hint of cinnamon.

"You're welcome," Jacq finally replied rather breathlessly. She so desperately wanted to wrap her arms around this man and lose herself in his effortless masculinity and strong limbs. But now was neither the time nor the place. Instead, Jacq looked down at her hands having to move them only inches to collect the tray and Thermos. Reluctantly, Garrett handed them over, their hands grazing in the process sending chills up her arms and down her spine. Garrett was forced to sidestep in order to bend down to collect the plastic container from the ground, his back still nearly pinned against the barn as door Jacq had not relinquished even an inch of real estate. Garrett was hopelessly drawn to how Jacq was tender and formidable at the same time. He was torn between wanting to know her better and not wanting to fall for the intelligent, gorgeous, intriguing, redheaded women standing before him, as he suspected he might easily do. She was, he reminded himself, returning to New York in a couple months. Confounding logistics and poor timing were the bane of his only two, somewhat serious, past relationships and would thwart a possible one with Jacq as well. Garrett sighed inwardly, as Jacq confidently and unhurriedly turned and reluctantly walked back to the house. Once again, Garrett leaned against the barn door and unabashedly took in the delectable view of Jacq's backside until she disappeared out of site.

Chapter 14

Jacq strode confidently to the house with a self-satisfied smile on her face. She had no doubt that she and Garrett were feeling mutual attraction and that he could be left feeling quite as unsettled as she had at times. Just as she walked through the door, she heard the chime of her cell phone indicating she'd received a text. "Would you like a ride to dinner tonight? I could swing by and pick you up." He was thinking about her too, just as she thought. "Sure, that would be great" she answered with a smiley emoji. "Pick you up at 6:30" was the reply.

The writing was on the wall—Jacq was going to have to decide whether or not to plunge in and see if the sparks between them meant anything or not. Even if it was only for a little while, it might be nice to enjoy the feel of a man's arms around her and the excitement that a new relationship brings. Or she could be honest with herself and face facts—she wouldn't be here for more than another couple of months at the most and if something did start to develop it couldn't possibly end painlessly. Jacq wasn't the type of person who flitted from one relationship to the next.

There had been a few very nice men in her life, but nobody that ever felt like "the one" and so no relationship had made it past the one-year mark. She had no desire to waste her time

108   **J. KIMALIE**

or someone else's. So why be tempted now? Perhaps it was the span of time without anyone that was prompting it. She had not actually dated anyone since losing her family. But after she stepped off the plane, she felt she had taken the first baby step toward healing and had started to think about opening up more with friends about how she was feeling. Could this be the beginning of being able to move on? Her parents had always encouraged her to "go with your gut" and not over think decisions that weren't absolutely life changing. Maybe she was making too big a deal out of this as well. She was drawn to the guy, so what would be the harm in a little flirtation if it felt right in the moment? The answer seemed easy—nothing at all.

A leisurely hot shower later, Jacq perused her closet and decided on a fitted, soft, rose-colored Ralph Lauren flannel shirt that looked good tucked into her skinny jeans. A belt and a pair of ankle high boots completed the ensemble and she declared herself to be dressed rural chic. Christopher would approve. She took a little extra time with her make-up, chuckling to herself about his comment that fussing with her make-up meant she had met someone she was attracted to. Chris knew her so well. Then, she finished up by clasping on a moonstone bracelet her mother had given to her for one of her birthdays and a pair of gold hoop earrings. She was pulling her teal colored, boiled wool jacket out of the downstairs closet when she heard a friendly knock at the door.

Garrett opened the door part way and leaned in. "Your driver is here," he called out in a cheery voice and then opened it wider for her when he saw she was near. "Dinner awaits us and I'm hungry enough to clean out the entire kitchen," he added gesturing her through the door with a cavalier flourish. He

THE WEDDING SLIPPER 109

walked her to his silver SUV and opened the passenger door for her. "Do you need an assist up?" he asked, as the vehicle had been raised substantially.

"No, I can manage," she replied hoisting herself up. "It's sort of like mounting a horse. I take it you need something that can handle off road conditions in your line of work?"

"You nailed it," he responded. "Sometimes the dogs and I have to go into some pretty rugged areas and the closer we can get to the last point of contact, the better." He closed the door securely and walked around to the driver's side. His car was fairly tidy and organized, just like his house and barn. It had a very slight but not overpowering scent of dog and she wondered if he had cleaned it up just for her tonight.

"So, you ride?" he asked as he pulled out of the drive and headed toward town.

"I haven't in a while, but yes, I grew up riding and have always enjoyed it, especially getting out on the trails. I don't know which is better, getting away from everyone and out into the forest, or watching the horses enjoy themselves when they get the chance to go on an adventure. It's all pretty wonderful!"

"When was the last time you went trail riding?

"Oh, it's been quite a while. I didn't get the chance to ride much while I was away at college and then I moved and my career became my focus, so it's been probably about seven or eight years. Maybe I'll get the chance again someday."

"Maybe I can help with that," he replied. "I rode all the time as a kid and had hoped I might have a chance to in some capacity in the army, but it didn't happen. I always knew I'd be around horses when I got out though. They go hand in hand with search and rescue operations here in the northwest and one day I'd like

110   **J. KIMALIE**

to take some of the rehabilitated horses from my equine rescue and put them to work. It seems like a natural fit."

Garrett continued to talk comfortably about his plans for his business and before long they arrived at the Longhouse. From the looks of the parking lot, the place was hopping, and an evening of fun appeared promising.

They went inside and saw that many of the gang had already arrived and commandeered a large table near the back. Lia and Brett were seated at the head of the table flanked by her parents on one side and Nicole on the other. Ian was parked at the other end with an empty chair on each side of him. Pitchers of beer, and ice water, along with a couple of carafes of wine congregated in the center and baskets of tortilla chips and platters of wings were within reach from each end. Jacq took the chair to Ian's right and Garrett sat down to his left. Ian spread his wings wide and rested them on the tops of each of their chairs in a sort of welcoming embrace. "Hey, ho you two, I thought you'd never get here," he announced, before removing his arm from only Garrett's chair and taking a sip of red wine.

"You're so full of it Gams, we're early and you know it," Garrett shot back at him. "Now how about passing a glass and some of that wine down this way, unless Jacq would like something else?"

"Red wine sounds great," Jacq noted and smiled at the twinkle she saw in Ian's eyes. "Ian, I wouldn't have taken you for a vino man"

"No?" he asked with a hand over his heart. "What do you think I should be drinking?"

"Well, anything you want of course, but you seemed to be sort of the Scotch whiskey type, or possibly Guinness. Probably

THE WEDDING SLIPPER   111

the power of suggestion from the kilts, but I think I'd guess that anyway."

"Well, you'd be right my dear," Ian replied. "I am a scotch drinker and occasionally I do enjoy a cold Guinness, but today I decided to take a walk on the vineyard side. Plus, now I have the added bonus of enjoying something in common with you."

"Such a ladies' man," joked Garrett. "You better watch out for him Jacq. He likes to pull out the charm whenever a pretty gal crosses his path and "working" here behind the bar when he's in the mood, well, you can imagine how often that happens."

Ian laughed and ran a hand through his wavy, red hair and leaned back in his chair. "I can't help it if I can't resist a pretty face. I don't mean to be charming—it just comes by me naturally."

Lia waved to Jacq to beckon her down to the other end of the table, so Jacq excused herself and left the guys to continue to tease each other.

"Brett and I want to thank you again for being the angel who's loaning us the barn," Lia said.

"It's really my pleasure," Jacq said, "plus it's nice to have the help getting the barn all cleaned up. Who doesn't like a good win-win?"

Brett stood up and pulled her into a friendly half hug. "We didn't have much of a chance to get to know each other earlier so I'm so glad to thank you in person too. I felt terrible about missing most of the work party today, but my work sometimes changes my plans at the last minute if a kid calls with a problem. It's sure nice what you're doing for us. We both appreciate it so much!"

Lia's fiancé had a warm, friendly nature that likely served him well as a high school counselor. He was taller than Jacq but didn't tower over her. He had dark hair and eyes, caramel skin, and looked as if he might have pacific island origins. She instantly felt comfortable around him and returned his hug. "It's my pleasure. I'm so happy for both of you and glad I could help." Brett and Lia both gave off such positive energy that it was easy to see that they made a wonderful couple. "I'm looking forward to the wedding. I never thought I'd have the chance to be part of such a special event having just arrived."

"You made my Lia's dream come true, so you're family now," he said seriously.

"Really, it was just good timing. One of those things meant to be," she told him with a pat on his arm.

Lia was beaming and gave her a hug as well. "Fate may have made our paths cross, but you made it possible, so please, enjoy dinner and drink up and just know that we're always here for you too," she added.

Jacq was pleased at the feeling of belonging that the happy couple bestowed on her and was smiling when she went back to her chair. Ian had stepped away for something and Jacq sat down to a welcomed glass of wine. With only two sips in, she heard the bar music stop, a pause, and then the old-time juke box kicked into gear. Next thing she knew, Ian was at her side with his hand reaching out to her. "Care to dance?" he asked.

She laughed and took his hand. "Sure," she replied, "this is a first for me. I'm wearing the pants and my dance partner is in the skirt."

He grinned broadly and led her out to the dance floor as the Righteous Brothers began crooning "Unchained Melody."

THE WEDDING SLIPPER 113

He snapped her into his arms and began leading her expertly in a dance that was something of a hybrid between a foxtrot and a rumba. She couldn't help but grin back and ask where he learned to dance like that. "Miss Sabrina Stevenson's Dance Studio," he replied. Jacq shook her head in wonder and enjoyed the dance. When it ended, he pulled her hand up to his lips and gave it a short, chaste kiss and then he curtsied. She in turn, batted her lashes at him with staged exaggeration and bowed, much to the delight of the table of patrons sitting closest to the dance floor.

"That was, well, something," she proclaimed.

"Thanks for the dance," he replied. "Although, I think you'll find that my friend wasn't too happy about it."

"I don't understand," she said with a puzzled look on her face.

"Garrett didn't like it," he said with a slight nod over his shoulder. "I saw the look on his face when I asked you out on the dance floor. You know, I have to say that I haven't seen my buddy care one way or the other who I dance with in...well, ever. I think he is rather taken with you."

Jacq wasn't sure how to respond so she simply asked, "Was it your intention to get to him?"

"He's the brother I never had and as good a guy as you'll ever meet. I wasn't trying to get to him, but I did want to satisfy my curiosity", Ian replied earnestly. Let's go back and put him out of his misery," he continued, and they headed back to the table. Garrett watched them approach but didn't give anything away. He continued to drink his wine and said that the table was ordering dinner now and he'd held their menus for them. Donovan and Emmett both arrived while Jacq and Ian were dancing. Emmett pulled up a chair and squeezed into the space between her and Ian. He looked relaxed and was enjoying a glass of beer, but rose up to greet her and, ever the gentleman, hold her chair when she sat back down at the table. Jacq thanked him and chatted a little about the past couple of days.

Everyone ordered what they wanted for dinner and the laughter grew as the beverages were emptied and refilled. When dinner was served the food was attacked and the buzz only diminished slightly. Once the plates were cleared, the glasses continued to get refilled, and conversations became a little more directed but still gregarious. Chairs got exchanged now and then so that everyone got a chance to talk to each other and the conversation flowed as easily as the booze. Jacq looked around and saw that the entire bar was full of tables where people were doing the same. Nobody appeared to be there to close a business deal or to see and be seen. Everyone seemed to be there to unwind from their day and enjoy the cozy camaraderie that exuded from one wide plank wall to the other.

She looked for the first time at the Native American art on the walls—rich colors of the earth with totem symbols screened onto framed prints as well as baskets, weavings with shells worked into the knots, and blankets hung on rods mounted to the wall. Here and there were various types of antlers—moose, elk, deer, and strangely, a small pair sprouting from a wild rabbit's head. Emmett saw the point of her attention and leaned over to speak into her ear so she could be heard over the noise. "That's a Pacific Northwest Jackalope," he informed her. "A very rare find because they are shy and wily, and they know how to hide themselves really well."

"You think I've never seen a Jackalope before?" She asked him with a wink. "Why, I've just never seen one so small. Back

THE WEDDING SLIPPER 115

east, Jackalopes are three times that size! Maybe that's why they aren't as shy, and we see them everywhere."

Emmett slapped her on the back and laughed and she chuckled along with him. Jacq couldn't remember when she had felt so comfortable with people as quickly as she did with this whole gang. They made it easy to fit in and she felt as though she'd know them for years rather than weeks. The thought of not seeing them again after she went back home tugged a little at her heartstrings.

Garrett was sharing stories with Donovan, but he managed to catch Jacq's eye and smile without breaking stride. She smiled back and felt that ever present tug a little stronger. After a little while longer, Lia announced that she was "pitifully pooped" and ready for her feather bed and down comforter. Jacq glanced at her watch and saw that it was after eleven already and couldn't tamp down a yawn that escaped with the awareness.

"That sounds like and looks like our cue," Garrett said as he reached in his back pocket and pulled out a billfold.

"Don't you even think about it buster!" Lia shot out at him, catching him before he could open his wallet. "You get to help us get the place ready, but that's all you're in for. Try it again and I'll have your hide!" The gang laughed and Garrett slipped the billfold back in his pocket.

"Okay, consider me educated," he quipped and held out Jacq's coat to help her into it.

Everyone else followed suit and as a group, they made their way outside and finished their goodbyes. Once again, Garrett held the door for Jacq and then got in and turned on the ignition. "We'll let it warm up for a few minutes," he said as he saw her shiver slightly. It wasn't too terribly cold outside, but there was a light frost on the windshield. "Did you enjoy the night out?"

"Very much," she answered. "I really like the whole gang and you and your buddies are pretty entertaining when you're all together."

"You seemed to find Ian rather entertaining," he said in a slightly inquisitive voice.

"Yes, Ian is a hoot. I can't help but wonder what he's like when he's not joking around. He made a point of telling me how much he values his friendship with you."

"We've been through a lot together," Garrett replied. "I don't think there's anything we wouldn't do for each other if it came down to it. We kid around a lot but we're like family in the end."

The night sky was lit up with a nearly full moon and stars galore. No clouds or bright streetlights dimmed their brilliance.

"It's chilly, but a pretty stunning night sky. Do you mind a quick detour on the way home? We can go straight back if you're tired and not up for it," Garrett said.

"No, I'm game," she said. She pulled her coat tighter and buttoned it all the way up.

Garrett was pleased with her response and drove down into town, past all the closed shops and turned into the entrance that led them to the marina on Liberty Bay. He parked the SUV, grabbed a blanket from the backseat and helped her down. Tucking her hand in his arm, he led her down by the docks and navigated to the end of one that had a bench that looked out over the entire bay. It was fairly quiet, with just the steady sound of the waves gently lapping against the boats and a nearby line clanging rhythmically against a pole or possibly a metal mast. Several docks over, there was a soft glow lighting up one of the

THE WEDDING SLIPPER 117

moored sailboats and she could see the silhouette of someone inside their cabin reading.

They sat down and Garrett tucked the blanket gently around her. "I like to come here sometimes and just absorb the moon and starlight," he said in little more than a whisper. "Especially after I come back from a difficult search and rescue."

Jacq didn't say anything but lifted the side of the blanket to offer him some of it too. He nodded and accepted. They sat quietly, side by side, comfortable without having to converse. Time passed by, but neither of them could have told you how long they had been sitting. Now and then, they'd see the dark shape of a seabird pass quietly across the low sky in front of them. In the distance, a small boat with lights chugged by, on its way to some nearby destination.

"Cold?" Garrett asked looking at her thoughtfully.

"Maybe just a little," she quietly replied, "but I'm not ready to leave yet."

He shifted closer to her and put his arm around her shoulders and nudged her into his warmth in a way that seemed caring and natural. She gently leaned her head on his shoulder, and they continued to take in the peacefulness and beauty of their surroundings. Being there at that moment with him, felt totally and completely right to Jacq. And being there at that moment with her, felt totally and completely right to Garrett. The growing trust between them created a sense of comfort. While the attraction had taken root, these feelings were something different and yet equally special. Try though she might, Jacq couldn't stifle a small shiver as a little more time passed, and the temperature dipped. "I can tell you're cold and I should take you home now," Garrett whispered.

118   **J. KIMALIE**

"I don't want to leave, but I think it is time," she whispered back.

They walked silently back to the car and headed home. Garrett turned on the stereo and acoustic guitar music resumed playing from whenever he'd last had it on. It was soothing and matched the mood of the moment perfectly. They listened to it all the way back to the farm where Garrett turned off the ignition and unbuckled his seatbelt but didn't immediately jump out. Jacq undid hers and waited for him to speak. There was no sense of urgency as the peaceful turn of the night still had them in its embrace.

Garrett turned toward her and softly lifted her hair with the back of his hand. His hand was warm, and he smoothed it over behind her neck and gently pulled her over toward him. There was no hesitation, just a slow steady movement as his lips descended toward hers. His kiss was tentative, light at first, and testing to see if she was receptive to it. She answered with a soft moan and parted her lips to welcome him further. He pulled her tighter and deepened his response, leaving no question that he knew how to kiss a woman and clearly wanted to be kissing her.

Jacq felt lightheaded as she melted into his embrace, nipping slightly at his lower lip when he came up for air. He smiled and kissed her once more soundly and then pulled back a little. "It's late," he said softly into her right ear, and then playfully tugged on her earlobe with his teeth.

"I think you found a way to help me warm up," she murmured and smiled back her face nuzzling against his cheek.

Garrett gently pulled back and opened his door, then came around to her side. He opened her door and lifted her down but kept his hands on each side of her waist for a little longer than necessary. "What would you say to going on a proper date with me?" he asked.

"Is that an invitation or a what if?"

"It's an actual invitation. Tuesday night at six?"

"I'd say you've got yourself a date," she said in a quiet voice.

Garrett answered with just a smile and walked her to the door. "Good night Jacq." He leaned forward and marked her forehead with a tender kiss and watched her step inside.

"Good night, Garrett. Thanks for the ride." She slowly closed the door where she watched the taillights of his car as far as they could be seen until he turned into his driveway and they went dark.

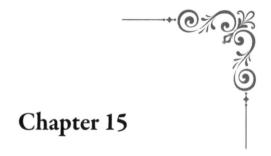

Chapter 15

Hearing the sound of a car in the driveway, Jacq looked up as she was preparing a refreshing pitcher of iced tea. Nicole was scheduled to come over to discuss the sale of Aunt Rose's property and, like her aunt had taught her, Jacq had prepared some savory bites and refreshing drinks to welcome her guest. She had asked Nicole to do some research to see if the property could be subdivided or if the farm needed to be sold in one piece. She hadn't told Nicole the reason for her inquiry. Given her talk with Garrett, she knew he wanted at least a piece of the property and Jacq thought she would try to make that happen if she could. What she didn't know is what kind of budget Garrett had for the purchase. He seemed to be doing well, but it undoubtedly took quite a few resources to be able to run a farm for the sole purpose of saving animals, some of which would never be adopted by other families due to the nature of their abuse.

"Come in," Jacq shouted from the kitchen when she heard the peal of the doorbell. The tap of high heels sounded on the entry tiles as Nicole made her way into the sunny kitchen. Jacq was just adding a lemon wedge to the rim of the tea filled glasses when Nicole peeked around the corner.

THE WEDDING SLIPPER 121

"Hey," Nicole said, "You must have read my mind. I need something to drink in the worst way."

Jacq chuckled, "Well I can get you something a little more hard-core if you need it," Jacq said handing Nicole a frosty glass.

"No, this is perfect. It's been such a busy day, I haven't stopped for a break in hours, so food and drink are most welcome," Nicole sighed as she removed her red denim jacket and draped it across the breakfast bar chair. Nicole looked her put together self with white jeans, a white gauzy blouse with large free-form black and red polka-dots painted on it, red strappy heels and the now discarded red denim jacket. Jacq noticed again Nicole's seemingly effortless talent of looking great under any circumstances. Jacq looked down at her dusty blue jeans and sweatshirt and grimaced. "Oh well," she thought, "I'm not the one meeting clients all day."

To Nicole she said, "Thanks for coming to the farm. I would have been happy to meet you at your office."

"No worries, I enjoy coming out here. It's quiet and there are no distractions. It makes a nice break in the day." Nicole sipped some iced tea and rummaged around in her briefcase. "I have the final comps we talked about. The market is on the upswing so I wouldn't think you would have a problem selling pretty quickly. I did check into your question of whether or not the property could be sub-divided, but it appears that the land is zoned in a way that doesn't allow for it to be parceled out, so we'll need to sell as one large parcel. It shouldn't be a problem though; the farm is beautiful and I'm sure we'll find a buyer soon."

Nicole pulled out her computer and a sheet of paper with descriptions of properties and price per acre numbers outlined in neat columns. Jacq's property was highlighted with a recommended sale price circled in red. "I did update my research of selling prices in the area and recommend we pinpoint the numbers on the high side of the properties because of the house, barn and green house that come with the land."

Jacq looked at the number and was surprised at the asking price. It was a lucrative number for her, but keeping her conversation with Garrett in mind, she doubted that was a number he was thinking when he mentioned his dreams to Jacq. She didn't know if Garrett had approached Nicole and wasn't sure if she should mention their conversation. Instead, she said, "Has anybody inquired about the property. It seems that news spreads fast in a small town and I didn't know if there was anybody you knew that might be a potential buyer?"

"No, I haven't had discussions with any serious buyers, but once we get it on the market, I'm sure we'll have our share of traffic to the website as well as to the open houses I'm planning." Nicole pulled a marketing plan up on her computer and explained her ideas for pushing the sale of the property out to the public. Jacq was only listening with half an ear, still thinking about Garrett's disappointment if it wasn't possible for him to purchase the property.

"Of course, I'll finalize the plan and then you can let me know when you want me to pull the trigger," Nicole continued. "I didn't know if you wanted to list it until after Lia's wedding."

"Having open houses and people walking through the house while trying to get ready for a wedding and clean out the house at the same time sounds crazy making," exclaimed Jacq, "Why don't we wait until after the wedding. That way it will give me time to clean and stage the house. If I get done with the clearing out quicker than I think, then maybe we could go ahead and show

THE WEDDING SLIPPER   123

the property by appointment and delay the open houses. That way I will have some flexibility on the timing of people stopping by." Nicole nodded and jotted down notes as Jacq brainstormed her ideas.

"Has Lia been by since the barn cleaning?" asked Nicole, stowing all the papers for the land sale in her briefcase. Jacq shook her head no. "It's fun to see her so excited about an old barn. Not that it doesn't have a rustic beauty, and it's perfect for her and Brett. Matt and I have discussed our venue and decided we would go a bit more formal. We've been contemplating the St. James Cathedral in Seattle. It's a beautiful, majestic building and fits into what I want my wedding to be like. We went to look at the possibility and I've got some pictures, if you would like to see them?"

Jacq nodded excitedly and Nicole proceeded to show her pictures of a beautiful Catholic cathedral with a central high alter and picturesque vaulted ceilings. It certainly would make a beautiful formal wedding, very different than what Lia had in mind. "Matt grew up Catholic and prefers getting married in the church. Other than that, I don't think he cares about the wedding details although he's been good about listening to my ideas. I just want our day to be perfect, you know; not only for us, but for those who take the time to celebrate with us."

Jacq listened to the love in Nicole's voice as she talked about Matt. Nicole described him as her rock and the person who could calm her down just by holding her hand. Matt's father was an ambassador to South Korea and his mother was an interpreter his dad had met when he was visiting dignitaries on behalf of the United States. According to his dad it was love at first sight, so he bundled up his beautiful South Korean bride and dragged her back to America. Matt's mom would just shake her head and with an indulgent smile tell Nicole the true story that it had been a couple of months before she could wrap up her work and move to America to marry. Matt had inherited his tall, lankiness from his dad and his mom's beautiful ebony straight hair and deep brown eyes. As Nicole, described what Matt meant to her, Jacq wondered if she would ever feel that way about a man and was a little envious of Nicole and Lia's impending weddings.

She didn't know much about her Uncle Thomas, Aunt Rose's husband, as she was really young when her uncle passed away of a heart attack. She had overheard her parents tell stories of Rose and Thomas over the years and it sounded like they, like Nicole and Matt, had found true love. Jacq recalled the book she had found in Aunt Rose's bed side drawer. She was sure it was a diary and thought perhaps the leatherbound book would hold some answers to questions Jacq had about her aunt's life. She vowed to herself that she would take the time to read the handwritten pages, if for nothing else, but to immerse herself in a piece of her family history.

"....and we'll both need a new dress," Coming out of her reverie, Jacq had missed the first part of what Nicole was saying.

"Why do we need new clothes?" Jacq asked.

"For Lia's wedding, of course. Weddings are always a good excuse for a girls' shopping trip. Although I don't think it will matter what you wear to a certain someone who can't keep his eyes off of you," smirked Nicole waggling her eyebrows in a Charlie Chaplin fashion at Jacq.

"I have no idea what you are talking about," Jacq stated squinting at Nicole with suspicion.

THE WEDDING SLIPPER 125

"Oh, come on, I've seen how Garrett looks at you when he thinks nobody is watching," said Nicole with a smile. "You definitely need a new dress, girlfriend."

"I don't know. Not about the new dress, but about starting anything that can't go anywhere. I have so many things going on, trying to juggle issues on two coasts, making my way through months of grief as well as volunteering to be a wedding host. It just doesn't leave time for romance," Jacq sighed.

"It may not leave a lot of time for romance, but just give it a chance," Nicole said giving Jacq a side-armed hug, "you never know what will come your way if you leave yourself open to possibilities."

Jacq smiled softly and let herself lean into Nicole for a second. "However, I do know the idea of a new dress has some merit. What do you say we take the afternoon off and go shopping?"

"I thought you would never ask. Just let me talk to the office a second and we'll head to Silverdale to see what we can find." As Nicole talked with her assistant, Jacq ran upstairs to freshen up and contemplated the fact that Nicole noticed Garrett's attention. She wondered if others had also noticed. She felt anticipation and a little bit of anxiety to think that Garrett might take their flirting to the next level. He still owed her for the tequila bet he'd lost, and she knew exactly how she would have him pay her back, if given the chance. She just hoped she could summon the courage to make her fantasy a reality. She already had a group of new friends that she was coming to cherish, how much harder would it be to open her heart to a handsome, gentle man who saved animals?

126

J. KIMALIE

"Let's go," Nicole said hooking her arm through Jacq's as soon as she returned and led her to the white-washed front door. Smiling to herself, Jacq followed Nicole to her car determined to find a dress that would keep Garrett's eyes on her for the entire wedding. Jumping into Nicole's Subaru they headed for town, talking all the way, while Nicole navigated the winding roads lined by maples, firs, and cedars.

"Has he kissed you yet?" Nicole asked out of the blue, startling Jacq who had been bobbing her head to the radio, enjoying the scenery.

"What?" asked Jacq stalling for time as she tried to think of what to say.

"Oh, yes you have!" exclaimed Nicole grinning.

Jacq continued to look out the window no longer seeing the scenery, but instead imagining Garrett leaning in to capture her lips. To Nicole, she said, "The thing about a first kiss is that you build it up in your mind, like how soft his lips are going to be, or will they be dry and chapped, or will he take his time, or suck too hard," Jacq sighed ruefully. "I wasn't expecting our first kiss to be one on the cheek, but it was perfect. Maybe because it was so unexpected. Maybe it's because HE is so unexpected" Jacq looked and saw Nicole was smiling at her. "Okay, he went on to do more than just kiss my cheek and, yes, it was excellent!" Their smiles grew until they both looked like love-sick fools and giggled. At the same time both turned back to look out the front of the windshield lost in their individual thoughts.

Reaching the dress shop, Jacq spied a beautiful emerald-green cocktail dress in the window. It was perfect for a barn wedding. The dress looked like it was made of silk with a fitted bodice and a flared skirt falling just below the knee. Fitted

THE WEDDING SLIPPER 127

elbow length sleeves complimented the sweetheart neckline. What really drew Jacq to the garment was the big peony painted on the fabric in hot pink, white and cream. Whoever had dressed the window had paired the garment with hot pink cowboy boots stitched in white. Jacq and Nicole stood outside the window and stared. "Do you think they have it in my size?" said Jacq in awe.

"God, I hope so," whispered Nicole, "because we can't leave without that outfit." Jacq grabbed Nicole's arm and dragged her through the beautifully etched shop door to seek out the perfect dress encased in the window.

Chapter 16

The waterfront restaurant Garrett chose was lovely with stunning views of scenic Hood Canal and surrounding woodlands. Nestled among the trees was a log structure with massive, soaring floor to ceiling windows on three sides of the building to afford panoramic views of the fjord which formed the western lobe and one of the main basins of Puget Sound.

As Jacq exited the SUV, the fragrance of Douglas Firs, cedars, and a plethora of other towering trees caressed Jacq's senses quickly followed by the scent of salty sea water wafting on the breeze.

Garrett opened the massive iron and glass front door for Jacq. She entered a voluminous space with three huge metal and glass chandeliers, made to look like a ring of candles flickering behind frosted glass chimneys, comfortably filing the upper portion of the enormous room. Two matching stone stacked fireplaces faced each other, one on the north side of the grand space and one on the south side like two giant sentinels keeping watch over the guests. Jacq's trained eye appreciated the oversized scale of everything that worked harmoniously together to create an impressively elegant and welcoming retreat with tables scattered discreetly around the grand room. The hard surfaces of glass, metal, and stone were softened and

THE WEDDING SLIPPER   129

complimented by wide plank wood floors, large native woven baskets, nature inspired tapestries, and potted dwarf Japanese maples, strategically positioned to enhance the privacy of guests.

Jacq and Garrett were shown to their table next to a window near the whitecapped dark blue water. The square table was angled with one point of the table almost touching the window. At the corner of the table sat a trio of metal and glass lanterns encircling a vase of fiddleheads ferns surrounded by smooth black stones. Two rustic, yet sophisticated, place settings were laid out on each side of the opposite corner of the table affording both Jacq and Garrett views out the window without turning their heads. The pleasing overall affect was intimate and relaxing, and the view of the calm waters and evergreen forest was soul soothing.

Jacq sighed appreciably and turned toward Garrett. "Thank you" breathed Jacq, "I didn't realize how much I needed a break."

"You have had a busy few weeks. You've already made impressive progress on going through your aunts' things," Garrett said knowingly.

"It has been a busy two years," Jacq responded matter-of-factly.

"What's kept you so busy?" Garrett inquired. Garrett's innocent question instantly focused Jacq's full attention on Garrett's handsome face.

"I thought Emmett would have told you," Jacq said.

Dreading what he might hear given Jacq's tone, Garrett tentatively asked, "Told me what?"

"It wasn't only my aunt that I lost two years ago," Jacq shared, "my parents both died in the same car accident."

Garrett was nothing short of gobsmacked. After a few seconds he leaned toward Jacq, gathering her hands in his and said, "I had no idea, I am so very sorry." His compassionate tone and tender sensitivity almost undid Jacq.

Her eyes filled with tears pooling in her lower lids, threatening to escape down her cheeks. Jacq noticed that Garrett's eyes were also glistening. For a couple long minutes, neither one spoke, and neither one broke eye contact. Garrett simply squeezed her hands a bit more tightly.

Clearing the lump from his throat, Garrett said, "Thank you for trusting me enough to share your story."

Jacq, still not steady enough to speak, just nodded and was relieved to see a waiter approaching. Jacq started to lean back in her chair and relax her grip, but Garrett's warm hands held firm not allowing a retreat. The waiter introduced himself and asked if he could get something started for them. Jacq ordered a glass of red wine and Garrett suggested the waiter bring the entire bottle. She leaned back in her chair more forcefully than before causing Garrett to reluctantly release her hands as he likewise settled back into his seat, patiently waiting for Jacq to engage.

"Well, I sure know how to put a damper on a perfectly good evening," Jacq lamented.

"You've done no such thing," Garrett firmly countered. Looking compassionately into her piercing green eyes, Garrett continued, "I asked you out to get to know you better and how could I know you at all without hearing about what must be the most seminal event in your life? You can share with me as much or as little as you would like."

"I will," Jacq replied more confidently, "but first I'd like to know more about you."

THE WEDDING SLIPPER   131

As Garrett took a deep breath and began to collect his thoughts, a huge, majestic, bald eagle soared past the window commanding the attention of everyone in the room in a shared moment of wonder. Once the eagle was out of sight, Garrett's and Jacq's eyes found each other's and they smiled – their evening felt as though it had just been blessed. From that magical moment on, the conversation was comfortable, easy, and uncharacteristically intimate for a first date.

The menu was a choice of three farm to table fixed four course dinners. Over a long, lingering, scrumptious meal featuring roasted pork that both Garrett and Jacq had each selected, and an exceptional bottle of Mark Ryan's cabernet sauvignon, they did indeed get to know each other better.

Jacq learned that Garrett had been lovingly raised by a single mom and her parents with whom they lived on an apple orchard in central Oregon. He had adored his grandparents who were quick to correct when he needed it and even quicker to love him regardless of whatever he had done. From a young age they taught him the habits of a firm handshake, proper manners, how to converse with adults, and the respect conveyed by liberally using "yes ma'am" and "no sir." His mom always reminded him that gentlemanly manners would take him a long way in life and with the ladies. As it turned out, it also served him well in the military. Garrett's grandparents had passed away less than a year apart after fifty-six years of marriage. Garrett's grieving mother sold the house and orchard and moved to Portland, Oregon, and Garrett joined the army. His mom enrolled in a medical training course and became a lab technician ultimately finding her niche as a phlebotomist. Garrett felt like the city suited his mom better than rural life ever did or could. Garrett and his mom remained close and connected regularly by phone or in person. Ironically, Garrett enlisted hoping to escape a provincial rural life only to return to one after his two tours of duty. After seeing more of the world, he realized he was content and even preferred to return to a quieter rural existence near his friends.

Jacq noticed that Garrett skipped over details of his years in the army, but she chose not to press him as the conversation had fallen into a comfortable rhythm that she did not want to interrupt, nor did she want to pry into a potentially sensitive subject.

Once the sun had set, the lanterns on every table were lit and the fires glowed brightly in the fireplaces. The space was filled with a warm luminosity, making each table feel like an island in a sea of serene flickering shadows.

Jacq began sharing her background with Garrett, feeling not exactly vulnerable but maybe a little fragile. After all, only recently on her way to Seattle had she opened up for the first time and shared much about the accident and aftermath.

Garrett listened attentively as Jacq recounted most of what she had shared with the caring lady on the plane. She found it easier talking about her story the second time although the most painful parts were still just as achingly difficult to say out loud. A few times Jacq had paused to get a grip on her emotions. As she looked up into Garrett's sympathetic eyes, she saw an understanding of what telling her story was costing her. His unwavering gaze also expressed reassurance that he was there for her on her terms which gave her the fortitude to press on until she brought her thoughts to a close.

THE WEDDING SLIPPER   133

"Enough of me and my sad tale. You'll have to wait another day for Jacq part one, life before the accident," she said attempting to lighten the mood.

Having verbalized that statement, Jacq realized she had mentally, and probably emotionally, divided her life into pre-accident and post-accident intervals. She wondered to herself if that distinction would ever change.

"I will wait for another day;" Garrett said cutting into her thoughts, "I sense hearing Jacq part one will be worth the wait. I'm just so terribly sorry that Jacq part two has been so life altering and painful," he added. "I feel like you just handed me part of your heart to guard, and I will," promised Garrett. This time it was Jacq that leaned into the table and reached for Garrett's hands to squeeze.

The waiter approached the table with a pitcher of ice water and Jacq took advantage of the break in the conversation to visit the lady's room. On her way back to their table she noticed that about a third of the tables that had been full as they entered were now empty. Glancing at the cell phone in her purse to check the time she was surprised by how late it was. She was halfway across the restaurant before she realized that Garrett was no longer at the table and neither was her green pashmina wrap that she had dangled over her chair. Her mind had just started to process options of what could have happened when she spotted Garrett heading toward her. He reached out his hand as he said, "I'd thought we would go someplace different for dessert."

Jacq took his outstretched hand, so warm and soft despite the work calluses on the pads of his fingers, letting Garrett led her to a secluded table by the fireplace. On it were two steaming mugs of coffee, a generous pitcher of cream, and an extra-large slice of hazelnut tart with two forks one on each side of the plate. Her wrap was gracefully draped over her chair. The cheery, crackling fire, and Garrett's companionable company was just what she needed to reset her heart and soul to be in the here and now. By unstated mutual agreement, she and Garrett stuck to light and funny topics as they polished off the decadent sticky dessert.

After a while they assumed they might be taking advantage of the waiter's good graces, so they rose to leave the restaurant. Garrett walked around the table to help Jacq with her wrap. From behind Jacq, he spread out the pashmina and from right above her elbows he drew it up around her shoulders his hands deliberately making contact with her upper arms the whole way. Jacq involuntarily shivered at his electric touch. He ever so gently leaned into her and whispered in her ear, "The green matches your eyes perfectly; I don't believe I have told you tonight, you look stunning." And with that, Jacq and Garrett exited into the coolness of the evening.

Hand in hand they headed toward the SUV, but Garrett detoured toward the inky water. The moon was high above the towering trees reflecting its light on the shimmering surface. They stood facing the water, each lost in their own thoughts. Jacq gradually turned to face Garrett and simply said, "Thank you!"

Garrett wrapped Jacq in a warm bear hug wanting so badly to safely cocoon her from anything painful that might yet come her way in this life. She sagged into him accepting the heavenly comfort he was providing. She felt him kiss the top of her head and for the second time that night she took it as a blessing of sorts. She did not want to move, nor did she for several minutes even as the wind whipped the edges of her wrap and the coolness

THE WEDDING SLIPPER   135

of the night slowly seeped into her bones. She just wanted to soak in his warmth, his humanity, his kindness. Just as her teeth started to chatter, Jacq felt herself starting to thaw from the glacial state she had been in for the past two years. Wordlessly, Garrett once again took her hand and led her to the warmth of the waiting vehicle.

Garrett pulled the SUV in front of the house and walked Jacq to the front door. Before she could reach the door handle, he gently cupped his hand under her chin and tenderly tilted her head up toward his. He leaned down and kissed her slowly and firmly, not with the passion of their first kiss but with the purity of a sweet benediction on their evening. He said, "Jacq, I would not have traded a moment of this evening for anything." He graced her with his most devastatingly heart melting smile and turned saying, "I'm sure I'll see you soon."

Jacq sighed audibly as she entered the quiet house tossing her wrap over a chair. Their evening was not what she had imagined; yet it was wonderfully restorative. On the drive back from the restaurant she had formed various scenarios of how their evening might end. Nothing in her amorous imagination matched the anticlimactic, yet sweet reality of the end to their evening. Alone Jacq headed upstairs. Emotionally spent, she was out when her head hit the pillow and she ended up getting the best night's sleep she had experienced in two years, two months, and eight days.

One house over, Garrett could not get to sleep. His mind was churning in several directions at once. On the drive to the restaurant, he had imagined various scenarios as to how the night might end and they all involved Jacq's glossy red hair splayed out on his pillow. What a Neanderthal he had been since the

136   J. KIMALIE

very first moment he had laid eyes on Jacq. Their whole first
encounter had been so ridiculous. Her, in those silly oversized
rubber boots and the queen bee night shirt she was wearing,
prompted his cheeky response and childish flirting. He wished
he could take back all the adolescent silliness. It wasn't even like
him to carry on that way with a perfect stranger. "She just, she
just, she what?" Garrett wondered. He tried to pin it down for
the hundredth time. She just got to him on a variety of levels.
He was so damn attracted to her; drawn to her inviting curves,
luminous mind, and, after tonight, her bruised but resilient soul.
Why was he torturing himself? Her life was on the east coast
and his roots were deeply planted here in the northwest. He
needed to get her out of his mind which only conjured up a few
senseless rounds of self-chastisement for his carnal thoughts of
her followed by more unwholesome thoughts about what Jacq
might, this very moment, be wearing or not wearing. There was
only one honorable thing to do. Garrett concluded that he
would back off from encouraging Jacq in any relationship. She
didn't need another person to care about and then exit her life.
He would only be there for her as a shoulder to lean on. In
a couple days he would go over to her place with a bottle of
Tequila, because he did need to pay off the bet, and he could
provide Jacq a listening ear. He definitely knew she could use a
friend right now.

As much as Garrett's body yearned to take advantage of
Jacq's vulnerable state, his gentlemanly sensibilities would never,
ever, let him go there. It would be easy enough, his uninvited
thoughts persisted, as there were enough sparks between them
that he was sure it wouldn't take much to ignite a blaze
consuming them both. He wanted so badly to experience the

flames. Even so, he doubted that would end well for either one of them when, inevitably, she returned to New York. Garrett vowed, from here on out, to provide brotherly companionship rather than what his body and heart craved every time he looked at her. Decision made; he drifted off into a fitful sleep.

Chapter 17

Several days had passed since Jacq and Garrett had gone on their dinner date. Although she hadn't anticipated having a conversation that would gather her emotions to the point of spilling over, she felt a profound sense of relief that it had occurred, and that Garrett now was aware of the total load she'd been working through. It was another weight off her shoulders and with each one removed, she felt lighter and more like herself. She hadn't heard from him since their date, but it seemed natural for some time to pass given where their conversation had gone, along with the fact that they were both very busy with some fairly big projects. She knew she needed to talk to him about the property now that Nicole had completed her market analysis and research. Their date didn't seem like the right time to bring it up, so she had held back on the information, but now it was important to let him know. She was rather hoping he would drop by or call and give her an opportunity to broach the subject, but she might have to be the one to create the opportunity. Better yet, Nicole might see him first and break the news to him.

Jacq finished up the chores in the greenhouse, smiling as she recounted for probably the tenth time the gentle but sensual way Garrett had helped her into her pashmina as they left the restaurant. Tonight, she was booked for a conference call catch up with her best friends back home and she was debating whether or not to tell them all that was swirling around in her head on the subject of Garrett. It would be nice to talk it out, but their relationship was so new she wanted to keep it a secret for a while.

Several of the wedding slippers had formed elegant buds that were about to burst open and two had actually produced blooms in all their delicate, blushing glory. It took years for a new orchid to bloom and this both celebrated and underscored the success Aunt Rose had achieved. The orchid her aunt had created really did produce blossoms that resembled an antique wedding slipper when fully opened. They looked like a delicate, handmade cloth slipper with its ribbon ties falling to each side. She held one up to eye level and marveled at the waxy bloom, touched that her aunt would dedicate, in her name, such a marvelous achievement. She put it back in its place, made sure all the slipper orchids were left with moist but not soaking wet soil, and did a quick sweep of the greenhouse floor. Order had been restored to the room and the glass had been cleaned inside and out. The dried up plants had been removed and the empty pots stacked neatly to the side. The sun warmed the entire space but was tempered just enough by a few open vents. In just the right light, like this morning's, some of the leaded windows functioned like prisms and sent rainbows dancing around the room to her great delight. She paused to take one last deep breath of the green, loamy, mossy fragrance that could only be experienced from inside a greenhouse before returning back to the farmhouse.

140   J. KIMALIE

Progress was clearly being made in this space as well. Jacq had completely boxed up and labeled all of the items from the first floor that were either being donated or sold from those that required packing. She had left out the essentials she needed to keep living there comfortably until the property was sold, and she had removed all of the items that needed to be disposed. That just left the furniture she'd use up until her departure and the few boxes of items she would ship back to New York.

She'd made quite a dent in the work upstairs as well, having sorted through most of the rooms applying the same "keep, sell, give away, toss" system that had been serving her well so far. Aunt Rose's bedroom would be the last frontier so to speak, and at the rate she was progressing, she'd be tackling that in the next few days. Once all of her work was done, she'd need to consult with Nicole to figure out staging and a schedule for showing. When she'd first got started, it felt like it couldn't happen fast enough. Now, she was wishing it wasn't happening quite so rapidly. Funny how easily perspectives can change.

Jacq carried an armful of linens she'd gathered from the second-floor closet downstairs to the washroom to begin what was likely to be a day of laundry. She had heard that Lia was starting her marriage with very little and could use linens and blankets. She wanted everything she gave away to be fresh and clean and the simple task of doing laundry grounded her. She plopped the pile down on top of the dryer and began opening the sheets and pillowcases, stuffing them into the washing machine that was filling with her favorite "spring scented" detergent and fabric softener. As she lifted one of the sheets, a folded piece of paper fluttered to the floor. She retrieved it and opened yet another handwritten note of poetry with two

THE WEDDING SLIPPER   141

pressed flowers, this time violets. "And timid violets in the shade, will know that they by love were made" it read, with the sweet simplicity that marked the similarity to some of the other notes that had been slipped between the pages of some of her aunt's books. Again, Jacq wondered why her aunt had these and who had written them as the handwriting did not resemble her aunt's as far as she could ascertain. She set it aside to add to the growing stack of notes that she was saving in a large cloth covered hatbox that she had found in her guest room closet.

At some point, she'd go back over all of them and see if she could make sense of whatever story the notes might tell. She was beginning to get the feeling that they were connected to a romance in her aunt's past. Strange that Aunt Rose had never talked about anyone. It felt like the kind of thing they might have discussed in front of the fire, sipping wine, during one of their girls' weekends away. They had certainly discussed her relationships in great detail, and she remembered the accuracy, in hindsight, of their collective wisdom. Thinking about it, perhaps this was a sign that a good group think was exactly what she needed on the subject of Garrett and so she was resolved to go ahead and talk about him during her friends' call tonight.

The rest of the day passed quickly as the chores were completed and Jacq felt she'd made some real headway. She folded the last load of laundry and decided to take a quick shower and make herself a light dinner before her phone call. A nice full glass of pinot noir was her reward for a day's worth of work and she was going to enjoy sipping it when she joined her friends. She'd found a little packet of shower bombs when she

142
J. KIMALIE

was going through the linen closet and decided to add one that was labeled "sweet orange" to her shower for an added treat.

An aromatherapy shower and a tasty deli chicken Caesar salad later, Jacq gave herself a generously poured glass of wine, grabbed the comfy afghan and phone, and settled onto the sofa for a long distance get together with her closest friends.

Right on time, the phone rang with Christopher initiating the call. "Hey there Miss Jacq, Miss Beth, are we all here?" Everyone piped up and cheered that the conference call had successfully begun. "So, Jacq, bring us up to date," Christopher said.

"Oh please, no, I want to hear all about you guys first," Jacq responded. "I am seriously feeling the distance and I need to get all caught up. I'll do my share of updating, I promise, but first let me just fill up on all that's been happening with you both."

"Sure," said Beth. "I'll go first since mine is easy. Nothing. Nada. Not a damn thing. I've been busy catering to needy clients all day, every day, and too many evenings. Same ol' same ol.' Then I come home, lose myself in a little mindless television, do a few things around the apartment, then rinse and repeat."

Christopher uttered a series of "tsk, tsk" sounds in quick succession. "Say it isn't so, come on Beth, there has to be more going on than that."

Beth sighed and lamented, "I'm afraid not. Here I am, thirty-five years old and a slave to my job. I can still remember when it was fun. I remember being excited about new clients, meeting up with everyone after work, and weekends—oh yes, I remember when it was all about weekends. Now I've supposedly arrived, and the fun has fled. I make pretty good bank and I'm managing my own accounts and I don't have a life. If it weren't

THE WEDDING SLIPPER   143

for both of you being here, I think I'd be shopping for a new job in a new place just to shake things up a bit. I don't just need a new life, I need "A" life. So that's it for catching you up on me. What's new with you?"

"Wait a minute Beth, let's not stop there. This isn't the first time you've been swamped at work and felt this way," reminded Jacq. "Remember a few years back when you talked about running away and going to culinary school?"

"Right," answered Beth, "that was seven years ago after I broke up with Kevin, the great pretender, and had my heart smashed into little bits. That was more about avoiding running into him than changing jobs."

"Oh yeah, I remember him," Christopher interjected with a snarl in his voice, "he used to always call me "dude". Really, me? Dude? Idiot probably couldn't remember my name."

Beth continued ignoring Christopher as if he hadn't said a word. "I've grown up a lot since then and now I know better. This is about figuring out how to support myself and still be happy while I'm young enough to make a change and old enough to know how to do it well," Beth continued. "Seriously, I am open to change. I just don't know what to do but I'm thinking about it. That's as far as I've gotten now but when you get home, Jacq, we're going to all get together and the two of you are going to help me figure this out, okay?"

Christopher chimed in, "You've got it. Hey, we may all be looking for something new. We don't know anything for sure yet, but it's sounding more and more like the hotel chain is changing ownership."

"What have you heard lately?" Jacq asked.

"Well, nothing concrete, but both the HR and marketing managers at corporate announced that they're leaving. Everyone's on their best behavior and there's lots of whispering going on. I think it's happening," he surmised.

"Hmm." Jacq thought about what he said. "It sounds like something's underway, but we also know how the rumor mill can get things going. Nobody's reached out to me yet and I'd think that would be something that would happen if it was getting serious."

"Not necessarily," Christopher responded. "The Exec's office has been pretty committed to leaving you alone to wrap up all that you needed to handle. I don't think they'd call you and interrupt or risk making you panic and run back unless it was a done deal."

"You might be right. We just have to wait and see. How are you feeling about all of it?" she asked.

"You know, I'm really okay either way," he said calmly. "I've been headhunted enough times that I'm not worried about finding something new. Plus, I'm fairly certain my boss will give me a good recommendation. After all, she relies on me most of the time." He paused for the anticipated snicker that followed. "Seriously, I'd really be okay with it. Besides, if I'm leaving, that means you would probably be too and so we could always market ourselves as a two-fer."

"So, there we have it," announced Beth, "we might all be starting over. Aren't we just the three musketeers?"

"Or the three blind mice," muttered Christopher.

"Everyone let's raise our glasses," ordered Jacq. "I assume everyone has one..."

"You bet." said Christopher.

THE WEDDING SLIPPER 145

"But of course," said Beth, at the same time.

"Here's to we three and whatever will be. Chin chin!" chirped Jacq and they all three drank to the future.

"Okay, okay, now can we finally get to the good stuff?" Beth probed. "Spill girl."

Jacq sighed and then paused briefly. "I'm not really sure where to start..."

"Start with the easy part then," suggested Christopher.

"Well, I'm making pretty good headway on the house. I've gotten past the halfway mark with sorting and packing. I'm doing a great job resisting setting too much aside to bring home with me and emotionally, while I have my moments, I'm managing that part fairly well too."

"It can't be easy," Beth said empathetically. "We know how much you treasured your aunt and all the fond memories you carry."

"Yes, but that's actually what's helping," Jacq explained. "I have so many good memories and I can hear her voice in my head. She actually speaks to me sometimes in my dreams. I don't need to keep a lot of her things to feel her close, so I feel I have her permission to let whatever I need to let go, go."

"I'm glad to hear that," Beth continued. "I don't know where you'd find space to put very many new things if you didn't feel that way. We'd have to find you a larger apartment and even then, who knows where you'd find room if Chris loses his job and tries to crash at your place long term. His wardrobe alone would take up half your space."

"What part of three musketeers did you not get?" countered Christopher.

"How much longer do you think you'll be tied up there?" Beth asked ignoring him yet again.

"I'm not really sure. While I've accomplished a lot of the sorting and packing, I still need to handle selling the items that need to be sold as well as clearing out the greenhouse and then, of course, selling the property. Speaking of the greenhouse, you should see it. It's really something special. Now that it's been cleaned up a bit, it's even more spectacular than it appeared in the photos I sent you. And then the house needs a good final cleaning and staged and marketed and all that."

"I thought your hunky neighbor might be making an offer," suggested Christopher.

"Well, there's that too," she muttered in response.

"Come on, dish," ordered Beth.

"My realtor just pulled the comps together and the good news is the place is worth more than I realized. The bad news is that the property can't be subdivided and I'm fairly certain it's going to go for more than he has the ability to offer. I don't look forward to talking to him about this, not when—well, when we've been getting along so well."

"And what exactly does that mean?" Beth probed.

"Okay, seriously now you guys, I need your help on this one. We went out and it was, well, it was nice."

"How nice are we talking?" Christopher asked, "like breakfast in bed the next day nice?"

"No, not like that," she answered openly. "He is a genuinely sweet guy. He didn't know about my folks—just about Aunt Rose. He was so tender and caring when I told him. We had already had a moment, okay—a kiss—before our first official date so I know the chemistry is there. He's had some tough times

THE WEDDING SLIPPER 147

in his life too, but I think it's shaped him into the sensitive and caring guy he is. And if you could see him with his animals. He's so patient, and so, well, tuned in and connected. This is someone I think I could fall for if I weren't..."

"If you weren't leaving in a month or two to come home?" Beth finished for her.

"Exactly," Jacq answered. "I thought a little fun and flirting would be harmless and a nice tonic for what's been ailing me, but now I worry that it could just make everything worse. However, I like him, and I'm feeling things for him. So, what do I do?"

Everyone paused to think about the question she put out there. It wasn't an easy one to answer.

"How good was the kiss?" queried Christopher.

"Very good," Jacq sighed in response.

"What does your gut tell you to do?" asked Beth. "Isn't that what you always say? Trust your gut?"

"Yes, but this time it's not talking to me. I keep asking and it doesn't speak up."

"So, if your gut isn't answering, what does your heart have to say?" Beth added.

"Heart's pretty confused and not really speaking up either."

"Okay then, ask your libido," Christopher suggested, "that's one opinion you can always count on to be heard loud and clear."

"Yea, well, you're right about that and to be honest, Miss Libido says full steam ahead, but we all know that her opinion is not always the best advice."

They all three acknowledged the truth in the statement.

"What do you think you should do, when you really look deep inside yourself and ask?" Beth asked quietly.

148   J. KIMALIE

"I told myself last week I should go for it, but after taking the first step I'm thinking I have to back away. I don't want to hurt him and I don't want to get hurt. And this back-and-forth flip flopping on the topic is ridiculous, I know it. I think we need to say it to each other out loud like the adults we are and move on. I'll be honest with you, if I was staying, this would be a different conversation. But, of course, I'm not and that's that." Jacq sighed again and was glad she'd said it out loud to her closest friends.

"I'm sorry," said Beth, "but sometimes you owe it to yourself to just let whatever needs to happen, happen. Just be sure you aren't over thinking it and denying yourself a chance to be happy even if it's not forever."

"Life can sometimes really suck," added Christopher. "We're here for you though and that's not ever going to change."

"I was hoping we'd talk and then I'd have all this clarity," Jacq said. "I love you guys even though you sometimes make me crazy."

"Right back at you sweetheart," Christopher replied.

"Wouldn't have it any other way," added Beth. "So, same time next week?"

They all agreed it was a date and said their goodbyes. Jacq knew she needed to choose a course with Garrett and speak openly to him about all of her thoughts. Maybe he'd been struggling with the same concerns as she had since she knew their attraction was mutual. She finished her glass of wine and decided to call it an early night. Tomorrow, she'd walk over and initiate a conversation if he didn't start one first.

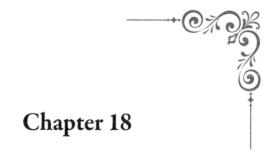

Chapter 18

Garrett sat in the visitors chair across from Nicole's desk, looking at her as his heart sank. She was exploring financing options for Jacq's land if he chose to buy it, but he knew he couldn't come up with the payments even with the hefty down payment he had saved up. The price was just too steep. Nicole went on to explain the reasons for not being able to sub-divide, but Garrett was only half listening, his brain working overtime for a solution. He needed at least a portion of the land. Nicole continued to explain the ins and outs of city planning regulations, looking up she realized that Garrett wasn't listening anymore, but looking out her office window at the street beyond. "Garrett," Nicole said getting his attention. He turned his head to look at her. "I know you are disappointed, but perhaps there is a way to entice investors or hire a person to work on bringing in donations?" Garrett turned his head to continue staring sightlessly out the window. He scrubbed his hand down his face and grimaced. "I'm not sure Nicole," he sighed, "Maybe I should just stick with what I have and forget growing the shelter, for now."

"Look, I'll keep thinking of potential ways to finance that may help. Don't give up yet. Jacq isn't ready to put the land on the market, at least not until she finishes going through Rose's things. There is still time," Nicole entreated.

Garrett looked at her with a slight smile and rose to go. "Thanks Nicole, I'll continue to think on it. I appreciate you taking the time to meet with me." Nicole came around the desk and gave him a quick hug and watched him walk out the door, sharing his disappointment.

Garrett slowly ran the curry comb over Angel's flank thinking about his meeting with Nicole. He had Angel cross tied in the middle aisle of the barn looking out the door at the pasture beyond. The day was gray and misty with rain, the kind of rain that, if you stood outside only a little while, could soak you to the bone before you realized it, so softly did it touch down. He loved the repetitive motion of rubbing with one hand to sooth and brushing with the other to stimulate the skin. The ritual was as relaxing to him as it was to the animal that was enjoying his ministrations. Sadie and Nitro were roaming around the barn sniffing into corners and then running outside playing a game only the dogs understood.

Garrett watched their antics with a half-smile on his face. Soon his thoughts went back to the phone call earlier in the day. The temporary shelter was looking for a home for another horse. He had to turn them down, he just couldn't shelter another animal without finding more room, a painful and disappointing realization. Angel blew a breath on his neck as he took a soft brush and rubbed it over her cheek. "What are we going to do Angel," he said as he scratched under her chin. The horse just stretched her nose out, guiding his hand lower along her neck where she wanted to be rubbed. "Some people would probably say that I have a hero complex, always wanting to save people,

THE WEDDING SLIPPER   151

animals, orchids..." he chuckled. "What do you think?" he asked the silent animal. Angels' ears twitched back and forth as if contemplating his words. "I just can't figure out how to make it work," Garrett sighed.

Angel was showing real signs of healing. Garrett could no longer see the indentations of her ribs, there was some muscle build up along her flanks and her mane and coat held quite a bit more shine than when he'd first seen her. Her eyes were brighter and more of her personality came out each day. You would think she would have a huge grudge against humans, but she was docile and seemed to like company. She still startled easily and didn't like being out in the pasture for long periods of time seeming to like the shelter of the barn better. He found it ironic that she was tied up in a small place for so long, but still liked the indoors better than wide open spaces. He wondered if she suffered from a mild case of agoraphobia or whatever the equivalent psychological ailment was for animals.

"I either have to find a way to heal animals quickly and find them new homes or expand someplace else," mused Garrett, "but minds and hearts can take an unpredictable amount of time to set the damage right and I don't want to push an animal out before it is ready, and I certainly don't want to move." Angel tossed her head in seeming acknowledgement of Garrett's logic. "But what are we going to do?" Garrett asked himself again. He had thought about asking his friends to brainstorm solutions to his land problem but was afraid they would offer him money. He suspected that they donated heavily to his cause already and he didn't want them to feel like they needed to do more.

Jacq stood just inside the barn in the shadow cast by the open barn door and listened to Garrett talk to the mare. At the moment, he was humming to the animal as he groomed her, but Jacq had caught the tail end of the one-sided conversation and suspected he was talking about needing more land to expand the shelter. Nicole called Jacq after Garrett left her office to let her know that he would probably not be able to afford to buy Aunt Rose's property. She had also told her how disheartened he seemed as he walked out her office door. Jacq was on her way over to Garrett's today anyway hoping to have a conversation about their budding relationship and maybe he would allow her to help him think through his options with the property. She wondered if Garrett already had company when she heard his voice coming from the barn. Jacq hadn't realized it was just Garrett talking to Angel until it became apparent, she was eavesdropping on a private conversation between man and beast.

"I am going to figure this out," Garrett paused continuing to rub down the mare. "Do you know how I got in this business?" Garrett asked the silent horse. "It's a long story, but I'll tell you the short version. I always loved helping animals as a kid and later I was working search and rescue in Nepal. An earthquake had devastated a good portion of the area. I was sitting against a wall resting with the dogs after a morning of activity and watched a young boy set up a makeshift animal shelter. People were stopping by his small tent and dropping off animals of every kind that had been lost in the rubble or wandering around the devastation. I don't know how the community knew he was there, but obviously the word got out. It dawned on me that pets were also victims of emergency incidents as well. Most of the time we think of the human or economic toll of earthquakes, but here was a young kid, with probably very little to his name, taking care of the animals that were displaced by the destruction.

THE WEDDING SLIPPER 153

As I watched, others would come by and, I assumed, they asked him if he had their animal. There were huge cries of joy when somebody was reunited with their pet. I still remember that kids face, with a smile as big as the world, when he handed over a rescued furry member of a family." Garrett was quiet for a moment. "I once was lost, but now I'm found," he whispered under his breath, his brow crinkling in concentration. "Anyway, I wanted to be that boy. It seemed like such a small service, but so crucial to the wellbeing of the community."

Jacq discreetly wiped a tear away from her cheek as Garrett finished his story. At least she thought she was being discreet, but her movements must have alerted Garrett he wasn't alone as his head snapped up looking directly at where she was standing in the shadows. "I'm sorry I startled you," said Jacq quietly, "I wasn't meaning to eavesdrop."

"No worries," stated Garrett as he turned back to the horse, "Angel and I were just reminiscing."

Jacq noticed the worry lines etched in Garrett's forehead. "Your story was beautiful. I never asked how you came to run a rescue shelter, but it all makes sense now." She walked to Angel's opposite side and looked at Garrett over the horse's back. "Nicole told me about your conversation."

"How much did she tell you?" questioned Garrett, not sure if he liked Nicole sharing his personal business.

"Not much, just that you left her office looking dejected."

Garrett threw her a half-smile. "Dejected, huh?" Garrett leaned on Angels back with his chin resting on his crossed arms, looking at Jacq. "Not so much dejected as perplexed. Since you're here can I ask a favor?"

Jacq nodded, "Anything."

"Can I borrow or more specifically rent some pastureland temporarily to shelter an animal? I'll need to put up temporary fencing, cut down the grass and set up a feeding and watering station. I was thinking the pastureland closest to me would work and I would pay for any upgrades. I'll also have my attorney draw up an agreement so we both know what to expect from the deal. I'll do the work quickly, so I don't interfere with the sale of the farm."

Jacq nodded again, "Of course, although if it's just temporary then there is no need to pay rent. We'll call it a donation to the animal shelter."

Garrett didn't say anything as he went back working on the mare. Jacq had thought maybe she offended him, when he said, "I think I'd rather pay you at least something, even if it is a token amount. I don't want any debts between us."

Jacq didn't understand where his attitude was coming from since they had seemed so trusting just the other night and was a bit hurt by his rejection of her offer. "If Aunt Rose was alive, would you have asked her to borrow the land?" questioned Jacq.

Garrett nodded, "I would."

"Would she have charged you rent?" inquired Jacq "Or would you be just as stubborn as you are being now and insist on a lease arrangement? I told you I would find a way to pay you back for taking care of her orchids and this is the perfect way. Or would you prefer that I be indebted to you, not the other way around," Jacq snapped, offended by her generosity seemingly being thrown back in her face.

"Whoa," Garrett said, quickly moving around the mare to grab Jacq's hand. "I didn't mean to offend you. I'm sorry. It's been a frustrating day and I wasn't careful with my words. Let's call it

THE WEDDING SLIPPER   155

even then. I get to temporarily use the land and your perceived debt to me is paid in full for taking care of the orchids," Garrett looked at her with the same worried expression he had on his face when she interrupted his conversation. He was holding her hand gently rubbing his thumb back and forth over her knuckles.

Jacq stuck out the hand he wasn't holding and said, "Deal."

Garrett grinned and shook her hand and stated, "Deal." They both looked at each other with goofy grins on their faces realizing they had just survived their first argument.

Still holding both her hands, Garrett said, "So what brings you out here on a day like today anyway? I wasn't expecting company."

Jacq realized quickly that this wasn't the right time to bring up their relationship, so she brought up the first thing that came to mind. "I wanted to ask if you came up with any leads on what I can do with the orchids. I need to clean out the greenhouse and the orchids deserve to go somewhere or to someone that will preserve their beauty."

"I checked with my florist friend and nothing panned out, but I've had an idea, I'm just not sure it will fly. I've always wondered about Emmett and your Aunt Rose," Garrett confessed.

Jacq looked at him with an eyebrow raised, but he was looking down at their clasped hands as he continued to speak. "I thought maybe they had something going. I could be wrong, and they could have just been good friends, but there seemed to be a spark there. Not that it was any of my business," Garrett said hastily looking up at her, "but I was thinking that maybe Emmett would like the orchids and if my suspicions are right, he would have something to remember Rose by."

"Do you think Emmett would want the responsibility of the orchids?" asked Jacq. "He's been taking care of them for so many years."

"That's the thing," said Garrett, "not once did I hear him complain about the work the flowers took. As a matter of fact, a couple of times we got our wires crossed and I thought it was my turn to feed and water the plants, but I found him softly singing to them."

When Jacq looked at him incredulously, Garrett looked at her with a fake frown and stated, "You can't tell him I told you that."

Jacq smiled and said, "Never," as she crossed her finger over her heart.

"Emmett's not the kind to let you do much for him and I thought it would be a nice gesture," Garrett shrugged as if the thought of doing something nice for his friend made him uncomfortable.

Jacq put her hand on Garrett's arm and said, "The orchids are his if he wants them."

Garrett released Jacq's hands and went back to Angel unhooking her from the cross ties and leading her to a nearby stall. The dogs came in from the rain happy to see Jacq, with Pirate trailing behind them. Garrett watched in amusement as Nitro and Sadie ran up to Jacq and shook their wet fur all over her. Jacq stepped back, but not fast enough to avoid being sprayed with rainwater. The dogs sat at her feet, tongues lolling out of their heads waiting for a treat. "You smell like wet dog," she said patting them daintily on the head. "And wet sheep," she continued as Pirate decided he would join the dogs to see if she could collect some goodies as well.

THE WEDDING SLIPPER 157

Garrett just chuckled and continued to settle Angel in her stall. "Okay, enough begging," said Garrett as he slipped up alongside Jacq and put his arm around her waist. He liked the way she leaned into his embrace. "Pirate, you stay here and keep Angel company. There is feed in her stall," Garrett moved away from Jacq and led Pirate to Angel who chuffed at the ewe's entrance. "Nitro, Sadie, let's head to the house and offer Jacq something warm to drink," Garrett finished looking at Jacq with a question in his eyes.

"I'd love that," Jacq said. Garrett grabbed her hand and headed out of the barn with the dogs trailing behind them.

Chapter 19

"That will be $45.10," Shirley, the clerk at the Silverdale Feed Store, said with a smile. "How's the little mare doing?"

Garrett smiled back and pulled out three twenties to pay for the food supplements he was picking up for Angel. "She's doing really well," he said and handed the cash to Shirley. "She's filling out nicely and she's beginning to lose that scared look in her eye now that she's relaxing and realizing that she's safe and can count on getting some square meals."

Shirley shook her head and sighed loudly. "It just guts me when I see an animal treated like that. Thank heavens for your rescue service Garrett, but I know that for every one you take in..."

Garrett nodded and stopped her before she finished. "I know, but I try to focus on the ones we can save. I really appreciate the discount you folks give me—it goes a long way to helping them."

He pocketed his change and gathered up his items.

"Do you want a bag for those?"

"No need, I'm headed right for my truck," he replied and nodded his appreciation as he turned and left.

THE WEDDING SLIPPER   159

It was late morning and he had already gotten quite a bit done. Although learning about the price of the farm he'd hoped to buy had been a disappointment, his time spent with Jacq earlier in the week had him still thinking about her and feeling excited about the prospect of spending more time together. He climbed into his truck and started to head back to the house when an idea came to mind. He doubled back and found a spot practically in front of Sluy's. Ten minutes and a full bag of pastries later and he was once again headed home. Although the day was cool and crisp, the sun was shining, and he found himself singing softly along with the radio.

Once he got home, he put a pot of coffee on to brew and then finished up the few chores at the house that had to get done before he could leave for a while. Filling a thermos of coffee and grabbing a couple of cups, he gathered these items along with the bag of pastries and headed out to the barn. Hoping that his idea for an impromptu date would work out, he called Jacq on his cell as he took his saddlebags down from the hook he stored them on.

"Hello, Garrett?" she answered sounding surprised.

"Hey there Jacq," he replied. "Are you too busy to take some time off for a coffee break this afternoon?"

"Well, no, nothing that can't wait. Do you want me to meet you somewhere?" she asked.

"No, just stay put and I'll swing by in a few minutes."

"Well, I need a little longer than that to clean up a bit and change. I've been going through more stuff at the house and let's just say that dust is the theme of the day."

"No need to change. Just freshen up so you feel good, but we're not going anyplace where you will see anyone," he assured her. "In fact, the dust will be quite comfortable where we're going."

"Hmmm, that sounds intriguing," she responded with what sounded like a grin.

"See you in about 10 minutes then," he said and hung up.

He saddled up Tony, a sturdy dun colored gelding that he often used on high mountain rescues as well as a very sweet-tempered red roan mare. Her name was Cindy and he had taken her in when she aged out of competition and his friend needed to place her where he knew she'd be well cared for in her retirement. She was still fit to ride as long as it wasn't too rugged a challenge and he was confident that Jacq would get along quite well with her. He secured the saddlebags behind his saddle on Tony and then mounted up and headed across the field to Jacq's place, leading Cindy by the reins behind him.

Jacq opened the door just as he arrived and the delight in her eyes as she saw what he had planned made his heart swell.

"Is this what I think it is?" she asked with the excitement of a young girl.

"You said you liked trail rides, so I thought we'd take our coffee out on the trail," he responded.

Jacq clasped her hands together in delight as she took in the sight of her handsome neighbor looking like a magazine ad in his faded jeans, shearling-lined leather vest and worn, felt cowboy hat sitting relaxed and at home on a beautiful horse that looked to be about 16 hands high. He held the reins to a smaller, but well-built mare that was clearly intended for her.

"Just give me a minute to go change from these loafers into a pair of boots and grab a hat and coat and I'll be right back," she said as she hurried away to get ready. She was back in a flash and

THE WEDDING SLIPPER 161

saw that Garrett had dismounted and was waiting to help her up into the saddle. "That won't be necessary," she assured him. "It has been a while, but I've got this down." She stretched up and touched the top of the saddle with her left hand and raised the stirrup up with her right until it stretched up to her armpit. "I think you got the length just right," she said impressed, and then lowered the stirrup, stepped into it with her left foot and gracefully pushed up swinging her right leg over the horse and settled into the saddle. "Yes, you did, this fits perfectly. "

Garrett gave her an appreciative nod and said, "You sure do look like you know what you're doing. It's just a short distance from here to a path that accesses the power line trail. It's a nice easy ride but also a pretty one and there are a couple of nice spots to stop and have coffee." He turned his horse to face hers. "Your mare's name is Cindy. I think you'll like her. She's about 17 years old and retired from rodeoing about a year ago. My friend asked me to take her in and he pays more than she costs to board, so she sort of helps to support my operation. She's still got a lot to offer, but she earned a good retirement from the really hard work. Don't worry, she has plenty of spunk and will be worthy of an experienced rider. "

Jacq reached forward and petted Cindy's neck. "I can't believe you invited me to do this today," she said enthusiastically, "I mean, I know I told you not long ago that I've missed riding, but for you to set this up already, well, it's such a nice surprise."

Garrett gave her a warm look as he nudged Tony forward, and Jacq and Cindy joined him. "I wanted to be sure you got to do this while you were here, and you never know at this time of year when you'll get another beautiful day like this. The horses love getting out and I'm lucky to have someone to help me give them some exercise, so thank you for that."

"Are you kidding?" she asked, "I love this too!"

Tony stretched his neck out in an arch to the side and grabbed a big bite of a tall fern that was growing along the path. Both horses had a little extra bounce to their step, excited to be out of the pasture and on an adventure, ears shifting right and left taking in all the sounds. As promised, they quickly reached the access to the power line trail. Jacq saw that it was wide enough for service vehicles to use, though a bit overgrown, enabling them to ride side by side. The horses had picked up a little speed now that they were underway and they walked on at a comfortable clip, their steps somewhat muffled by the damp earth and foliage underneath them. Now and then a critter scrambled out of the brush ahead of them and they also startled a gorgeous ring-necked pheasant and its mate.

"How often do you ride up here?" Jacq asked.

"Not often enough, unfortunately, but when I can it makes for a nice break for me," Garrett answered. "Until I get to a point where I can hire some more help, there is only a few of us trying to do everything and by the time it's all done, I don't have enough daylight to get out on the trail much. Sometimes when I'm caught up early or one of the guys has pitched in, I can squeeze a trail ride into the end of the day even if just for a couple of hours. Nitro likes to join us too, but I left him home keeping Angel company today," he grinned. "Besides, I sort of wanted you all to myself."

Jacq felt herself flood with warmth at the comment and looked at him so he could see that his words hit home in a good way. "You couldn't have come up with a better idea for spending

THE WEDDING SLIPPER   163

the afternoon together. I was ready for a break myself, so your timing is also perfect."

"Sometimes you just need to make time for things like this," Garrett stated. "Tell me about when you used to do more riding. You look pretty much at home in a western saddle, so I assume that's what you're used to?"

"I've ridden a little English style too, but mostly Western," she explained. "I went away to camp one year when I was a kid where we took lots of organized trail rides and then I got hooked. We didn't really have a place for a horse, so I didn't have my own, but my parents could see how much I enjoyed riding and there was a stable fairly close to our house that I could go to for lessons and pleasure riding. Once I passed the skills test, I could go out onto the trails that were close to the stable as long as I went with one other qualified rider. I had a couple of friends who also rode and used the same stable and we rode every chance we could. We rode different horses, but we all had our favorite mounts. Mine was a gelding named Oliver who was as steady as they come. I swear, a bomb could go off next to him and he wouldn't bolt. We covered miles and miles together and thanks to him, I felt safe and became a very confident rider."

Garrett listened to her and nodded as she continued to talk about growing up around horses.

"When I got older and went away to college, I had to let go of my membership at the stable and I really missed Oliver and the others, but it wasn't something I could continue. I always hoped to get back in the saddle, but other than an occasional opportunity, it just hasn't happened. "Jacq shrugged her shoulders, then looked around and took a deep breath. "I was so lucky to have parents that supported me in everything I wanted to do. That's the kind of mom I want to be some day. I was always encouraged to try new things and go after what I wanted." Jacq gathered a little bit of Cindy's mane in her right hand and fiddled with it as she was momentarily lost in her thoughts. She turned and gave Garrett a wistful look. "I miss them so much, but I know how lucky I was to have them."

Garrett nodded solemnly and said, "I know exactly what you mean. My grandparents did a fair amount of parenting to me. My mom's great too, but my grandfather spent a tremendous amount of time with me as a kid and taught me a lot about being in the mountains, being around horses, being responsible. "He grinned big and looked away for a moment. "Let's just say he also taught me the consequences of being irresponsible as often as needed until I learned all about that too. I think he taught me more than my gran, my mom, and the Army all put together."

Jacq smiled back at him and noted, "I wish I could have met him. For what it's worth, I think he did a fine job."

"Do you feel like giving them a good stretch?" he asked. Jacq nodded so Garrett clucked to his horse and picked up the speed to a controlled gallop.

Jacq loved the feel of the wind in her face that a good gallop always provided. She could feel that Cindy wanted to really fly, but she held her in a bit. "Not today sweet girl, this isn't the right place for full speed." They kept up the comfortable pace for at least five minutes giving the horses a good workout and then Garrett reined in Tony and slowed to a walk. Jacq had kept pace and was right behind him, so she slowed to a trot until she was back alongside him. Both horses were breathing hard, but clearly had plenty of gas left in the tank. The run was exhilarating for them and they danced a little in place hoping to speed off again.

THE WEDDING SLIPPER 165

"Follow me," Garrett said veering off the trail and walking them through a little break in the trees. This trail was narrower, and they had to continue single file. They rode for about a half mile and then he led Jacq up a slight hill to a small clearing that looked out over the valley below. In the distance, she could see a little bit of the rooftops of the buildings in town. Garrett dismounted, so Jacq followed suit, and they tied their reins to a couple of saplings. Garrett reached into his saddlebags and carried the contents over to a fallen log that had a nice mossy cover that cushioned it forming a comfortable seat. He unrolled a small blanket and laid it over the moss and invited her to join him sitting side by side on the log.

Jacq inhaled and raised her brows. "Are those pastries I smell?"

Garrett chuckled and unfolded the bag, leaned his shoulder against hers, and waved it around a little in front of her so she could capture the full impact of the aroma.

"Sluy's pastries?" she enquired.

"Nothing but the best for my riding partner," he declared.

Jacq clapped her hands silently together as he handed her the bag and began pouring coffee into the mugs. The white bakery bag was chock-full of delicious, flakey pastries. "You've brought enough for at least a couple more trail rides," she noted.

"I didn't know what your favorites were, so I had to bring an assortment," he explained as he handed her a cup of hot coffee. The steam from the mug rose, carrying the scent of the coffee joining that of the pastries making her mouth water.

"How can I pick a favorite when they all look so tasty?" she asked, reaching into the bag for one that was heavily dusted with cinnamon sugar.

166   J. KIMALIE

"You can always do what I do and work your way through them 'til you know," Garrett added with a wink.

"Well, yes, I could," Jacq said thoughtfully, taking a bite of her treat, "but think about poor Cindy who would have to carry me home twenty pounds heavier."

"I'm sure she could manage," he responded noticing a little speck of cinnamon sugar that had settled invitingly just above the corner of her lip. He considered whether or not he should do something about it. Deciding he couldn't resist he leaned in and kissed her, finishing with a little flick of his tongue in the vicinity of the cinnamon. Success, cinnamon gone, and Jacq seemed to be pleased with his spontaneous action. "There was a little something-something from your pastry," he explained with another grin. He rubbed his pointer finger above his own lip indicating where it had been.

"We can't have that, now, can we?" Jacq said in a sultry tone, as she took a slow, deliberate second bite, leaving yet another errant smudge of cinnamon near her mouth.

Garrett didn't need further explanation and he made sure that each subsequent cinnamon smudge was well dealt with.

After polishing off a couple of pastries each and sharing more fond memories from their youth, Garrett glanced at his watch and said it was unfortunately time to head back.

Jacq saved the last bite from her pastry for Cindy who sniffed it and then gladly took it from her flattened hand, her big soft tongue licking up the last few crumbs. Cindy put her head down and let Jacq rub all around her ears. "I could fall for this good girl," she announced as she leaned her forehead back against Cindy's.

THE WEDDING SLIPPER   167

"I could fall for this good girl too," Garrett whispered to himself as he packed up the remainder of the pastries and coffee supplies.

They both mounted their horses and headed back to the trail to return home. They didn't encounter another soul on their way back other than the chipmunks, birds, rabbits and what looked like a well-fed coyote off in the distance. Garrett entertained Jacq with some funny stories about Army boot camp and the jokes the guys played on each other. Jacq told Garrett about her early days in the hotel business and how she met Christopher and Beth, and all the support they had given each other as they launched their careers. They clearly had made friends for life from each of their post college endeavors. Jacq told Garrett how much she liked his friends and that she wished Christopher and Beth could have made it out west so he could have met them as well. "Maybe one day," they both said at the same time and laughed.

They covered the remaining distance home in what seemed like a couple of minutes, although it was a distance of about three miles. The conversation was so comfortable and friendly, each of them enjoying recounting some of the best times from their past. It had been a perfect afternoon. When they finally arrived back at Aunt Rose's, the afternoon sun had taken on that hazy, end of the day hue and an early moon could be seen rising above the peaks of the Olympics.

Garrett dismounted and walked over to meet Jacq. She handed him Cindy's reins and then opened her arms to invite him into an embrace. He held both sets of reins in his left hand and then pulled her in close with his right arm. They held each other snugly and Jacq kissed the side of his face.

168   **J. KIMALIE**

"Best surprise date ever," she said. "Thank you for such a lovely day Garrett."

Garrett loosened his hold and reached up to cup the side of her face. "Best trail ride ever," he said leaning in to capture her lips in a slow lingering kiss.

Tony snorted and tossed his head a little, jangling the bridle. He knew he was close to home and was anxious to return to the pasture and check the feeder for some grain.

Garrett gave her one last quick kiss and said, "I guess that's my cue that it's time to go home and feed. The natives are getting restless."

Jacq gave Cindy one last pat and waved goodbye. Garrett was right. This was the best trail ride ever.

Chapter 20

The week before Lia's wedding, Jacq could not help but notice the buzz of activity in and around the barn. When Jacq asked if there was anything she could do to help in the preparations, Lia asked if she would do a final walk through of the wedding venue on Saturday, about three hours before the wedding once things were set up to see if she had forgotten anything. Lia was insistent that Jacq, having allowed them to use the barn, had already been generous enough and Jacq was a guest, not a worker bee.

Late morning on Thursday, a knock at the front door surprised Jacq. A hefty delivery man asked where she wanted the tables and chairs dropped off. Over the man's shoulder Jacq could see a large white paneled truck with *Grand and Intimate Occasions Party Rentals* painted on its side.

"In the barn please," Jacq replied, suspecting that is where Lia wanted them. "If there is anyone in the barn, they may have more specific instructions for you," Jacq added.

Early Thursday evening, a group of vehicles arrived at the barn around six in the evening. Jacq assumed that Lia had taken her advice to have the rehearsal on Thursday night rather than on Friday as the day before the wedding is often hectic enough with last minute preparations without adding a rehearsal to the

170   J. KIMALIE

mix. Less than an hour later, Jacq heard all the vehicles drive off, presumably to a rehearsal dinner. While Jacq was grateful, she had not been roped into a week of wedding prep, it was a little odd to be on the sidelines of an event especially when it was being held on her property. At the hotel she was always in the thick of things ensuring that every last detail was as the bride and groom had envisioned. Jacq realized she really did enjoy bringing the vision of an event to a beautiful and successful conclusion. Not only did it do her heart good to see her clients so pleased, but she was also simply good at doing it which brought her a feeling of contented satisfaction.

About the time Jacq was fixing her second cup of coffee on Friday morning, she looked out the kitchen window surprised to see a full court press happening at the barn so early in the morning. Across her property she could also see Garrett loading bales of hay into a pick-up truck. He was wielding a large hook in each hand and he would simultaneously thrust a hook into the ends of the bale, lift the bale to his thigh, then hoist the bale with the use of his leg while swinging the bale onto the tailgate of the truck. His movements were fluid, rhythmic and very sexy as he was wearing chaps that highlighted some particularly attractive looking muscles he was using. Why did he have to have chaps on she mused? She was stirred by seeing a man in chaps like some women were by seeing a man in uniform. Jacq remembered the strength of his arms when he had embraced her and at that moment she would not have minded feeling the strength of his thighs in a different kind of embrace. It took him no time at all it seemed, to Jacq's disappointment, as she was enjoying the show, to load up a couple dozen bales of hay. He then got in the truck and drove the short distance over to her barn. He then reversed

THE WEDDING SLIPPER   171

the process and unloaded the bales into neat rows perpendicular to the barn doors leaving a gap in the middle of the row, creating an aisle.

Before Garrett returned to his property, a swarm of ladies were already draping colorful quilts over each bale of hay. Apparently, the chairs were not going to be used for the ceremony but instead around tables for the reception. Jacq idly wondered who all the people were there helping Lia, how nice it would be to have such a large community to draw upon when needed. Jacq glanced in Garrett's direction, but to her chagrin he was nowhere in sight, so she decided it was time for her to tackle her own projects for the day.

Around nine the next morning, an excited Lia came calling asking Jacq if it was a good time for her to do the venue walk through. Lia was wearing her dress cowboy boots and a hot pink robe. Her dark blond hair was down in soft curls that had not yet been combed out. As they walked to the barn, Lia exclaimed, "Oh Jacq you won't recognize the place."

"I bet not," Jacq replied, "you've had a small army over here working all week."

"We lucked out," Lia added, "I've been closely tracking the weather and yesterday and today the weather was predicted to be cloudy with sun breaks and tomorrow is back to light rain."

Jacq chuckled saying, "Only in the Northwest do weather forecasters report when sun breaks are anticipated on cloudy days."

"We take it when we can get it," Lia retorted, "and every time the sun peaks out through the clouds I'm taking it as God smiling down on our day."

As Jacq and Lia neared the barn, lovely details emerged – the venue had indeed been transformed. What looked like sage green and pale-yellow plastic lunch bags with the tops rolled down contained exuberant bouquets of colorful flowers that graced the end of each hay bale row along the aisle. The riot of color of the flowers mirrored the variety of colors in the quilts that topped each hay bale. The overall effect was charming and cheerful.

Two large metal tubs holding much larger bouquets were situated one on each side of the open barn door beckoning guests to enter but would also beautifully frame the wedding party. As they entered the barn and Jacq's eyes adjusted to the darker interior, she let out a gasp. Rows of breezy ivory tulle draped from the barn's rafters. Rows started at one end of the barn and ended at the other. Every other row of tulle began one rafter in creating graceful offset scallops transforming the interior of the barn into airy wonderland.

"How enchanting," Jacq breathed, and she meant it.

Lia was bouncing on the balls of her feet. "Jacq, I can't thank you enough for making my wedding day dreams come true," she said for the dozenth time. "Seriously, this is exactly how it looked in my dreams."

"It's simply gorgeous!" Jacq said, "And I love how you tied the table and chairs into the theme; it grounds the space well." Each table had flower petals randomly scattered on the tabletop covered by the same ivory tulle that hung from the ceiling.

"We just stretched the tulle taunt and duct taped it to the bottom of the table," Lia added with just a touch of pride. The table legs show but I think it works in the rustic barn setting."

THE WEDDING SLIPPER　　173

"Oh, it does," Jacq assured her, "And the posy of flowers tied with sage green ribbon hanging on the back of each chair is such a sweet touch." The table center pieces were duplicates of the aisle decorations surrounded by tea lights in pint size mason jars. Jacq declared the look as "unfussy rustic elegance."

"Okay, so what have I forgotten," Lia soberly asked. Jacq quickly, but with practiced expertise, scanned the venue taking inventory. The DJ was set up at the south end of the barn and food serving tables were already laid out with plates, cutlery, napkins, and large serving trays and bowls were located toward the north end. Large tubs of drinks were already staged on each side of the interior barn doors just waiting for ice. A huge grill was outside and just out of site of the west barn door and downwind to avoid smoke funneling into the barn. Further down from that were the portable facilities.

"Where's the cake?" Jacq inquired.

"It should be arriving anytime now," Lia stated.

"What I meant to say is where will the cake be displayed?"

Lia paused for a beat before calmly saying, "Oh no, I forgot the table."

Jacq began a mental inventory of Aunt Rose's tables. All of them were either too big or too small. "I don't think I have anything that will work well for the size you need," declared Jacq.

"Shall we call Garrett to see if he has anything that will work?" Lia produced her cell phone from her robe pocket, and calmly dialed Garrett's number. Jacq heard just one side of the conversation explaining the cake dilemma and soon Lia said, "that sounds perfect."

"Ask if he needs any help?" Jacq silently mouthed to Lia.

174   J. KIMALIE

"Jacq's here and wants to know if you need any help," Lia said into the phone. "Okay, she'll be right over," Lia conveyed to Garrett while nodding her head affirmatively to Jacq. "Garrett has a wine barrel with a glass top that should work for the cake," Lia explained to Jacq. "It will save him a trip if you carry the glass over while he wheels over the barrel."

By the time Jacq arrived at his back door, Garrett was loading the barrel onto a hand truck that he had cushioned with a towel.

"You're a lifesaver," Jacq announced upon greeting Garrett.

"Well, that is what I do after all. Sounds like this emergency qualifies as only a rescue, no searching required." Before, they reached the barn a bakery van pulled up.

"Looks like a timely rescue," Jacq said. The cake table could not have been a more perfect addition to the reception venue nor a more perfect size for the modestly scaled three-layer cake.

"Thank you, Garrett," Lia enthusiastically exclaimed stepping on tip toes to kiss him on the cheek. "I wanted ivory frosting and simple decorations on the cake, but the cake looks almost too plain. Your fancy wine barrel helps elevate it," Lia stated, while eyeing the cake with a look of mild disappointment.

"That's easy enough to fix," Jacq stated with certainty, "I'll be back in a flash."

Garrett and Lia watched Jacq walk with purpose to the greenhouse returning with a handful of long stems full of beautiful orchids. Jacq looked at Lia, inclined her head toward the cake and hitched her eyebrow in an unspoken question. Lia nodded her consent. Jacq plucked off pristine individual flowers from the stems and gently pressed the stems into the frosting careful not to touch or bruise the delicate flowers. Lia and Garrett watched in awe as Jacq artfully cascaded the orchids

THE WEDDING SLIPPER 175

from the top layer to the bottom at an angle so the flowers adorning the cake reached half-way around.

"That is exactly, just exactly, what the cake needed," Lia cried. "I've never seen those beautiful orchids before, what are they called?"

Garrett and Jacq glanced at each other and at the same time said, "Wedding Slippers."

"Until today, there are probably only a handful of people who have ever seen those orchids," Garrett added reverently. "Rose hybridized those orchids dedicating them to Jacq."

Lia walked over to Jacq and hugged her fiercely saying, "In addition to everything else you've done, thank you for giving me part of yourself and a part of Rose to weave into my memories of our wedding day. Honestly, Jacq, you're better and more resourceful than a fairy god-mother!" The sweet moment was interrupted by a very loud bleating. All three turned toward the sound, Garrett and Jacq were horrified to see Pirate casually eating the flower arrangement at the end of the last row of hay bales.

"Oh no, I must have left the gate open" Jacq realized, as Garrett raced to redirect Pirate from the flower buffet she was enjoying.

Lia laughed out loud, and said, "That's got to be lucky or something."

Garrett and Jacq each thought, "Or something" but both said aloud in unison sounding reasonably convincing, "It's definitely lucky!"

Jacq promised to disguise the assault on the arrangement by pilfering flowers from the other arrangements on the aisle to fill out the decimated one. "No one will ever know when I'm finished," Jacq pledged, and Lia was sure no one would. Happily, Lia tucked away the story, and the mortified looks on Garrett's and Jacq's faces, in her mind as a little treasure for telling at a later date.

Lia excused herself to finish getting dressed and headed the short distance to the RV she was using as the gals dressing room and the place she and her dad would emerge from to walk down the aisle. Once Pirate was corralled and the flowers restored, Jacq and Garrett headed to their respective homes to get ready for the wedding now less than two hours away.

Chapter 21

Most of the guests arrived about fifteen minutes prior to the wedding and were busily catching up with one another as Jacq unobtrusively joined the group. The first person Jacq noticed was Ian, resplendent in a dress kilt complete with a traditional silver and fur sporran around his waist and very fancy wool kilt hose reaching just below his knees. He looked formidable and ready at a moment's notice to protect either the highlands or whatever brand of Scotch he likely had in a flask hidden away in his sporran. Ian was holding court with several ladies when he noticed Jacq and without a break in his conversation, he blew her an exaggerated kiss followed by a mischievous wink. She couldn't help herself; she broken into a grin and shot an air kiss back at him.

Several of Lia's relatives whom she had met at the barn cleaning, made it a point to walk over to Jacq, say hello and to introduce her to other family and friends whom she had not yet met. Jacq was warmed by the sense of community she felt with what amounted to be practically strangers. Of course, over the years, she had established a group of friends and colleagues in New York but the community she was already a part of here felt so welcoming. In New York there always seemed to be a vetting of status, fashion labels, desirable zip codes, or acceptable

178   **J. KIMALIE**

university pedigrees before you were really welcomed into an inner circle. Maybe her New York group was more clique than community.

Before she could continue her comparative musings, Brett, the groom, his best man, and a groomsman filed into the barn followed by Donovan looking extremely handsome, in fact, head turning handsome, in a black slim fit mandarin collared jacket with matching black slacks. Donovan's tailored look was adorned with elaborate brightly colored Native American necklaces almost covering his chest area. The arrival of the men signaled the imminent start to the ceremony. Conversations were quickly brought to a close and folks moved to find seats. Jacq turned to the row nearest her to find Garrett already seated and looking expectantly up at her. "Please take the aisle seat," he said, "I have it on good authority that if you get hungry the flowers make a delicious low-calorie snack." Jacq stifled a giggle as the mother of the bride, appearing from seemingly nowhere, came walking down the aisle on the arm of the father of the groom, who also had his wife, the groom's mom, on his other arm.

When the three parents were seated, a man, decisively Hawaiian looking, in the second row on the right stood and began playing a ukulele as he hummed an upbeat tune unfamiliar to Jacq. A young bridesmaid, the groom's sister, if Jacq recalled correctly, and the maid of honor, Lia's sister, made their way down the aisle, chiffon skirts dancing in the breeze and took their places up front. The ukulele paused, just for a moment, as the man, whom Jacq later learned was a cousin of the groom, began playing *What a Wonderful World*. His clear tenor voice sang out the familiar tune. All guests stood as a glowing Lia on

THE WEDDING SLIPPER 179

her father's arm made their way down the aisle. Lia was not a blushing bride; she was a beaming one with a smile directed at her groom so genuine it was almost too intimate to witness. The groom could not take his eyes off her, his tears welling as she came into his full view.

Lia looked beautiful! Her ivory lace dress was contemporary but harkened back to a fitted silhouette from the 1950's. Her treasured cowboy boots turned out to be the perfect accessory to the dress and accompaniment to the setting. Her light brown hair was pulled back into a loose twisted boho braid with fresh flowers woven into the casual style.

Donovan began the ceremony with a greeting in his tribal tongue. It was doubtful anyone, other than Donovan himself, actually understood a word of what he was chanting. Donovan raised his face and arms to the sky, stomped his foot on the ground twice and used both arms to, what looked like, gather spirits to himself, the message was clear enough, albeit somewhat open to interpretation. Jacq was surprised by his graceful, fluid movements and decided they were downright poetic. Jacq looked left and caught a nonplussed expression on Garrett's face. He shrugged his shoulders, leaned toward Jacq's ear, and whispered, "I thought he only knew swear words in his tribal tongue." Jacq looked into his twinkling blue eyes as a slow smile bloomed on her face. At some point the ceremony had switched to English, but when, Jacq could not quite pinpoint as she was caught up in the dramatic and unexpected opening to the wedding.

The ceremony would prove to be a seemingly random collection of traditions that Lia had solicited from friends and family. The next surprise was a tradition that Ian had

180   J. KIMALIE

contributed. Donovan asked what token Lia and Brett brought to symbolize their commitment to each other; both produced a ring – not the surprising part. Donovan explained that a Gaelic wedding ceremony tradition is the warming of the rings. He explained that the rings would be passed around by the guests as the ceremony progressed. Lia and Brett wished for each person to briefly hold the rings in their hands while saying a short, silent prayer or blessing for the couple to enjoy a long and happy marriage. Ian came forward, undoubtedly the most Gaelic looking person in the crowd, carefully collected the rings and walked down the aisle handing the person in the last row the rings. Ian, as discreetly as he was able, positioned himself on the ends of rows to ensure the rings were passed in an orderly fashion as to not miss anyone. His role was not unlike shepherding an offering plate in church, so that every guest had a chance to "warm the rings." Meanwhile, the ceremony continued with Lia and Brett exchanging vows.

Lia passed her bouquet of red roses surrounded by a profusion of multicolored flowers to her maid of honor. She turned her body to face Brett and took both of his hands in hers. "Yesterday was our past," she began. "Our past is where we met and fell in love. Our past is where we learned from our parents, family, and friends how to truly love in a way that is patient and kind and seeks not its own. The best parts of our past we will always carry with us. Let's agree not to let the worst part of our pasts define or confine us. Our present is here and now, and I couldn't be happier," she gushed. In an automatic gesture with no care for tradition, they fell into each other arms in a long, sweet embrace. They stayed in each other arms unwilling to release the other but after a time she continued her vows. Their embrace so

THE WEDDING SLIPPER   181

tight, Lia had to arch her back and tilt her head back to look up into Brett's face. "Our tomorrow is unknown. What is certain is that we will come to many crossroads in life. Since you are more fearless, I will lean on you to guide us on our chosen path and in turn offer support to you just as two trees in the forest do as they grow toward each other, their roots intertwined and supporting the other, each less likely to succumb to a raging storm. I promise to search for joy in all circumstances and love you until my last breath."

Her vows complete, Lia stood up on tip toes and kissed Brett like no one was watching. Before the moment could get uncomfortable for guests, from the side aisle, Ian boomed in a sing-song voice, "We're all still here." Everyone in attendance broke into hearty laughter.

Donovan patiently waited for the guests to settle down and turned toward Brett. "Good luck topping that," said Donovan, earning a few more chuckles from the guests.

Brett, on the other hand, took Donovan's words as a serious challenge, and with Lia still in his arms he dipped her low, so sudden, and unexpected were his movements that a cute little squeak escaped from Lia's lips before Brett's lips crushed hers into silence. This time everyone present broke into both uproarious laughter and enthusiastic applause. The photographer's camera began clicking to memorialize the moment. Somehow Donovan managed to still look distinguished as he waited for the near horizontal couple to right themselves.

The remaining ceremony was just as untraditional and charming as it had started out. The only mishap, to put it as delicately as possible, was only witnessed by just a few people in the front rows and hopefully not the photographer; although no one who saw it would ever forget it. Lia's grandmother had dropped the groom's ring during the ring warming hand-off and Ian dutifully bent over to retrieve it from the barn floor. With an "Oh my" from a startled grandmother whose right hand flew to her chest, Ian, once and for all, conclusively revealed what men wear, or don't wear, under their kilts.

Donovan ended the ceremony with a Native American blessing. "While this is not from my tribe", Donovan explained, "this Apache blessing is my favorite and it seems apropos for the occasion:"

"Now you will feel no rain, for each of you will be shelter for the other. Now you will feel no cold, for each of you will be warmth to the other. Now there will be no loneliness, for each of you will be companion to the other. Now you are two persons, but there is only one life before you. May beauty surround you both in the journey ahead and through all the years. May happiness be your companion and your days together be good and long upon the earth."

As Donovan was coming to his concluding remarks, he had Lia and Brett face their family and friends. Lia's sister handed the bouquet back to her and Lia literally began bouncing on her toes in anticipation of the close. "And now, it is my great pleasure to present to you Lia and Brett, husband and wife." You may seal the ceremony with...," before Donovan finished his statement, Lia launched herself into Brett's arms. In one fluid movement that looked like a practiced dance move, he caught her, but just barely, as he was not expecting his new wife to vault toward him. Brett effortlessly swung her up into his arms catching her legs just under the knees before the newly married couple did indeed seal the deal with a kiss. Throughout the kiss,

THE WEDDING SLIPPER   183

Lia's boots could be seen from under the hem of her dress kicking rhythmically back and forth. When Lia and Brett finally tore their lips and eyes from each other, they looked to see their family and friends standing in an enraptured ovation. When Lia spied a cluster of her girlfriends standing together grinning like a pack of schoolgirls, on impulse she surprised everyone, including herself, and tossed her bouquet in a high arc over to the group of friends. She was off target just a bit, and the bouquet landed in the lap of a shocked Nicole who was saying something to her fiancé, Matt, and hadn't realized there was an incoming projectile.

Jacq couldn't help reflecting on the hundreds of weddings she had seen at the hotel, each probably costing many multiples of this event. But none had been so joyous, authentically reflective of the couple, or as fun as this wedding had been, and the party was just getting started. From the back of the barn, the DJ had the music going before the guests had finished hugging it out and congratulating the bride and groom.

As Garrett and Jacq started to move toward the bride and groom to add their congratulations, Donovan walked toward them down the aisle. "Well done" Jacq praised. "No one could have convinced me an amalgamation of so many different cultural wedding traditions could have come together so beautifully," she admitted. "I had to see it to believe it."

"Yes, that was all well and good," Garrett added, "but is their union actually legal."

"It will be once I mail in the license," Donovan assured them.

"You never cease to frighten me Donovan with what I don't know about you," Garrett stated, eyeing Donovan with an air of suspicion.

184

"You try saying no to Lia," Donovan retorted, "it's impossible when her mind is made up."

Ian walked over making it a foursome. "Ian," Donovan stated with more volume and animation than usual, which stopped Ian in his tracks and derailed a rather good line he was about to unleash on the group. "You could have given Lia's grandmother a heart attack," Donovan said in an accusatory tone completely out of character for him. A baffled expression washed over Ian's face. "I'm just glad you were not facing me when you bent over to retrieve the ring," Donovan went on to explain, "but you mooned grandma and anyone else with a sightline to your big ass."

"I did no such thing," Ian exclaimed indignantly, "all I did was reach down..." and he started to demonstrate when a desperate chorus of "Don't," and "Whoa," came from his three companions. Their hands moved in unison to cover their eyes to be saved from the unenviable site which would be permanently emblazoned in their memories.

Just then Emmett walked up and said firmly, "Gams you have got to stop giving anyone looking in your direction a show when you bend over. What the hel...heck," he hastily amended for Jacq's benefit, "was with the blue ribbon I saw dangling from your," Emmett paused and decided to end the sentence short with, "I saw dangling?"

"Oh," a remorseful Ian said, "I guess you did get a peek."

"I didn't peek," Emmett said in disgust," it was more like I was flashed. To peek is to initiate, to be flashed is to be victimized," Emmett clarified in an unnecessary distinction as the group had already sorted through the difference for themselves.

THE WEDDING SLIPPER   185

Jacq could not hold it together any longer, she had been biting her lower lip to keep from laughing but how long was a gal expected to keep it together especially given the blue-ribbon reference from The Drunk Scotsman song. The more irritated Emmett and Donovan became the funnier the situation was to her. In welcome release, she threw her head back and laughed with her whole being not even trying to contain her amusement. Her delight was so contagious the angst in the group quickly evaporated. "Let's go get a table and something to drink," Garrett proposed, and the group headed that way. Jacq barked out another laugh when from behind her she heard Emmett get in the last word when he grumbled, "try and keep it under wraps Ian."

Nicole and Matt ended up joining their table and the conversation throughout the evening never lagged for a moment. A wood plank of charcuterie, with a decidedly Hawaiian twist in homage to the groom's side of the family, had been placed on every table. Guests munched on meat, cheeses, dried mangos and pineapple, macadamia nuts, and other assorted treats. Guests hopped from table to table catching up with relatives and friends in an informal buzz of activity. Lia and Brett were deliberately visiting each table to acknowledge and thank each guest. Jacq realized that probably everyone in the room contributed in some way to making this event a wonderful expression of love.

When the chuck wagon bell announced lunch, folks leisurely headed to the serving tables. While not the variety of choice Jacq was accustomed to seeing at weddings, the offerings provided were outstandingly delicious and plentiful. The menu offered a choice of mouth-watering salmon or steak straight off the barbecue along with three salads and homemade Hawaiian rolls that literally melted in your mouth. Jacq thought it was smart to keep the menu to a manageable number of items as there were no kitchen facilities.

After lunch dancing began in the most unorthodox way. If there was a theme to Lia's wedding, unorthodox would have summed it up nicely. The bride and groom had moved away from all the guests to the darkest recessed corner of the barn presumably for a private word or kiss. Before long, Brett was twirling Lia in slow circles to the music that lead to their own "private" first dance as husband and wife. If they thought they had escaped the notice of their guests, they hadn't, but what they did accomplish was to signal that dancing had begun. Both set of parents made their way to the center of the barn followed by two-thirds of the guests and the dancing began in earnest. A father-daughter and a mother-son dance would no doubt occur sometime in the afternoon, but it would happen naturally at a time that suited the moment opposed to an announced spectacle that guests were obligated to watch. Jacq found the lack of a timed program and scripted events unfolding in a predictable sequence incredibly refreshing and relaxed. The society weddings she was accustomed to in New York, and in fact had helped to produce dozens of times, felt more like watching a well-choreographed performance rather than participating in an organic experience. Jacq was thoroughly charmed by the simplicity and authenticity of the day. Any thoughts she may have had of feeling like an outsider among such a tight knit group of family and friends had vanished early on.

Since Jacq and Nicole were outnumbered by the men at their table, the gals were kept rather busy on the dance floor.

THE WEDDING SLIPPER   187

Tablemates were not the only ones to keep Nicole and Jacq on the dance floor; Jacq was sure she had danced with every one of Lia's male relatives including two who were not old enough to shave. Emmett and Ian turned out to be superb dancers, Donovan and Matt were practiced and enthusiastic dancers, and Garrett had not yet asked Jacq to dance.

When the DJ slowed down the music, probably to avoid sending guests into cardiac arrest, Garrett appeared at Jacq's side. He looked at Ian and said, "Check out her dance card buddy, this one is mine." Garrett's look and tone left no doubt that he was going to win if it came down to a contest of wills. After a beat, Ian dramatically kissed Jacq's hand and stepped back from her executing a princely bow that earned a collective groan from the table behind Ian. Thankfully, almost everyone was on the dance floor and so Ian's modesty was only marginally compromised. Jacq and Garrett had also heard the groans and didn't need to look to verify what had happened. Garrett was shaking his head and chuckling in resignation of his friend's eccentricities and Jacq was unabashedly laughing, her head tilted back as they came together in a dance embrace.

It was all Garrett could do not to kiss her exposed neck, but his thoughts were forcibly interrupted when Jacq's body, not just her shoulders, heaved and her laughter intensified. Garrett swiveled his head to see what had completely captured her attention and noticed that Lia's grandmother had asked Ian to dance. Her hand was scandalously low on his back and slowly dipping. Within their line of site and behind Ian, Emmett was watching the spectacle and had an incredulous "go figure" expression on his face. Garrett couldn't help but join Jacq in her exuberant laughter.

188

J. KIMALIE

Triumphant in their struggle to regain their composures, Garrett pulled Jacq tightly into him instantly recapturing her full attention. "I was going to say you look good dancing, but you just look good," Garrett said in an extremely convincing tone a bit lower than his normal speaking voice.

Nicole and Jacq's shopping trip for a new dress for the wedding had been a great success. Jacq was wearing the peony adorned, emerald-green cocktail dress she had seen in the shop window with nude colored lace ankle boots, in lieu of the hot pink cowboy boots the mannequin had been sporting. Nicole had deemed the lace boots both sexy and practical for a barn setting. From the front of the dress, the sweetheart neckline did not hint at the back of the dress that was open down to Jacq's waist exposing her toned muscles and soft skin. The appreciative look in Garrett's eyes affirmed her choices. Jacq paired the dress with dangling pearl drop earrings and a long gold backdrop necklace that strategically placed a large teardrop shaped freshwater pearl low on her exposed back. When she had been dancing earlier to up-tempo songs, she could feel the pearl swinging around and bouncing against her back and she had questioned her choice in jewelry. But now as Garrett was ostensibly exploring the gold chain by lazily running his hand down the links, his warm fingers making contact with her back the entire length of his exploration, she was no longer doubting her jewelry selection. A shiver ran from her toes, in her lace boots, to the top of her head at his protracted touch. Jacq had always thought a shiver from head to toe was just a saying, but she was wrong, she could feel the top of her head and everyplace else in her body that had nerve endings vibrating.

THE WEDDING SLIPPER   189

"This thingamajig has been driving me crazy all night," Garrett confessed as he fingered the teardrop pearl low on her back.

"Well then we're even," Jacq countered.

"How do you figure that," Garrett inquired, having switched to exploring more exposed back than necklace.

"Yesterday, I saw you moving hay into your truck, and you were sporting a pair of chaps and those always make me a little crazy," she confessed.

"I was bucking hay, not moving hay, that's what we call it," Garrett informed her, "bucking hay."

"Great, now I have a new image to go with the one of you clad in chaps that is not going to help me sleep better," she informed him, "but my dreams might be more interesting," she added with a wicked grin.

The first moment Garrett had seen Jacq in her alluring dress, his resolve not to encourage her in the direction of a romantic relationship started to give way, like sand and pebbles on the fringe of a cliff when a hiker came to close to the edge. Dancing with her in his arms, he felt like a hiker who had completely lost his footing and was irretrievably sliding down into the abyss. Garrett removed his hand from Jacq's waist and reached up gently taking her right hand that had been resting on his left shoulder and pulled it down and behind her back allowing even closer body contact between them. In Jacq's mind Garrett's dance score just went way up along with her temperature.

Now dancing almost cheek to cheek, hip to hip, and chest to chest, Garrett spoke softly in her ear, "Jacqueline Rose Reed, if you were not going home in a month or two, I would work very hard to make all your dreams come true." His words, which could have sounded corny, pierced her heart given the sincerity of his declaration and the expression of longing on his face.

She leaned her head into his and audibly sighed, "I don't suppose you ever have a reason to be in New York?" she asked already knowing the answer.

"Not really," he said, the words grudgingly spoken aloud seemed to seal their fate. "I'll come visit," he vowed," if you would wear this thingamajig" he said as he flipped the dangling pearl at her back. He had attempted to lighten the mood, but his words only succeeded in reminding them both that their lives were on opposite coasts. With a shared look of regret and in unspoken resignation they both headed back to their seats mid-way through the song.

Rejoining her table mates, Jacq realized that it must be later than she had realized as the sun was about to set which she assumed would bring the party to a close. She could not have been more wrong. Someone drove a pickup truck to the west door of the barn and headlights served to illuminate the space enough for the party to continue unabated. She noticed the tubs had been refilled with drinks and ice and the DJ once more cranked up music and the tempo. Garrett took drink orders from everyone at the table and left to bring back another round of refreshments.

Nicole leaned toward Jacq, tilted her head toward the dance floor and said, "That looked very chummy until it didn't."

In a deflated tone, Jacq replied, "I don't deny there is chemistry between us, and he seems like an authentic guy I would love to get to know better, but soon there will be 2800 miles between us and I think we both just acknowledged the implications of that fact."

THE WEDDING SLIPPER 191

"You're killing me Jacq, I just know you and Garrett would be perfect for each other," Nicole proclaimed.

"You and Matt seem pretty perfect for each other," Jacq said desperately needing to change the subject.

Nicole looked toward Matt and smiled. "Yeah, we are opposites in many ways, but we are better together, I know we'll make a good go of it. When you were dancing with Garrett, Matt asked Donovan if he could marry us here and now and I think he was only half kidding. I'm the one who wants the big Seattle wedding and Matt thought an intimate wedding like today's would be perfect," Nicole confided.

"Well, I have to say," Jacq stated with conviction, "I've never seen a more joyous wedding, and everyone seems to be having a great time. I had my doubts that the old barn could look this picturesque, but the flowers, tulle and candles turned this place into a charming backdrop for a pretty remarkable celebration."

"Maybe you should keep the place and turn it into a party venue," said Nicole in an offhanded remark.

"But then you would lose a sales commission," Jacq responded back just as flippantly.

Garrett returned with the drinks and soon the gals were back on the dance floor. In between songs, Emmett approached Jacq to claim a dance. "Your Aunt Rose would have loved your dress and you look stunning in it," Emmett declared as he twirled Jacq in time with the song.

"Of course, she would have preferred an orchid painted on it, but the peony suits you," Emmett added wistfully.

"Thank you" Jacq responded noting Emmett's pensive expression. "I can see I'm not the only one who is missing her," Jacq tentatively stated looking meaningfully into Emmett's eyes.

192   J. KIMALIE

"I won't deny it, I miss her something fierce. We became close," Emmett acknowledged. "When I saw the Wedding Slippers on the cake, which was a lovely gift to Lia by the way, I couldn't help but think how delighted Rose would have been to see her orchids make their debut at a wedding. Although, I think she might have been saving that honor for you Jacq." The touching revelation brought tears to Jacq's eyes. "Did you know that it took ten years for the orchid to bloom for the first time?" Emmett inquired. Jacq, unable to speak, shook her head indicating she had not known. "She was a rare, patient and thoughtful woman, your Aunt Rose," Emmett proclaimed. For the remainder of the song, they danced in congenial silence. Jacq began to contemplate the nature of Aunt Rose and Emmett's relationship.

When Jacq returned to her seat, Lia and Brett were serving cake to their guests, one table at a time. When they arrived at Jacq's table Brett was carrying a large tray loaded with plates, each topped with a slice of delicious looking cake. Jacq had never before seen a bride and groom serve their guests cake, it probably wouldn't be practical at a wedding with lots of guests, but it was such a thoughtful touch and munificent way for Lia and Brett to honor their guests. Lia mouthed "thank you" as she handed Jacq her piece of cake. Looking down, Jacq saw a generous slice of carrot cake surrounded by orchids.

No one seemed sure when the bride and groom slipped away for the evening, but in true Lia fashion it happened with no fanfare or announcement. Hopefully, the photographer captured their clandestine escape. The enthusiastic dancing and visiting went on for another hour or so before guests started saying their goodbyes and gradually departing. Lia's folks made

THE WEDDING SLIPPER   193

a point to seek out Jacq and thank her again for the generous use of the barn. Lia's mom told Jacq that before Lia and Brett stole away Lia had shared with them, "Today was everything I dreamed of and more for my wedding. I feel like I lived my personal fairy tale and ended up with the prince of my dreams." Jacq felt humbled to have played a part in making Lia's dreams a reality.

Garrett offered to walk Jacq back to her place and Jacq gratefully took him up on his chivalrous offer as the night was dark with just a sliver of moonlight that did little to illuminate the uneven ground back to the house. She was grateful for Garrett's sturdy arm guiding her along. "May I have one last dance here under the stars?" Garrett asked, just before they reached the backdoor. His words fell upon Jacq like a giant weight, the phrasing laced with such finality was soul crushing. Jacq dolefully realized this probably would in fact be their last dance together. Without a word, because Jacq didn't trust herself to say anything that wouldn't be accompanied by tears, she turned to face Garrett and laid her head on his shoulder. They slowly swayed, in perfect rhythm, dancing to an unheard melody.

When Garrett felt goosebumps rising on Jacq's arms and back, he realized she must be chilled. With much regret, Garrett brought their private dance to a close. When his feet stopped moving, Jacq looked into his eyes. "Would you like to come in?" Jacq asked, her words posing more invitation than question.

"Oh yes ma'am, I would indeed, but would and should are two different things. I think I'd better say goodnight right here." Garrett lifted both hands and placed one on each side of Jacq's lovely face, his thumbs caressing the gentle curve of her jaw line. His hands slid around to the back of her neck in an upward path until her silky hair was flowing through his fingers like water. He twisted his fingers around her hair and gentle pulled her head back. His kisses started at Jacq's exposed throat and with maddingly slow progress he worked his way up until their mouths hungrily found each other's. Jacq sighed as Garrett slowly intensified the kiss, pulling their bodies together until they were hip to hip. Their kiss started with urgency and passion but ultimately dissolved into resignation of what was, rather than what would be.

Chapter 22

The day after the wedding, Garrett was called out on another search and rescue that would take him east, across Puget Sound, into the Cascade Mountain Range. He had acquired a diverse set of skills in the army that made him a highly sought-after member on any Search and Rescue Team. He was certified in Wilderness Survival, Trekking in Harsh Environments, Rope and Climbing, First Aid, and Navigation among others, but he knew his dogs and their skills set him apart as an elite member of any group. While most Search and Rescue Teams were largely made up of volunteers, Garrett was on paid retainer with a number of Washington Sheriff's Departments and the US Forest Service which over saw numerous Ranger Stations in the area.

After receiving a rescue call out, Garrett was normally on his way within 10 to 20 minutes as his gear was always packed and his satellite phone always charged. In this case, he had a ride coming for him in 40 minutes, never a good sign he thought to himself steeling his emotions for the task before him.

While he was sure that Jacq would not mind his ride landing in her meadow, he ran to her house to apprise her of the situation and to secure her permission. His field was large enough for

196

J. KIMALIE

the helicopter to land, but it was closer to the animals than he preferred.

Garrett was in mission mode and all business when he reached Jacq. As he knew would be the case, Jacq, without hesitation, gave permission for use of her property.

"How long will you be gone?" Jacq inquired.

"I'm never quite sure, at least a couple days I would imagine," Garrett replied. "Emmett will hold down the fort, so don't worry about the animals. When I get back, we have two pieces of unfinished business to conclude, we'll figure out the home for the orchids and I'll pay off my bet."

"Don't worry about either one of those things, in fact, I forgive you your debt," she added hastily. Garrett's mind was too preoccupied to see the color rising from her neck to her cheeks.

"Anything I can do to help out while you're away?" Jacq asked.

"Emmett will let you know if there is," Garrett said in response, already turning for the door.

Through the kitchen window Jacq saw the helicopter set down. Within seconds, Garrett and the dogs were loaded, and the helicopter rose and streaked east. Jacq felt silly when she realized she was waving—a totally wasted gesture with no one to witness her sendoff.

Jacq was relieved that their first encounter after last night's kiss had not been awkward. She wanted Garrett in her life to the extent that it made sense. He had already proven himself to be a standup guy and had become a friend. She would always be grateful for his caring sensitivity on their date as she exposed her story and heart to him. If nothing else, he had played a willing

THE WEDDING SLIPPER 197

part in her healing journey whether he recognized it or not. For that she would always be thankful.

Three days passed with no word from Garrett, which Emmett assured Jacq was not unusual. She found herself uncharacteristically edgy and needing to work out tension in her shoulders, neck and back. While she did not have a yoga mat with her, she made do with an area rug to stretch and soothe tight muscles. To keep from thinking about Garrett, she poured herself into her work.

The next afternoon, Jacq had piled the miscellaneous contents of her aunt's desk on the kitchen table and was sorting through all manner of mail, receipts, and odds and ends. Neat piles were emerging when she heard a sturdy knock at the door. "Come in" she shouted marveling at how naturally the phrase came out of her mouth when she would never even consider leaving her door unlocked in New York or yelling for someone to enter without knowing who was at the door. To her surprise, a dejected looking Garrett walked in carrying a brown paper bag.

"Hello" said Jacq by way of greeting, "when did you get back?"

"Late last night," Garrett said, his eyes looking tired and worn. His demeanor, resigned and rigid.

"I'm sure I was asleep," Jacq said, "but I can't believe the helicopter didn't wake me up."

"That's only a one-way ride, when time is of the essence." Garrett explained, "I was driven back by one of the guys in the search team."

"Given the look on your face, I take it things did not go well," Jacq gently inquired.

198   **J. KIMALIE**

Garrett said nothing but indicated no with a shake of the head. The broken expression of his sunburned face jarred something loose in Jacq's heart.

"I am so, so sorry Garrett," Jacq replied. "Come on, sit down and I'll get you a drink."

"I could use one," Garrett stated flatly, "so I'm here to kill two birds with one stone. I came to pay off my debt," he announced as he pulled out of his bag a bottle of Patron and a dozen limes neatly corralled within a mesh container. To Garrett's questioning eyes, Jacq stared at the bottle like she had never before seen Tequila. "I never welch on a bet, so I need you to show me how you do your fancy New York shots."

Jacq couldn't find her voice and when she finally did, she stammered, "but I forgave your debt."

"True," Garrett replied, "but like I said, I never leave a debt unpaid when I lose fair and square and this debt I can dispatch rather painlessly. So, are you ready to show me your New York technique?"

When Jacq did not immediately reply, Garrett quizzically studied her. The look on her face was inscrutable. He noticed that Jacq's exposed skin of her neck and throat had turned beet red. Darn he wished he could read her better. Was she upset he had stopped by unannounced, embarrassed for some reason, and why had she been struck dumb?

"Come on," he coaxed, "a shot's a shot, it can't be much different from how we down them here."

After more of the uncomfortably long pause, Jacq sputtered, "You might be shocked then."

Garrett was confused as Jacq was just standing there looking as though he had asked her to contemplate the mysteries of

THE WEDDING SLIPPER 199

the universe as she seemed so lost in her own thoughts. Why wasn't she saying anything and why was she just frozen in place not moving a muscle? In fact, it didn't look like she was even breathing.

Garrett waited with growing uncertainty as to what he had unintentionally set in motion. Jacq was battling between not being altogether sure that she wanted to commit to Garrett in this way and knowing she could help Garrett take his mind off whatever he had experienced during the rescue attempt. Did she want to start something that may be a delectable diversion in the short term but may prove to be a mistake in the long run? She was concluding that a diversion from her ordeal and his more recent one may be just what they needed when Garrett broke the silent tension by asking, "Shall I grab a couple of glasses?" Again, no response immediately came from Jacq and Garrett was unsure she was even tracking with the conversation.

This was not the first time Garrett wished he could read a woman's mind. To Garrett's grateful relief, Jacq decisively said, "We won't need glasses," as a resolute expression replaced her unreadable one from a moment before. Now completely self-composed, Jacq took charge and directed Garrett to cut a lime in half and grab the saltshaker. She left the room returning with a well-worn quilt and picked up the bottle of amber colored liquid.

"Why don't we head to the barn since it is such a nice day?" Jacq suggested.

"It's sunny but a little cool outside," Garrett warned.

"That's okay," Jacq responded coyly, "Tequila shots have a way of warming one up."

Once the blanket was laid out with hay beneath it, giving it a little extra cushion, Jacq gracefully sat down, and Garrett athletically dropped down across from her.

"Okay," Garrett said, "show me the big city way of doing shots."

"I never said it was the big city way of doing shots, I said that I learned the best way to do Tequila shots in New York."

"Go on then, enlighten me," Garrett quipped.

Jacq was sitting up, legs bent, with her arms around her legs. Last chance she thought, last chance to back out as she managed a long slow exhale. Jacq looked up into Garrett's amused and slightly puzzled face and realized that she didn't want to back out, in that instant she knew she wanted to be all in. She directed Garrett to fill the bottle cap half full of Tequila. As Garrett turned to dutifully comply with her instructions, she laid down flat on her back and began slowly unbuttoning her blouse. Garrett turned back toward Jacq spilling the contents of the cap, startled by her sexy and very unexpected actions. Garrett was fixed in place, jaw dropped, his mind desperately trying to catch up with the unexpected turn events had taken, his body well into processing her actions all on its own.

"Uh, oh, we're going to need that Tequila GoGo," was all Jacq said.

Somewhere in a small, recessed, part of Garrett's mind he realized that it was the first time Jacq addressed him by his call sign and he was inexplicably pleased. The rest of Garrett's mind and every inch of his humming body was fully engaged and mesmerized, utterly transfixed by Jacq's beautiful form emerging button by button.

THE WEDDING SLIPPER 201

"I'm ready for that Tequila GoGo," Jacq prompted again seductively.

With uncharacteristically unsteady hands, Garrett repoured a half cap of Tequila and handed it to her. Jacq carefully and ever so slowly poured it into her belly button. Garrett unconsciously licked his lips. "The lime next," Jacq coaxed.

Garrett reached to his left patting around for the half lime never taking his eyes off the hard and soft parts and the receding and protruding places of Jacq's shapely body. Once he secured the lime, he stretched out his hand to give it to her. Rather than immediately reaching for the lime, Jacq deftly opened her lacey bra by unhitching a hidden front hook and then she placed her hand over his. At her touch, Garrett's building desire rocketed through him. He had never experienced anything so enticingly erotic. They never broke eye contact as Jacq guided his hand over her left exposed breast and squeezed his hand resulting in juice trickling onto her inviting flesh. When the cold juice hit her hot skin, she shivered, and Garrett was instantly untethered from the past few difficult days and was fully tied to the moment. She calmly asked for the salt belying her own racing heart. She dipped a finger into the bottle of Tequila and rubbed a little on her right breast creating a bullseye for Garrett. Then she sprinkled it with salt.

"OK, GoGo, it's time to lick, drink, suck and pay off your..." he was moving on top of her before she finished the sentence his fatigue from the past few days having vanished. No additional processing time was needed as his carnal thirst for her took over. He may have covered the distance to her in record time, but he took things slowly, enjoying his "New York style" shot. He was downright determined to savor every drop.

Both were left panting and wanting more when Garrett had all too soon satisfied his debt. He generously offered her the next shot.

"I haven't lost a bet," she teased.

"I can remedy that," Garrett replied. "I bet you can't get through me taking two more shots without losing all control," he taunted in a husky tone. "And this time around, I get to decide how to use the salt and lime," Garrett added with hungry eyes and a wolfish grin.

"I'll take that wager," she enthusiastically countered and then Jacq wholly lost herself in losing the bet.

In due course when Jacq's muscles stopped quivering in delight, she lay back for a moment to catch her breath. Just as her lungs were finally able to take in deeper and slower breaths, Garrett's breathing became more frequent and shallower. In growing desperation Garrett grabbed the bottle, laid back and urgently splashed some Tequila in the vicinity of his navel. Jacq took the none too subtle hint and spent some blissful time happily working off her obligation in full. After the scales were better balanced, they lay in each other arms fully spent, no longer focused on their burdens and no longer thirsty.

Chapter 23

Jacq felt as limp and relaxed as a rag doll. She didn't want to move a muscle, just remain in the snug, warm place within Garrett's arms for as long as it could last. Neither had spoken for the past twenty minutes or so. They just existed in the special place they'd created, under the faded old quilt that smelled like it had been dried in the summer sun. The late afternoon light crept in all hazy and golden in the barn with the wedding tulle still dancing in the breeze that penetrated the old wooden walls. The quiet was broken only by the occasional creaking of the barn, Pirate calling out in the distance to one of the other animals, and the quiet cooing of doves that had returned after the wedding activity to roost up in the high rafters.

Garrett was the first to move, shifting his arm just slightly under her. He whispered, "I don't want to lose this moment, but I'm afraid my arm is beginning to fall asleep."

Jacq turned her head slightly to look directly in his eyes, forehead to forehead. "Let's get you more comfortable then," she murmured and lifted up so he could pull his arm out from under her. She then lay down on her back.

He shook his arm awake and then placed it alongside in between them, taking her hand in his. Their fingers intertwined, he gently massaged her hand and said, "Today was rather unexpected, but entirely fabulous. I had no idea when I lost the bet that I would end up winning the jackpot."

Jacq laughed, nudged him softly and replied, "JACQ-pot?"

Garrett joined her with a chuckle and nudged her right back, "I'll say!"

"I can admit that I wasn't sure I would go through with it in quite this way at the time we made the bet," she admitted. "Enough time has passed, and I've had a number of thoughts churning around in my brain."

"You and me both," he confirmed. "I've fantasized about being with you, I won't deny it, but I never expected something so, well, like I said—unexpected. I've also never had anyone call me "GoGo" who made it sound so sexy before either, of course, I guess up until now I've only had army buddies call me that. "

"GoGo" fits you. I hope you don't mind my using it."

"Not when you use it the way you did today," he answered huskily. "You continue to surprise and delight me at every turn Miss Jacqueline Reed. It would be incredibly easy to fall for a woman like you."

"I've obviously had some thoughts about being with you as well Mr. Garrett Olsen." Jacq turned toward him again so she could see his face. She moved her leg so that it could rest partially on top of his stretching her foot out so she could wiggle her toes against his. "I must say that you exceeded my expectations. It would not be hard to fall for a guy like you either."

Garrett kissed her softly and told her, "I think I'm already beginning to fall. I know how to handle repelling off a 100-foot cliff, or diving from a plane, but this type of falling isn't the kind of thing where I've had much practice."

THE WEDDING SLIPPER

Jacq closed her eyes and absorbed his words. "I don't think either of us was prepared for the feelings that came with this. I flew out here to the west coast to settle my aunt's estate and try to find some peace after everything that happened. I never in a million years thought I would meet someone like you. Why did I have to find you so far away from home?"

Garrett pulled Jacq on top of him and wrapped his arms around her again as she lay her head on his chest. "Isn't the important thing that we did find each other? We don't have to figure anything out today. Maybe we should just enjoy the moment and not focus on the distance between our home addresses for now. Why don't we just enjoy getting to know each other better and not worry about what's going to happen."

"Funny, but that's exactly what I've been telling myself ever since a few days after we met. It hasn't made it any easier for me," she admitted, "Today may have been unexpected, but I really don't do casual, and never have."

"I'm not someone who does casual either," Garrett added. "I've been thinking about what would happen if we tried to have something more serious too but was worried there was no point with the distance thing and, quite honestly, the timing. You've gone through so much these past two years, and I don't want to rush you into something if you aren't emotionally ready."

Jacq didn't say anything for a minute, so Garrett continued. "Only you will know when the time is right for you. That said, today felt pretty right to me. I just don't want to see you get hurt any further and I sure don't want to be the one responsible for making that happen."

Garrett's cell phone suddenly rang full volume cutting into the conversation like a machete. "You have *Hot Legs* for a ring tone?" Jacq asked as Rod Stewart rocked the barn.

Garrett let the call go to voicemail, made a face, and said to her, "Two guesses."

"Oh, of course, it's got to be Ian," she said hitting her head as if she should have known.

"You've got that right. We planned on getting together for a few drinks tonight and debrief from the rescue. I sort of got sidetracked and forgot all about it. He's probably calling to find out where I am."

"Why don't we talk about this later? Go see Ian," she said even though she wanted to remain curled up in his arms.

"Are you sure? I can call him and cancel."

"Absolutely. It's probably best we take some time anyway. Today was wonderful, but I think it would be good for us both to think things through a bit on our own." Jacq made herself get up, turn away, and rein in the tears that were threatening to slip loose. It had felt so good to be held. She wasn't ready to think logically and talk about it, so she just tried to keep it all together and got dressed.

Surprised at how quickly the mood had changed, Garrett slipped back into his clothes as well, laced up his boots, and tried to make light of what felt like an awkward moment. "I can always count on good ol' Gams for butting in at the absolute worst moment."

Jacq turned back to him, managed a shaky smile, and said, "We can't blame Ian for this one. You guys had plans, and as you said, today was unexpected. Besides, the conversation was starting to get serious real fast. Maybe he did us a favor."

"I suppose you're right, but we do need to finish talking about this." He pulled her into one last embrace, kissed her soundly, and finished smiling lips to lips as Pirate called out from just outside the barn door. "Okay, how the hell did she get out again?"

Jacq gathered the quilt up and they walked out of the barn. Garrett assured her he would call the next day and then led Pirate by her kerchief back to his place. Jacq walked slowly back to the farmhouse, thinking about all that had transpired. "Oh Jacq," she thought, "you've gone and started something that now you're going to have to finish."

Garrett texted Ian at the Longhouse to let him know he was running a little late. When he arrived, he quickly spotted his friend sitting in the back at a corner table, reading on his phone and sipping a scotch. Today, Ian sported a khaki utility kilt and a long-sleeved camouflage printed T-Shirt. There was a glass of red wine waiting for Garrett across the table from him. Garrett took his seat and thanked him and didn't hesitate to gulp some of the wine. Ian put his phone down and reached out to bump fists.

"Another tough one?" he asked.

"Yep, but we got through it. Any recovery that involves a kid is a particularly tough one for me, you know that."

"How'd the dogs do this time?"

"Great. They did everything we needed them to do. Sadie may be getting a little older but she's still holding her own, and Nitro seems to be stepping up. When I think of all the people they've located since we began doing this, I wish I could come up with a better reward than hugs and dog treats, but that's what they want. Plus, they seem to share the joy when the mission is successful or the relief at recovery, even though it's sad, along with the rest of us."

"Too bad more people aren't good dogs," Ian stated matter-of-factly.

"Cheers to that," toasted Garrett, taking another sip of his burgundy.

Garrett gave Ian a long, detailed recap of the rescue while his friend listened attentively. When he finished, Ian ordered them each another round and then sat back and looked directly at his best buddy.

"Make mine a coffee please," Garrett said. "I had some, uh, some tequila earlier so I'm done for the day."

"Tequila huh. So, what went wrong?" Ian asked.

"Nothing that I could have changed. Why would you ask that after I just told you everything that happened?"

"You don't usually go into such minute detail," noted Ian, "Particularly when things don't end the way you hoped. In fact, you usually sort of downplay all the things you had to do. Either something wasn't quite right, or you are trying to focus on the rescue instead of whatever else is eating at you. So, what's up?"

"Nothing's up and nothing's eating at me. I just thought you wanted to hear all about the trip," Garrett responded a little irritably. "That's all."

Ian took a slow sip of his second scotch and leaned back in his chair. "Okay, that's fine. I don't want to get into your business if you don't want me there. And I don't think you were drinking tequila because you were celebrating your rescue turning out okay. Just remember, we've been through hell together, literally. I'm here for you anytime you want to talk. I know we joke

THE WEDDING SLIPPER 209

around a lot these days, but don't forget I can do more than just joke with you. You're my best buddy and I think we both know what we've put on the line for each other in the past and always will. Just sayin.'"

Garrett thought about what Ian said and clinked glasses once again.

"I know that. I guess I've just got some stuff on my mind. I will if I need to."

"Damn straight," chirped Ian. "So, do you need to?"

Garrett grinned and replied, "Not really, but maybe."

"Business?" enquired Ian.

"No," said Garrett.

"Ohhhhh, I see," said Ian.

"You see what?"

"Jacq. Tequila. You've fallen and you can't get up."

Garrett grimaced and didn't acknowledge his friend's flippant remark.

"Look bro, I'm serious. I've seen how you look at her. She's gorgeous but there's a lot more to her than a pretty face. I get why you're drawn to her. If you hadn't seen her first, I might have approached her myself. I can tell there's chemistry between you two—in fact, everyone can see it."

"What do you mean everyone? Are you guys talking about us?" Garrett asked a little ruffled.

"Nothing much, just noticing that something's in the air. We aren't blind and you wouldn't want any of your buddies making any moves in that direction so of course we are aware and respectful. Is something wrong with that?"

"No, of course not. I'm just trying to figure out how to handle this. She's not going to be in town that much longer and she's had a rough couple of years. The idea of getting into something just to have to turn around and end it seems sort of pointless and insensitive. I've got to stay focused on trying to expand my place and the animals. I don't have time to run back and forth to New York and I don't want to lead her on and then end it."

"Who says you have to end things if they start? And what makes you think she's even willing to go there with you?" Ian asked.

Garrett said nothing but looked at him in resignation.

"Well, I guess this is a bit of a dilemma," said Ian. "I must say though, I haven't seen you show any interest in a woman in a very long time and the last time you did, you didn't seem all that happy with your choice. Look, it's not my place to tell you if you've chosen well or not Grasshopper, but I wouldn't be a very good friend if I didn't at least share that I think you've chosen well. Very well indeed!"

"Well, that's certainly helpful," snapped Garrett. "Now if I decide it's best to back away, I'm potentially hurting someone you think is wonderful."

"That's not why I said it," Ian added thoughtfully ignoring Garrett's irritation. "I just want you to remember how rare it is to meet someone special enough to capture your interest, and rarer yet for them to return it, as she has. Maybe you should give some deep consideration to how much you're willing to give to have any kind of relationship with her."

Garrett ran his hand across his face and thought about what Ian said. "You know me probably better than anyone Ian. You're right, I'm just not sure what to do with all of this quite yet."

"What does she think?"

"We haven't been able to have a complete conversation about it yet."

"But you're not avoiding it?"

"No. We started to talk about it, but I had to run to go meet this crazy, kilted Scot friend of mine."

"Seriously? You bloody idiot. You couldn't just text me and say something had come up? I'd have understood."

"I could have, yea, but we realized it might be good to think about if before we got too far with the conversation. It was a good call."

"Okay, if you say so."

"Maybe a distraction is what I need. Want to shoot some pool or play a couple of rounds of darts?" Garrett suggested.

Ian was uncannily perceptive. "Isn't darts what launched this conundrum?"

"Let's play eight ball," said Garrett.

Jacq had agreed with Garrett that it would be good to think things through and she took the task to heart. She thought about their afternoon together all the way back to the farmhouse and again over a light dinner. She thought about it some more while she took a long, slow, warm soak in the divinely deep vintage claw foot bathtub. She tried to take a break from thinking about it while she sipped a cup of chamomile tea and watched the ten o'clock news, but her mind kept going back to Garrett, so she never really did register what had happened in the world today. An hour later, she was still thinking some more about it as she lay in bed under a down comforter with moonlight streaming through the gap in the curtains that she liked to leave just a little bit open. It was the last thing she remembered thinking about before finally drifting off, and the first thing she woke up thinking about after a restless and dreamless night's sleep.

Waking up earlier than usual, Jacq felt tired but unable to return to sleep, so she got up and auto piloted her way to her morning coffee. She went into the living room and sat in an overstuffed chair that offered her a vista of the side field with the Olympics peaking above the hills in the distance beyond. A hawk was slowly gliding patterns around the field hoping to catch breakfast before the sun created shadows enabling it to be spotted from below.

Jacq was tempted to call Beth and talk about all that transpired, but somehow telling anyone about what happened in the barn didn't feel right. She could talk to Beth about almost anything, but her barn encounter felt too private to share. She'd already talked to her friends about her conflicted feelings and fear of entering into a more serious relationship with Garrett and she knew what they thought, so there really wasn't anything new to hear. But she felt so alone in the moment. Garrett understood that she was still working through the loss of her family. She was beginning to realize that no one ever actually heals from so deep a loss. One just gets better at containing emotions and making space for one's own life to happen. She wasn't just feeling alone in the moment, she was feeling the aloneness that had become her new normal.

Jacq was grateful to have her two devoted and close friends in her life, truly, but family was something that grounds a person even deeper, and she no longer had family. Did that mean that developing any new relationship was going to come with added pressure for whoever she dated? Would any man she got close

THE WEDDING SLIPPER   213

to think that he had to handle her with kid gloves? Was Garrett reflecting on their encounter yesterday and now wondering what he had gotten himself into?

It was just a few days ago that she had concluded it was best to curb things before they went too far. She knew at the wedding that her heart was stepping out in front of her head, yet against her better judgment, she let herself go there. She had tried to let Garrett off the hook for the bet and thought that would be the end of it and she could just stay friendly and maybe have a sweet kiss goodbye at the end of her stay, but no! She had to just give in to the moment. She had to fulfill her tequila fantasy—she'd acted so cosmopolitan, *Sex In The City* cool, but in truth, had never done shots that way before. Yes, they had both enjoyed it, clearly, but what must Garrett be thinking today.

Jacq poured a second cup of strong coffee and put the last, slightly stale pastry on a plate and warmed it in the microwave. Even a little stale, a pastry from Sluys beat anything hands down from her usual stop at the deli back home.

The microwave beeped a couple of times in harmony with the tone announcing the arrival of a text on her cell phone. She gathered the warm pastry and coffee and went back to the living room to see what was likely to be a message from Christopher on the other coast given the early hour.

She was wrong. It was a message from Garrett. "Good morning beautiful. We need to finish our talk. When can I see you again?"

Jacq couldn't bring herself to respond to him quite yet. Probably not her finest moment, but he didn't expect her to be up yet anyway, and she wasn't ready to face him so soon. What if he was primed to get out before it got too serious? What if he wasn't? When he showed up yesterday with the tequila, she just went with it. Maybe her instincts assumed that an afternoon of friends with benefits would get him out of her system, but if that was the case, her instincts were dead wrong. Garrett was the perfect balance of strong and gentle. He was the kind of guy she'd always hoped to meet. He was the kind of guy that getting close to and losing would surely break her heart.

She was still recovering from loss, but not reeling from it anymore and loving someone new didn't take away any of the love she had for the family she'd lost. It may not be so much a sense of wrong time, but it was definitely the wrong place. Given his commitment to his work and hers to her career, the distance was a deal breaker. That wasn't a conversation she was looking forward to having. She didn't want to hear that this wouldn't work from him. She needed to take control and responsibility for herself and inoculate her heart against the hurt that inevitably was coming. He may have been the one to ask her out, but she allowed things to go as far as they did, and she asked him to pour the tequila. This was on her. Maybe if she ignored the text for a while the right words would come to her. Maybe.

She decided to go to town on the rest of the house and see if she could lose herself in distraction. She still had to tackle her aunt's bedroom. If that couldn't help her escape these thoughts for a while, nothing could.

Chapter 24

Jacq leaned against the door frame of Aunt Rose's bedroom staring out the bay window beyond the bed. The view was a rain drenched blur with indistinct greenery in the distance. The bedroom was the last room Jacq needed to tackle, but she needed to stand still for a minute to get up the courage to go through her aunt's most personal things. She smiled when she remembered her aunt commenting on the fact that whoever found themselves cleaning out her bedroom after she was gone, the first activity they needed to accomplish was to clean out her underwear drawer and just throw everything away. She hadn't wanted strangers pawing through her underthings or heaven forbid, buy them at an estate sale. Aunt Rose was so adamant about her underwear drawer she made Jacq and her parents swear it would be the first thing they did if they found themselves in the situation of being executor of her will. Her Aunt Rose wouldn't be happy that it wasn't the first task that Jacq had done, but she would uphold the spirit of her promise by throwing her underwear out today. Jacq's smile faded as a feeling of loss and remorse filled her chest. Every time she started going through Aunt Rose's possessions she was hit with the overwhelming truth - she would never laugh with her aunt again.

216 J. KIMALIE

Pushing off the door frame, Jacq walked further into the room trying to shuttle aside the feelings of grief and loss to look critically at all the items that needed to be sorted. The bedroom was a little old fashioned. A king-sized four poster bed was the focal point that dominated the room. The posts where whimsically carved with grape vines and leaves with a cluster of grapes rising in relief in the middle of the headboard. The bed was covered in an old-fashioned quilt in sea green, gold, cream, and hot pink. The quilt was made up of a series of Northumberland star squares in various solids and patterns. Although quilts weren't really to Jacq's taste, she could appreciate the work that went into making such a piece of art. She reminded herself to do research on heirloom quilts as she was sure she could find a buyer who would treasure the not quite pristine, but well-loved quilt. Above the bed hung a triptych of individual orchids embroidered in gold silk. Aunt Rose had found them on a trip to China and, of course, since they depicted orchids, fell in love with them. Framed in simple mahogany, the flower on the right was done in lavender and purple thread with evergreen leaves, the left was in soft and hot pinks and the center was in creams, whites, and soft reds. Jacq wondered if the center orchid was the inspiration for the Wedding Slipper. She decided the stunning pictures would accompany her back to New York as a memory of Aunt Rose's undying love for the unique flowers.

Jacq knew the nightstands were full of personal keepsakes Aunt Rose kept close. Most notably was the journal she had found her first day in the house. There were some expired medications needing to be disposed of carefully as well as dog eared paperback romance novels. Jacq could picture Aunt Rose

THE WEDDING SLIPPER 217

sitting in her window seat rereading the steamy pages of her favorite books.

The window seat sported a thick green flannel seat cushion, perfect for rainy-day reading. Jacq walked over to the seat cushion, curious if she would find a storage cabinet. Sure enough, underneath the window a secret compartment was revealed with additional quilts and wool blankets. Jacq decided she would start her clean-up duties there as it would be easy to weed through the many coverings.

Jacq pulled out the thick wool blanket on top and shook it out to make sure moths hadn't eaten through the design. She realized Aunt Rose used dried lavender to keep the moths away when lavender pods flew all over the room. Sneezing, Jacq chuckled to herself thinking it was a good thing she had already found the vacuum. Looking down into the cabinet she spied a small piece of folded paper. Kneeling down, she gently lifted it out of the indent in the blanket where it was cocooned, she read, "Your laughter lights my days, and your passion fills my nights." The note was signed simply E. Putting the note aside, she hurriedly pawed through the rest of the blankets scattering dried lavender on the floor and seat cushion. Not finding anything else, she stood up and began to methodically unfold each of the quilts. By the time she was done, three more notes had been uncovered from their hiding places.

"Come grow old with me, the best is yet to be."

"Our souls sing to each other in the rain."

"Every moment we are together, my soul whispers to yours in words too beautiful to express."

Each of the notes were signed with a simple E.

218

J. KIMALIE

Jacq walked out of the bedroom to retrieve the hat box where she had placed all the other notes found around the house. Sitting cross-legged on Aunt Rose's bed, she laid them out in neat rows side by side. They were romantic, funny, touching, and beautiful. She mused whoever sent the notes was obviously in love with her aunt. They were much too personal to be given in just friendship. Since Garrett had mentioned his thoughts about Emmett and Aunt Rose, she was convinced, more than ever, Emmett was the author. If it was Emmett, her heart broke for him and the loss he had suffered.

Carefully sliding off the bed, so as to not disturb the notes, Jacq walked to the closet. She assumed she would find other love notes. It seemed logical Aunt Rose would keep the most romantic notes in her bedroom, but why were the others scattered all over the house? Why didn't Aunt Rose put them in one place like Jacq did as she collected them? Shaking her head, knowing she would never know the answer to that particular question, she continued sorting through the blankets deciding that all of them could go. She would hold onto the quilts until she could research their worth and decide the best way to sell them.

Deciding she better get to the underwear drawers, Jacq grabbed a roll of trash bags and moved on to the closet. Aunt Rose had a walk-in closet, lined on one side with built in drawers and cabinets in a warm walnut with various rods on the other side holding hanging clothes. In true northwest style, much of the closet was taken up with boots, sweaters, jeans, and t-shirts. Everything was organized by type of clothing. Jacq laid out three trash bags designating the keep, toss and donate piles. She began with all the shirts. As she sorted through the various pieces of

THE WEDDING SLIPPER   219

clothing, Jacq checked every pocket she came across. Jacq felt like she was on a scavenger hunt. Not finding anything in the shirts she moved on to pants. Here she found a note in the front pocket of what looked like Aunt Rose's favorite jeans given the frayed hem and the holes in the knees. The note read, "The beauty of your orchids can never compare to your smile." Jacq chuckled at the badly drawn happy face with a big cheesy smile nestled beside the signature E.

Methodically going through each of the pockets so she didn't miss anything, Jacq found two more notes in the hanging clothes. One was tucked in the built-in bra of an evening gown. Jacq pictured Emmett, at least by now she hoped it was Emmett, handing it to Aunt Rose as they shared a romantic evening dancing under the stars. Jacq didn't see any evening bags, so she imagined her Aunt Rose tucking it near her heart so the sentiment would never be lost. Taking a quick break from the closet, Jacq lined up the small notes on the bed where the others rested. Between all the discovered notes and the pressed flowers, she had come across in books weeks ago, the collection was starting to tell a romantic tale.

After grabbing a can of grapefruit infused sparkling water, she began to tackle the opposite side of the closet. For a while she got lost in the jewelry Aunt Rose kept in the top cabinet. Necklaces, bracelets, and earrings sat on lush cream velvet that lined the thin top drawer. Aunt Rose preferred semi-precious stones. Tourmaline, opals, jade, peridots, and garnets winked up at her in a variety of settings, some whimsical and others more simple. She picked up an emerald cut garnet in a gold setting. Jacq tried it on the ring finger of her right hand and discovered one of the things she and Aunt Rose had in common was the size of their fingers. After almost a half hour of trying on various pieces, Jacq decided she should leave the jewelry until last so she could admire every piece before deciding what to do with the colorful gemstones. In this, she and Aunt Rose had similar tastes and, for now, Jacq would put it all in the keep pile.

Jacq retrieved a separate trash bag from the roll sitting on the floor of the closet and dutifully threw every piece of Aunt Rose's underwear away. Bras, panties, camisoles and spanx went into the toss pile along with all the work clothes that had seen better days. Tucked in among the lingerie was a small black lacquer box inlaid with mother of pearl along the edges. Jacq pushed at the top to open it and discovered it was locked. She had a hunch the small key she had found on Aunt Rose's key ring would perfectly fit the lock. Jacq took the box out of the closet and set it on the dresser for closer inspection later.

After going through the rest of the closet, Jacq went back to the jewelry drawer and tried to pull it completely out of the cabinet where it rested. She wanted to take it to the kitchen table, examine every piece and wrap them up to ship home. She had a suspicion she wasn't going to be able to part with any of the jewels, but wanted to examine the various pieces with their beautiful gemstones and intricate designs. As she tried to pull the drawer out, it stopped about two thirds of the way and refused to go any further. After several yanks that did nothing but jumble the contents, she walked into the kitchen to grab a butter knife out of the drawer to use as leverage to pry out whatever was holding the drawer partially shut. Jacq pushed, pulled, and jiggled until with a swipe of the butter knife a navy-blue velvet ring box popped out. Opening the box, Jacq was disappointed that it was empty of any jewelry. Turning the box

THE WEDDING SLIPPER   221

this way and that, Jacq noticed, tucked in the top of the white satin interior, was a piece of paper. Unfolding the small note, Jacq read "Will you marry me?" signed E.

Chapter 25

Jacq placed the tiny marriage proposal at the end of the last row of love notes. She didn't realize she was crying until a tear fell on the corner of the small piece of paper. Laid out before her was a love story in three-by-three short poems and love quotes. Jacq sat on the edge of the bed letting feelings of elation and devastation engulf her—elation that Aunt Rose had found love again and devastation that her new love story had such a tragic ending.

After what seemed like hours, but was probably only a few minutes, Jacq wiped her hands across her cheeks, slowly rose and walked to the nightstand to retrieve the journal she remembered spotting that first day, hoping the volume might reveal the identity of the poet who had captured Aunt Rose's heart. Sitting in the window seat, she thumbed through the first few pages of scientific orchid names and hand drawn diagrams with notes about this stem and that petal. It was obvious, Aunt Rose was putting together the recipe to create a new flower. Jacq continued to turn the pages until she spied a date in the top right corner.

"I spent the day in the greenhouse watching the orchids; sometimes I feel like I can actually see them grow. I wish that were the case as I'm anxious to see my new creation. I hope it

THE WEDDING SLIPPER   223

is as beautiful as I envision. This one is for my favorite niece. I hope it will bring her love and happiness and maybe some good whoopee with a handsome man." Jacq gave a snort of laughter at her aunt's words. She wondered if the moments she spent with Garrett qualified as "whoopee" in her aunt's eyes. Since Jacq was her only niece, she assumed her aunt was talking about her. A few pages later another entry read, "I'm thinking that the new flower is a bust. The leaves are not as robust as the other species. I'm going to give it a few more weeks, but I may need to start over." Jacq didn't read disappointment into her aunt's words but rather the thrill of a creative soul discovering a new country.

Thumbing through a few more pages of orchid doodles, scientific terms that meant nothing to Jacq, a picture of the greenhouse with measurements and happy face doodles, another entry caught Jacq's eye. "I thought I would never look or feel for a man the way I looked and felt about Thomas. But lightening does really strike twice." It was just a few short words, but the first clue to the mystery man that tended to pore out his heart in tiny poetic comments.

Jacq sat the journal down in her lap and looked out the window thinking of Aunt Rose, Garrett, the friends she made here and the friends back at home. Her feelings were a jumble of half formed dreams and wishes. Jacq sighed and stood up from the window seat thinking a cup of tea would help her find her equilibrium. On the way out of the bedroom door, Jacq grabbed the black box off the dresser and carried it into the kitchen.

Jacq set the box down on the dining room table. Walking into the kitchen, Jacq filled the bright red metal tea pot with cold tap water and set it on the stove to heat. Soon the kettle set off a shrill whistle indicating the water was ready. Poring hot water into one of her favorite mugs, Jacq stood at the counter dunking her tea bag, staring at the black lacquer box. Leaving her tea bag to steep, Jacq picked Aunt Rose's key ring off the hook by the kitchen door and walked to the dining room table with the small key clutched in her hand. Fitting the key into the lock, she opened the box curious as to what was so important to Aunt Rose that she had hid it in her lingerie drawer. Inside was a black and white picture of Aunt Rose and Uncle Thomas on their wedding day. They looked young and in love. Digging deeper into the box there were other pictures of life with Thomas as well as a folded legal sized vellum envelope. Jacq was strangely reluctant to unfold it, wondering if the contents would bring her more grief or would prove to be a keepsake to treasure. Flattening the envelope, Jacq noticed written on the front was "to my Jacqueline Rose." Taking a sip of her quickly cooling tea, Jacq ran her fingertips over the writing knowing that what was inside could change her life. Jacq gently picked up the envelope, took two sheets of thick stationary out of their casing and began to read.

My dearest Jacqueline,

I hope this letter finds you well and happy. I've been meaning to put this note in the mail for a very long time, but never seemed to get around to it. Your Mom keeps me updated on your success in the city, but I always knew you would make your mark on the world. You do know, you are my most favorite niece.

Jacq smiled at those words again. It was the way her Aunt Rose would end their phone calls. There was never a good-bye, just "remember you are my most favorite niece."

Though it seems we never get to spend enough time together, I think about you often. So often, that my latest project is a special

THE WEDDING SLIPPER   225

flower that I plan on presenting to you on a special occasion, maybe even your wedding day. You know how I love to hybridize my orchids and I think I've hit upon the perfect combination of feminine and flirty with the beautiful blossom. It is only a bud now, but I know one day I will walk into the greenhouse and it will be there, an extraordinary specimen for my beautiful niece. If everything goes according to plan and it looks the way I think it will, I'm going to call it the Wedding Slipper. That is another reason why I haven't mailed the envelope, I'm hoping I can include a picture of my latest creation.

Jacq realized, time must have passed between the first and second part of the letter because the ink Aunt Rose was using changed from black to blue. It appeared her aunt had taken a long enough break from writing that she wasn't able to find the original pen she had been using.

The bud doesn't seem to want to open. I've been out in the greenhouse encouraging it to show me its face. Emmett has told me I have to stop being pushy. He thinks the flower is not going to want to meet me if I keep up my nagging. For such a quiet and stoic man, he sure has some fanciful thoughts.

You probably remember Emmett. He was Grace's husband. Emmett and Grace were good friends to Thomas and me. Since both Thomas and Grace's passing our relationship has deepened. Emmett is incredibly handy and has helped me around the farm as well as playing a huge part in putting my heart back together after Thomas' death broke it to bits. Hopefully, I have helped him along the way as well.

I didn't mean for this letter to turn morbid. Just know that I am doing really well, I have a lovely man in my life, but that doesn't keep me from missing the joy in your smile.

226 J. KIMALIE

Lately I've been thinking about the future and have decided to leave the farm to you. I know your life is in New York, but perhaps you will find this place a sanctuary where you can come to gather solace for your heart and mind, when needed. Or you may decide to sell it. Whatever you decide to do, know that I support you always.

I think of you as my bright and beautiful friend. Make sure you always cherish all of life's moments. Stop and smell the flowers and if you see any orchids, pause, and think of me. Let love find you and when it does, hold on to it with both hands and never let it go. Most of all always remember you are wrapped in my love.

Aunt Rose

Jacq reread the letter twice and turned to the second sheet of paper on the table. It was the official notice from the International Orchid Registration detailing name and genus of the Wedding Slipper under Jacq's name. Feeling numb and restless at the same time, she wandered out the kitchen door with the letter held loosely in her hand. The greenhouse door was open, so she walked in not really seeing the empty pots, thriving plants or hoses snaking along the walls. There was movement in the back, and it spoke volumes about Jacq's state of mind that she didn't even notice there was somebody else visiting the farm.

As Jacq approached the place where the orchids were housed, she saw a silhouette leaning over the flowers. Hearing her footsteps, Emmett turned from feeding and watering the plants. Her anguish must have been written in her red-rimmed eyes and trembling lips as Emmett took one look at her and simply opened his arms. Jacq slowly walked into them with a quiet sob.

THE WEDDING SLIPPER 227

"Ah sweetheart," he whispered enfolding her in his embrace. Not saying anything else he just held her tight as she wept on his cotton-clad shoulder.

With a hitch in her breathing and face buried in his chest, Jacq asked, "Did you love her?"

She felt his muscles tense and then relax, with a deep breath that lifted Jacq's head on his chest, he answered, "I did. Very much." Jacq stayed in his embrace for several minutes composing herself.

Emmett relaxed his hold, as Jacq slowly pulled away. Reaching beyond her, he tore off a paper towel from the roll sitting on the potting table. She took the substitute handkerchief and worked to wipe the evidence of grief off her face.

"Why didn't you tell me?" asked Jacq looking into his sky-blue eyes that reflected sadness back at her.

He shrugged, "I don't know. I guess I didn't want to intrude on your grief." They looked at each other remembering the woman who unknowingly had brought them together.

"Did she say yes?" Jacq asked giving him a small sad grin.

Emmett's eyebrows rose in surprise. Then his face broke into a joy-filled smile even though his eyes were bright with unshed tears. "She did."

At that moment, Jacq realized what a good-looking man he was when a smile lit his face, and with his poet's heart, she could see why Aunt Rose found him so attractive.

Jacq held out her hand to him, Emmett took it as she tugged him through the greenhouse door. "Come with me, I think I've found the book you wanted, and I want to show you something."

Walking through the kitchen door, Jacq laid the letter on the kitchen table and led Emmett into Aunt Rose's bedroom where the notes were laid out on the bed. Emmett looked at the paper collage and slowly approached the bed shaking his head.

"I had no idea she had kept all of these. It was a small joke between the two of us. She began to expect to see them at least once weekly. If I got busy or just forgot, she would let me know that she expected a note to arrive any day," he chuckled.

"It's obvious she loved you," Jacq stated, "I'm so glad she had you in her life."

Jacq picked up the journal and handed it to Emmett, "I haven't read through the whole thing, but I think you should have this."

Emmett took the journal. He looked at Jacq and said "Thank you. I don't know exactly what is in here, but I do know a couple of times Rose said she was going to record some of our experiences so we could laugh about them later. I wasn't sure she should write them *all* down," Emmett grinned. He looked down at the book in his hand with a soft smile and Jacq was surprised to see a blush appear along Emmett's cheeks and wondered at the memories the book had ignited.

Emmett looked up his eyes shining, "Your aunt was a special woman, and I was truly blessed to know her. Thank you for this." Emmett said. Gripping the book, he walked out of the bedroom, squeezing Jacq's shoulder as he went by.

Jacq let her eyes take in the room, the old-fashioned furniture, the beautifully embroidered pictures, and the view of the trees beyond. She was finished with the bedroom and essentially finished going through Aunt Rose's life. She realized, in the process, she had come to know her Aunt as a kind, gentle and loving soul that apparently engaged in "whoopee" with an extremely handsome older gentleman. Taking a deep breath and

THE WEDDING SLIPPER 229

one last look around, Jacq closed the bedroom door saying a final good-bye to a woman who had left her mark on the world through her flowers and the people she'd loved and left behind.

Chapter 26

Lately, most days seemed to fly by for Jacq, but not this one. After Emmett left, she kept starting jobs only to get sidetracked by her thoughts of Garrett and then would need to start something over again. It was already well past noon, and she hadn't accomplished anything of substance which was very unlike her. She also hadn't responded to Garrett's text. The right thing to do was to text him back and set up a time to meet and finish their conversation. Doing the right thing wasn't usually such a challenge for her. Even difficult conversations were in her wheelhouse, whether they were work related or personal. In fact, Jacq mused, her ability to face things head on and discuss them in open, direct ways had been a barrier to finding the right man up until now.

Most men that got past the "flirting and asking her out stage" seemed to find her too "business like" and "intimidating" for their comfort or else they embraced her strength but couldn't come close to matching it, leaving her to make all the tough decisions. She never mourned the loss of any of them as she seldom felt a strong enough pull toward either of those personalities. Now, she finally found a man she was attracted to who didn't back down from any conversations and didn't depend on her for carrying the dialogue. Now she was the one

THE WEDDING SLIPPER   231

having a hard time stepping up. If she had a therapist, this would definitely be a topic for a session she mused. Jacq had never thought of herself as a wimp and wasn't going to start behaving like one, but the fact that she was procrastinating on this told her that she was more emotionally invested than she thought possible after just a couple of months.

She heard her phone chime again, indicating another text. Sighing to herself, she picked it up intending to respond to Garrett this time, however, it was a text from Christopher with two lightning emoji's—their code for urgent. Jacq quickly opened it up and read the message, "OMG, hotel has sold. Call me ASAP!"

Jacq didn't have an immediate emotional reaction to the news. Strangely, she didn't feel a sense of dread or fear, just a little bit of concern for Christopher and of course, curiosity about what was coming next. She refilled her coffee, grabbed a pen and notepad just in case she needed it, and sat down at the kitchen table. She punched in Christopher's number and he answered instantly.

"Jacq, it's all happening," he said somewhat breathlessly.

"Okay, slow down and tell me what you know," she responded.

"When I got in this morning there was a strange feeling in the air and everyone was just heads down, doing their jobs. Then we got called into a group meeting and we were told that the hotel had sold, and the deal had closed overnight."

"The Chinese buyer?" she prompted.

"No, it was a real estate investment group with a hotel branch out of Boston. Never saw that one coming. We heard that they are small but planning to expand. Nobody knows if our jobs are safe, but we were told that initially there would be only limited staff changes. Oh Jacq, I don't know how to tell you this, but there was a man at the meeting who acted like he was the new manager."

"Was he introduced as such?"

"No, but we could sort of tell. I don't want to work here for anyone else but you."

A window popped up indicating another text message had been received. This time, it was from the hotel director's admin.

"Hey Chris, I just got a ping from Berkley's office. Guess we're going to know more shortly."

"I like the team the way it is. I can't imagine being here if you left," he insisted. "I also hate for you to have any more stress to deal with Jacq. When is it going to end for you?"

"I like our team too, but you know if I'm out, it's all fine. I'm really not stressed about this. Between my savings and my inheritances, I'm financially sound and can spend my time figuring out what comes next. It helped that you gave me a heads up a couple of weeks ago and I've had time to think about it. I've had so many changes in my life in the past couple of years, what's one more? Might even be good for me, you know."

Christopher paused a moment and then said, "I can always follow you to a new venue. Nothing tying me down here."

"That's right, but let's not get ahead of ourselves. Let's keep an open mind and see what develops. How's everyone else doing?"

"I think okay, for now. It's not like the hotel is going away and there wouldn't be a reason to bring in new people for most of the jobs, so I think it's just the top dogs who are squirming.

THE WEDDING SLIPPER   233

You better call Berkley back and hear what he has to say. You are going to let me know right away, right?"

"I will if I can."

"And even if you can't!"

"I'll get back to you as soon as I can. Don't worry Chris, we're going to be fine."

"From your lips..."

"Don't worry."

"Okay, I won't. How's everything else going?"

"Everything else is going fine. Don't worry."

"I worry when you say, 'don't worry' too much."

"Okay, then keep chill. I'm on the home stretch here and I'm not going to stress about work."

"Well, maybe that's because you've got a hero GI-cowboy to help manage your stress."

"Yeah, well, that's another story that we can discuss after I find out what's happening in New York. I better make that call before it gets too late since you're three hours ahead."

"Right, better do that. I'll be waiting for your call."

"Hang in there," she encouraged him, "we're going to get through all of this with flying colors."

"Okay girlfriend, we always do."

Jacq ended the call and checked the text from the director's office. His assistant wanted to know if she could take a 4:30 call, so 1:30 her time. It was nearly 1:30 so she texted back that she could and waited for the call. She meant what she said to Christopher—she wasn't stressing about it and was resolved to just absorb whatever the news was and move on from there. That's the thing about losing the people you love most in life. It puts all the other stuff in perspective, and you realize that a job is just a job, an apartment is just an apartment, and life is really about the experiences you have and who you share them with. Change can hurt but it can also energize you.

"So, bring it on!" she said out loud to herself and the universe.

The universe responded and her phone rang almost immediately. Jacq answered and Daniel Berkley, the Vice President of Operation's assistant asked her to hold for his call.

"Jacq, how are you? I'm sorry to interrupt you during your leave," Berkley said in a friendly tone.

"Hi Dan, I'm doing fine, thanks. It's been a busy couple of months, but I've accomplished a lot and shouldn't be too much longer. I have heard through the grapevine that things are happening on your end too."

"To put it lightly! You may have heard that the hotel was just sold. It's been bought by Hughes and Benack, a real estate and investment firm out of Boston. "

"The name sounds a little familiar to me," she interjected.

"That may be because they bought the Harrison two years ago. Their hotel branch isn't too big, but it is expanding slowly, and they target upscale boutiques like us. They have a reputation for being strategic and thoughtful about their investments and they are growing steadily. I think they'll do a great job here. I believe I'm leaving the running of it in good hands."

"They've let you go?" she asked with a concerned note.

"No, they've asked me to come to Boston to help manage the entire hotel branch. I've accepted the position."

"Congratulations Dan, I'm very happy for you! It won't be the same without you though."

THE WEDDING SLIPPER   235

"There aren't going to be a lot of changes, but the senior management team is going to look very different. I need to tell you that this affects you too Jacq."

"I knew it was a possibility. I've learned so much from you over the years and I'm sure I'll find something new."

"Well, you already have if you're open to something different. We want to talk to you about a couple of new options. You've done a great job over the years and, if you're ready to dive back in full time, we'd like to offer you the chance to move up. It could mean a move to Boston or another location though. "

"I'm certainly intrigued. What more can you tell me?"

"Plenty, but this should be done in person. When can you come home for a face to face?"

"I could probably get a way for a few days late next week. I'm close to a point where I'd just need to return to sign papers when the property sells. I can check on flights and confirm tomorrow—would that be okay?"

"That works. Just coordinate with Joan and get something on my calendar by the end of next week and we should be fine. I'm headed to Boston the following week and after that I'm doing a facility tour that's going to tie me up for at least three more weeks. You will need to jump on this if you're interested."

"Understood. I'll get moving on this. I want you to know that I really appreciate the opportunity and your support. I'm anxious to hear more."

"It's all good and you earned it. I'll see you next week then."

The call ended and Jacq leaned back in her chair and shook her head. Not what she expected. If she wanted to kick her career into high gear, this was certainly the opportunity. She decided she wasn't ready to talk to Christopher but needed to give him something, so she sent him a brief text. "Nothing clear yet, but I'm not without a job. I'm going to be flying back to discuss. Will send you more details when I have them." She ended with a smiley emoji and called it good. If only the message to Garrett was that easy.

Running a rescue ranch is not a job for anyone who isn't willing to roll up their sleeves and deliver a full day's work, each and every day, unless they have the resources to hire plenty of help. Maybe someday Garrett would, but for now, he was the entire staff, supplemented by a little help now and then from his caring friends. With so much to do, it was easy to get lost in the chores and not worry too much about how long it was taking Jacq to get back to him. He knew she'd be in touch and the time leading up to that was good for reflecting on what he was going to say.

Garrett shoveled out the stalls and freshened up the wood chips that made good bedding for the horses and had the added benefit of controlling the odor. Angel stood patiently outside her stall while he cleaned it, whistling a tune that she seemed to like as her ears were pointed forward and her stance was relaxed. The conversation with Ian the previous night was at the forefront of his mind and he considered the questions that had been posed. "Who says you have to end things if they start and how do you know if she even wants to go there?"

He didn't know if she wanted to start anything serious. He hadn't given her any reason to think he was offering more either. He didn't know for certain what she was looking for in a relationship. They had a connection that went deep; it just didn't include a lot of history and facts about each other. That said,

THE WEDDING SLIPPER 237

this was the first woman in a very long time that inspired him to remember every little detail that she shared.

Garrett had not been involved with many women. He was rather reserved and focused on studying during his college years and then came the army. He and his close circle of army brothers were all single and subscribed to the belief that it was best that way given the combat danger they were in every day while they were overseas. None of them wanted to risk leaving a fiancé, wife and possibly kids to face the news that they were permanently disabled or gone as so many of their comrades' families had been forced to face.

There was one time when Garrett had let his heart rule over his head. Her name was Lydia. She was from Atlanta, a reporter with Turner Broadcasting, who was on a several month assignment to do stories on the troops overseas. She was a peaches and cream blond with a seductive southern drawl. Nearly all the men, except Ian for some reason, were drawn to her, but she didn't seem to notice anyone but him. He was instantly smitten and dove in headfirst. She had him wrapped around her well-manicured little finger and he was ready to leave the unit as soon as his first tour was up just to be with her. When her work came to an end, she tearfully told him she had a fiancé back home and her family would disown her if she didn't follow through as they both came from old southern families and reputation was everything.

Garrett reacted like any normal guy would—he walked away and took comfort in a bottle of whatever was closest at hand. Unfortunately, the closest at hand was a bottle of apricot brandy that someone had left out in the barracks. It made him sick as a dog and left him with a raging headache. Ian couldn't help but tease him a little, given the choice of drink, but he knew his best friend was hurting and so did his best to commiserate and help. Garrett never forgot how Ian didn't say "I told you so" when Lydia had wounded him, but from that day forward, whenever she was discussed Ian referred to her as "Lied-to-ya" instead of her actual name. The experience left Garrett hesitant to ever rush into a relationship thereafter, except with animals. They always showed you exactly who they were from the first.

Angel walked back into her stall and rested her chin on his shoulder. Garrett reached up and scratched her behind her ears, her favorite place, and then ran a hand down her long neck and patted her withers. "You're starting to feel comfortable and at home here now, aren't you girl?" he asked realizing that she had been with him about the same length of time as Jacq. Jacq was starting to feel like home to him too. He may not have had a lot of deep conversations with her, but he'd had enough time to sense that she could be trusted. He felt a pull toward her that didn't include any sense of danger. He couldn't imagine giving up the rescue operation and the animals after all the effort he had already put into it, but a future with Jacq, if there was one, could be a once in a lifetime opportunity. Yet how could he ask her to give up a successful career to stay with him and find out where things could go, if he wasn't equally open to starting over on the east coast to accommodate her?

Garrett pushed the wheelbarrow out of the barn, emptied it, and took his gloves off to pet Sadie who had come over to shadow him. As usual, Nitro was only a few steps behind. Garrett sat down and poured a cup of coffee from the thermos he usually prepared mid-day and enjoyed a few moments of down time with the dogs. They could move anywhere with him and do their jobs just as happily, no problem. Garrett certainly wasn't risk adverse, not when you consider how he had spent the last decade of his life. Risking your life shouldn't seem easier than risking your heart, but oddly enough it was. Could it be possible the first woman he'd met who was worth the risk had just popped into his life? And did he have the courage to find out? He was beginning to think he did. He just needed to gauge her reception before he took the leap.

He decided it was time to man up and speak up. He would tell her how he felt after he finished all his chores. "Come on dogs, we've got some post holes to dig." Garrett got up, shook the last drops of coffee out, packed up his cup and thermos then fished his phone from his pocket to check it. Somehow, he'd missed a text from Jacq. "I'll be home this evening. Why don't you come over around 7:30 and we can talk?" She didn't give him any clues as to how she was feeling, but no matter. He had set his course and was ready to see where it would lead. Fortunately, there was nothing like digging post holes to work up a sweat and distract a man from over thinking things.

Jacq had to kick into gear after talking to her director, so she created a punch list of things that had to be done before she flew back to New York to meet with him. She added a quick timeline to each of the tasks and decided she could complete the most time sensitive items, and probably a few more, soon enough to leave by next Wednesday. That left Thursday and Friday open as options for the requested meeting. She went online and booked a direct flight that would not force her to get up at the crack of dawn but gave her breathing room on the other end so that jet lag wouldn't be too bad. She left the return trip open so that she could be flexible depending on what came of the meeting.

After texting both Christopher and Beth to let them know, she was returning home for a few days and could get together with them over the following weekend, she finally took a beat and slowed down. She needed to wrap her head around the conversation with Garrett that was going to happen in another hour. Fate sort of took control of things and made it clear that her career was taking off now and this wasn't the right time to get in too deep. She'd been leaning toward that decision all along, but each time she was around him it was easy to push it away given how he made her normally level head swirl and her pulse race. There was no putting it off any further though, she had to let him know that she'd be leaving. She could own up to her very real and solid attraction to him though, as she felt she owed him that much.

Jacq made herself a quesadilla for dinner with some fresh salsa she had picked up at the country store the day before. She washed it down with a sparkling water and then cleaned up the few dishes from the endeavor. There was a chill in the air despite the fact that the days were growing a little longer and a bit warmer, so she lit a fire in the living room fireplace and adjusted the music to an all-acoustic instrumental channel that made the environment more inviting but didn't distract with lyrics.

Even though she was expecting him, Jacq twitched in surprise when she heard Garrett's knock at the door. She went over to greet him and felt her heart skip, as usual, when she saw him smiling at her. He had on his leather vest with the sheepskin collar and a cowboy hat and, if possible, looked manlier than ever. Removing his hat, Garrett stepped in, shutting the door

THE WEDDING SLIPPER   241

behind him, and instantly wrapped her in a firm, steadying hug without saying anything. After a minute or two, he kissed the top of her head and then stepped back, smiling at her with ease still holding her arms in his big, strong hands. "Hello gorgeous. I'm glad you invited me over tonight."

Jacq smiled back at him a little wistfully and rubbed his shoulders briefly before disengaging and leading him inside. "What can I get you to drink—a glass of wine perhaps?"

"Sure, if you're joining me," he answered, noting that she seemed a little more reserved than normal and didn't quite meet his eyes.

Jacq had a bottle of Pinot Noir opened already so she poured them each a glass and gestured toward the living room sofa that was facing the fireplace. They both sat down, and Garrett stretched out his long legs, crossing his boots in the process and took a sip of his wine. It was full bodied, velvety, and smooth. He looked at Jacq and simply said, "Tell me about your day."

"Such an easy thing to talk about on most days," she responded, "but not so much today."

Garrett sat up with concern and enquired, "Is everything okay? I noticed it took you awhile to text me back, but I just assumed you were busy with estate business."

Jacq took a bolstering sip of her wine and met his gaze. "Yes, I'm fine, no worries. I have been busy with the estate of course, but some stuff has come up with work. I'm going to have to go back to New York next week. I talked to my boss about it today and it's not something that can wait."

"But you'll be back, right?" Garrett asked keeping his voice calm.

"Yes, but I'm not sure when and I don't know how long I'll be staying when I return." Jacq looked down at her wine glass and swirled the red liquid a few times before meeting his eyes again. "The hotel has sold, and things are changing for me. The new owners are based out of Boston. Apparently, I still have a job if I want it, but it won't be the same. Dan, my current boss, indicated they were prepared to offer me a really good opportunity, if I was flexible. I took that to mean location."

Garrett absorbed the information and then nodded. "I'm happy for you Jacq. I know your career means a lot to you and if you have a chance to advance, then I'm sure it's a great opportunity you won't want to pass up. No idea where you'd have to move?"

"No, not yet; possibly Boston as that's where the new owner is located, but I really don't have any more information yet. She took another long, slow sip of wine. "It's time for me to finish pulling myself together and get on with my life. It's what my family would have wanted for me. A new position, especially one at a higher level, is going to mean long hours and dedicated focus. I wasn't expecting this, it actually caught me off guard, but I have to go check it out."

"Of course, you do. I've got to admit that although I am genuinely happy for you, I wish this had come just a little later in the year. I feel like we're just beginning to find the connection that's been hinting at us since we met." He leaned back again and looked at the fire as if it held answers, somehow, as to what he should say next. Unfortunately, it didn't.

Jacq's eyes were now focused on the flames as well. They both let the crackle of the fire fill the void for a moment and thought

THE WEDDING SLIPPER 243

about how much more to reveal. Jacq knew she needed to speak up first.

"We were. We are. We are just beginning to connect. You must know by now, especially after our tequila shots in the barn, that I feel something special for you Garrett. I've been thinking for a while now how nice it would be to have the time to find out what we might really have together. I've been so tempted to take the leap because I know you are the kind of man I'd always hoped to meet, but I also know that living on two separate coasts is not a way to sustain a good relationship. I also know that the work you are doing here is too important to abandon. I can't ask you to leave the animals and your dreams to come to the east coast, to some city I don't even know the name of yet, to be with someone who in truth, you hardly know. It doesn't make sense. And even if I was tempted to hit the pause button on my career, and I will tell you that I have been tempted, but the phone call today made it clear to me that this isn't the right time," Jacq's voice waivered a little on the last comment.

Garrett's heart hurt at hearing Jacq's explanation, but he reached for her and she let him pull her into his arms. She knew it wasn't fair to draw comfort from him when she was telling him things were over before they had barely begun, but her need to be held by him was too great and his arms were too inviting.

Garrett soothed her and rubbed his cheek along her temple. "It's okay, it's going to be fine," he said in a husky whisper in her ear. "I've been going through the same thought processes. It didn't feel right to ask you to abandon your career and New York friends to come out here and take a chance on a 'country boy' like me, but I was hoping it might just naturally go that way. There is clearly something happening between us and it feels like it could be strong, but you're right, the signs seem to be saying we don't belong on the same coast. That doesn't mean we have to give up our friendship though."

"No, of course not," she said straightening up and backing out of his embrace. "But like I told you before, I don't do casual."

"I didn't mean that we..."

"I didn't think you did," she interrupted putting her hand on his forearm. "It's just that I'm not sure how we go from what we feel right now to just friends without some time to adjust."

Here he was foolishly thinking they could make a go of their relationship and she was giving him up. Garrett closed his eyes as the pain in his heart increased ten-fold when he realized that he might never hold her again. It was all he could do to hold back the tears.

"I understand." He stated trying to keep his emotions reined in. "Maybe it's best if we limit time with each other."

He downed the rest of his wine and looked at her again and smiled sadly. "I'll never be able to drink tequila again without thinking of you city girl."

Jacq felt the slow creep of blush bloom on her face again, but bravely held his gaze.

He stood and asked, "So when are you leaving?"

"I've got a flight out next Wednesday," she answered. "I don't know when I'll be back. It all depends on what I find out about the new job and what Nicole tells me is needed once the farm sells. I think I can have just about everything done by then if I crack down and work double time." She so wanted to hang on to him and make this knot in her stomach go away, but after all that had been said she knew better than to reach for him again.

THE WEDDING SLIPPER   245

"Do you want me to look after the orchids while you're gone?"

"No, no worries. I've already asked Emmett to do that for me."

Garrett got up and reached for the wine glass to go rinse it out.

"Don't worry about that, I've got it," she said and placed his empty glass next to hers. "I'm really sorry that it all happened this way."

"Me too." Garrett looked down at her like he could inhale her, then closed his eyes and briefly sighed. He looked at her again with that half smile of his and said, "You're going to accomplish great things, I just know it."

"And you already are, and I'm so glad we got to know each other," she replied, realizing how awkward it sounded the minute she said it. Jacq walked Garrett to the door and opened it to find the garden bathed in bright luminescence. The moon was full and it lit up the garden enough that the crocuses and other early bloomers that lined the walkway could be seen in its shafts of light.

"You always look beautiful, but in the moonlight, you are absolutely stunning," declared Garrett. He leaned in and kissed her chastely on the cheek. "Goodbye city girl." He turned and walked out across the field toward his house.

Jacq stood on the porch with the door open, the fire crackling merrily behind her, and watched his form growing hazier and hazier. "Goodbye country boy," she whispered hoping she made the right decision.

Garrett walked slowly home and fought the temptation to look back. He wasn't sure he could resist turning around and retracing his steps so he could try to kiss some sense into her, if she were still there watching him. Ian was right, he was a bloody idiot. He should have told her yesterday while she was lying in his arms that he was ready to commit to her, if she'd have him, but he had chickened out. He hadn't faced the fact that he had fallen in love with her until he had lost her. And when you loved someone, you had to put their needs before your own. Her career was important to her. He needed to be strong so that she wouldn't be distracted while she was following her dreams. He knew now that he was walking away from his.

Chapter 27

The next afternoon, Garrett was startled when the insistent loud knocking began at his front door.

"I'm coming," he yelled as he made his way across the entry. Garrett opened the door to a distraught Nicole. "What's wrong," he asked as he ushered Nicole into the living room and had her sit down on the couch plopping himself down beside her.

"It's Matt," Nicole muttered before her composure crumbled and tears started to flow. Garrett was momentarily relived that whatever the crisis it had nothing to do with Jacq and then was abashed his thoughts had even gone there as he saw the distress in Nicole features.

"Tell me what's happened," Garrett prompted.

Nicole sat frozen for a moment before the story came tumbling out. Matt and his college buddy, Mason, had gone for a hike around ten in the morning and were now more than three hours overdue. Garrett's muscles involuntarily relaxed a bit that the news was not worse, given Nicole's anguished look.

"When were they due back?" Garrett inquired.

"Matt was supposed to pick me up at one o'clock and he never showed, and he is not returning any calls," Nicole explained.

248   J. KIMALIE

"Why are you so sure something is wrong?" he asked. "Maybe the guys extended their hike or went to get something to eat afterward."

"Matt wouldn't do that to me," Nicole insisted. "I didn't want him to go on the hike because we had a one-thirty appointment with our wedding planner. He promised me we wouldn't be late for the appointment." At that pronouncement Garrett's initial concern returned. Garrett had never known Matt not to keep his word once he made a promise.

Without looking at his watch, Garrett knew that darkness would be falling in about an hour, so he picked up the pace and urgency of his questions.

"Who have you notified that he's missing?" Garrett asked.

"No one except for you so far."

"Which trail were they going to?" Garrett queried.

Nicole's face fell as the guilt rose in her for only half listening to where Matt said they were going. After a seemingly endless pause, Nicole responded, "Howl Ridge, I think." Garrett did not press for a more definitive answer as he knew someone's first answer was in most cases the right one.

"Upper or lower trail head?" Garrett probed.

"I don't know," Nicole replied chocking out a sob. Her eyes starting to glass over.

"Nicole, look at me," Garrett gently commanded, "you are doing great. I have just a few more questions before I go find them."

"Whose car did they take?" Garrett asked.

"Matt's," Nicole quickly responded.

"You're absolutely sure?" Garrett entreated, wanting to get Nicole into a comfortable flow of answering questions. Garrett

THE WEDDING SLIPPER   249

knew one of the best ways to do that was to have someone confirm a question they sounded sure about.

"Yes," Nicole responded, gaining a bit more control over her emotions.

"He drives a blue Jeep, is that correct?" Garrett continued.

"Yes, that's right." Nicole confirmed.

"Do you know what the guys are wearing?" Garrett went on, seeking information as quickly as possible.

"I don't know about Mason," Nicole replied, "I only saw him as he waved from the front seat. Matt had on his bright blue North Face hiking gear. He took his winter weight jacket."

"Give me a description of Mason," Garrett urged.

Nicole eyes looked up as she was conjuring a mental image of Mason. "He's about two inches shorter than Matt and built heftier but in good shape. He has grey eyes and has very pronounced dimples. He's African American with short black hair, not a buzz cut but close. No tattoos or piercings that I've ever seen."

"Good job Nicole," Garrett praised. "Do you have anything in your vehicle that Matt has recently worn?" Garrett inquired.

"No, I always...," Nicole paused, "wait, yes! His hoodie is in the trunk. I'll go get it."

As she started to rise, Garrett put up both hands, "No, you shouldn't touch it before Nitro gets a good whiff. Here's what I want you to do, call Jacq and see if she can come over to be with you. I don't want you driving anywhere. Stay here, this house has good cell reception, and we will make it the communication hub. I have a couple calls to make and then I'm leaving before it gets dark."

250

J. KIMALIE

Garrett's first call was to Donovan. He rapidly explained the situation and asked if Donovan could quickly get to the trailhead and back him up on the search. Garrett would let him know which specific trail head as soon as he found Matt's car. Donovan's cat-like grace and agility allowed him to run trails on uneven ground like he was running a marathon on smooth concrete. The darkness would slow him down but not by much. Even with the head start Garrett would have, Donovan would likely catch up with Garrett less than an hour down the trail. Hopefully, by then the hikers would have been found. Garrett didn't need to tell him to bring a head lamp or provide any other instruction, as Donovan had experience backing up Garrett and knew what to do.

The second call was to Sheriff Avery's mobile phone. He once again quickly and efficiently communicated the information and both men agreed to hold off organizing a formal search party given the likelihood that Garrett and Donovan would quickly locate them. Since Matt's planned hike was only two hours, Garrett and Donovan would likely find the hikers before volunteers from surrounding areas could be gathered and organized. At this point, Garrett was more concerned about alerting Sheriff Avery to the possibility of needing medical assistance. If needed, Garrett wanted medical attention available without delay.

Garrett hurriedly changed into his orange, reflective, search and rescue clothing and boots. He paused just for a moment before grabbing the smaller of his two pre-packed go bags. Like any prepared hiker, Garrett had to balance weight and utility against speed of movement. Knowing that Matt was an experienced hiker, he didn't worry that he would have kept

THE WEDDING SLIPPER 251

hiking if lost or hurt. Matt, he was sure, would have the good sense to stay put and not make a search and rescue more difficult. At least that is what he kept telling himself and why he had grabbed the smaller pack.

Jacq must have run from her house to his after Nicole's call as she was already comforting Nicole on the couch as Garrett and, an already harnessed, Nitro, entered the living room. While Sadie was the more experienced tracker, Nitro was the better choice for the rougher terrain of this mission. Sadie had already curled up at Nicole's feet who was stroking her golden fur without thinking, allowing the gentle dog to calm her as much as possible. Jacq and Garrett's eyes met for a long moment, communicating volumes before Garrett nodded his head once and asked Nicole to open her trunk. They all exited the house from the front door and Nicole popped her trunk with the key fob. It was not until after Nitro finished sniffing the hoodie that Garrett picked it up. From here on out it was a game for Nitro to find the owner of the jacket and earn his favorite treats as a reward. For Garrett, it was a far more personal mission.

Garrett turned toward the women, his eyes moving past Jacq's face. Even at a quick glance he could see concern etched upon it, before his gaze stopped to look directly into Nicole's terrified eyes. "We have a lot going for us," he said. "First, Matt is an experienced hiker; second, the planned hike was only an hour or so up the trail and an hour, give or take, back down to the jeep so they shouldn't be too far up the trail and easy for Nitro to locate; third, Donovan is going to back me up and he can track anything and knows the trail inside and out; fourth, the weather is on our side tonight; and, finally, I'm determined to find him. I'll call as soon as I know something." With those final words he turned and had already finished compartmentalizing his feelings as he and an excited Nitro jumped into his SUV.

Garrett phoned Ian as soon as he was on the road. He once again succinctly relayed the situation and asked if Ian could head over to his house to coordinate communications and lend support to the gals. Ian responded that he could be there within the hour. Call complete, Garrett stepped on the accelerator wanting to take advantage of the fleeting sunlight.

Because Matt was an experienced hiker, Garrett headed first to the more challenging upper trail head and immediately found Matt's empty Jeep, the only vehicle in the parking area. He phoned in the information to Donovan and Sheriff Avery asking Donovan to phone Ian with the information. Odds were that Garrett and Donovan would find Matt and Mason in the next two hours, if not, a formal search and rescue would need to be organized.

Garrett adjusted his headlamp, checked the time, shouldered his pack, and let Nitro lead the way up the trail. Nitro was in his element sniffing the plethora of woodland scents searching for Matt's specific scent. The focused dog kept Garrett moving at a good clip across the uneven ground, muddy in spots but not as bad as Garrett had anticipated. Given the time of year and the fact that this trail was known to locals but not as well known or advertised to tourists, the trail was in about as good as shape as he could have hoped; although, not as well maintained as the popular trails in the area. About every 50 yards, Garrett would briefly stop and yell Matt's name hoping for a reply. Even if Garrett couldn't hear one over the sounds of wind and moving water, Nitro's canine ears would pick up even a feeble reply. At forty-three minutes into the search, Nitro began barking and

THE WEDDING SLIPPER 253

Garrett could tell by the bark he had found them. It wasn't until Garrett almost reached Nitro that he could hear a muffled voice yelling "down here." The voice was almost drowned out by the night's forest sounds and the running water of the creek that paralleled the trail about 20 feet below. Garrett did not recognize the voice as Matt's, so he yelled, "Mason?"

"Yeah, I'm Mason," relief obvious in his voice.

"What's the situation?" yelled Garrett.

"Just up ahead, part of the trail gave way and Matt, tumbled down ultimately falling into the creek. He managed to get his feet pointed downstream, but his body got wedged between a rock and tree trunk. I heard a crack while I was still up on the trail right before he screamed. I'm pretty sure his leg is broken. I knew I was going to have to help him out of the water, so I slid down the hillside on my butt and managed to pull him out. I think he passed out from the pain when I was hauling him out of the creek. I don't know if he has internal injuries, but I don't think he hit his head. He's been going in and out of consciousness," Mason concluded.

"How long was he in the water?" Garrett asked.

"It seemed like forever," Mason yelled up, "but probably less than 5 minutes."

"Give me a minute to call in our location and order a Stokes basket to get you both out of there," Garrett yelled down.

Garrett retrieved his satellite phone from his pack and called Sheriff Avery to apprise him of the situation and conveyed the equipment needed for the rescue. He also requested an ambulance be positioned at the trail head.

Garrett next called Donovan repeating his report and was reassured to learn that he was probably less than 10 minutes to Garrett's location.

Finally, Garrett called Ian. He repeated the report, emphasizing that the extent of Matt's injuries was still unknown. Just as soon as Matt was on his way to a hospital, Garrett said he would let them know where he was being transported. Ian volunteered to drive the women to wherever Matt would be going. Garrett let him know that it would probably be two hours before Matt would be in route.

Garrett yelled down to Mason that help was on its way and asked if they had any supplies or water. Mason let him know that what little they had brought with them had been lost in the fall. Hearing this, Garrett opened his pack and quickly jettisoned the items he wouldn't need. In the pack he left water, protein bars, a whistle, a flashlight, a lightweight blanket made of polyethylene terephthalate sheet coated with a thin aluminum layer and a couple other things immediately helpful to Mason. He tied his pack to a rope and let Mason know it was headed his way.

Mason was most thankful for the blanket and water. He was cold to the bone and knew Matt would be too as Matt was in the water longer. Mason had done what he could for Matt to keep him warm given their precarious position. He had given Matt his beanie that had miraculously stayed on Mason's head through the water rescue. He had laid down next to him to shared body heat and covered them both with dry leaves and fallen pine branches within his reach. But Mason could not risk moving around too much without sliding back into the water. His efforts to warm them both seemed to do little against the elements, but he was hoping it would be enough.

THE WEDDING SLIPPER 255

Garrett yelled down to Mason asking him if the slope down to the creek was less steep on the trail ahead of them where Matt had fallen, compared to where they had ended up downstream. Mason said it was less steep, but a further distance down to the creek and warned Garrett that it was still treacherous. Mason had cut his hands and forearms sliding down the embankment on his butt in a semi-controlled descent.

Garrett put on his helmet, grabbed his satellite phone, heaved some climbing gear over his shoulder and went to inspect the slope grade further up the trail where Matt had fallen.

Garrett carefully approached the spot where there were clear indications of someone having recently gone over the side of the trail and down the slope taking the edge of the trail with him. As Garrett was looking up to his left for a tree or something to use as an anchor point, Nitro began barking wildly just before Garrett sickeningly felt the ground under his feet dissolve way from him. Unbeknownst to Garrett a corroded culvert had failed a few inches beneath the soil where his feet had been planted just a second before. The ground, weakened by Matt's mishap, gave way under Garrett's full weight. As if in slow motion, he, and a good chunk of the trail around him continued shifting and falling. Dry and wet soil, rocks, roots, moss, decayed vegetation, and Garrett, limbs flailing, began hurtling down the slope. The satellite phone in his hand was lost in the cascading debris. Unsuccessfully, Garrett desperately fought for purchase to slow his decent. His last thoughts turned to Nitro, hoping he had escaped the slide, and to Jacq for whom he wanted to survive. Garrett's growing sense of dread abruptly ended when his head smacked against something unyielding, and everything went black.

Chapter 28

Nicole, Jacq, and Ian's initial relief at hearing that Matt and Mason had been located quickly turned to impatience and irritation at not receiving additional updates. What was taking so long they wondered? Nicole could not sit for more than a minute or two as her nervous energy and growing anxiety had her pacing incessantly around the room. Nicole wanted to go to the trail head and Ian let her know that would not be helpful to the rescue operation. Ian firmly insisted that they would, at best, be in the way and, at worst, might actually interfere with or, slow up rescue efforts. Nicole was not placated and every minute that passed she became more harried.

Jacq made coffee and set out some peanuts she had found in the pantry. Everyone gladly accepted a warm mug of brew, but no one actually drank it, three cups growing cold as time dragged on.

While not voicing his concern, Ian was surprised that Garrett had not telephoned with an update as it was out of character for him. If he was too busy to make the call, why hadn't Donovan called, he wondered. Cell phone reception would be an issue on the trail, but Garrett had his satellite phone. Twice, two hours apart, Ian had gone to the bathroom under false pretenses to ping Garrett's phone to check his location via GPS.

THE WEDDING SLIPPER   257

Both times, the GPS location identifier had showed the same exact location. Now it had been three hours since Garrett had called letting them know the guys had been found. Ian was not yet alarmed per se by the lack of information and fixed GPS location of Garrett's phone, but as each minute ticked by, he had an increased feeling of foreboding.

Ian went to the kitchen and poured three glasses of water. He handed one to Jacq and then went to Nicole. He took her hand, led her to the couch and said, "Drink," in a kindly tone. "It's going to be alright" he added, giving Nicole a squeeze on her upper arm before putting a reassuring arm around Nicole's shoulders.

Nicole leaned into Ian, tears silently running down her cheeks. Nicole's normal in charge disposition and pulled together looks were crumbling by the hour. As Jacq watched Ian pull Nicole into a hug, she was glad that he was there to lend support.

Jacq had only experienced Ian as the life of the party at social gatherings. He was always jovial and quick with a witty remark. The big man was also exceptionally tenderhearted and sensitive to the moods and needs of others, Jacq realized having observed him over the past few hours. When he had arrived, he burst through the door startling both Jacq and Nicole. It took, Jacq a beat to recognize him as he was wearing hiking gear with reflective patches on both jacket and pants. Jacq had never seen him in anything other than a kilt and suspected he had dressed to join the search if called upon. When Ian came through the door he went directly to Nicole and, without a word, enveloped her into a bear hug. After a long minute, he removed just one arm and stretched out a hand to Jacq. When she took his hand, he pulled her into a comforting group embrace. In the hours since Garrett's call, Ian let Nicole dictate the amount of conversation, giving her space to be alone with her thoughts yet engaging with her when she posed a question or shared a thought. In silence or when conversing, Ian was a calming presence. A couple times when Nicole's composure began to slip, he would serenely ask her a question to guide her away from her tormented thoughts.

Even with Ian's best efforts, the tension in the room seemed to be rising with each passing second.

"Why did Garrett say this would be the communication hub when no communication is coming our way," Nicole demanded.

"I don't know." Ian said truthfully, "I thought by now we would have heard from either Garrett or Donovan. We just have to trust that they will call us when they can." An anxiety riddled silence descended on the room once again.

Jacq decided to take a note from Ian's playbook. She turned to Nicole and gently said, "You've never told me how Matt proposed to you." A momentary smile passed over Nicole's face, before the grim reality of the evening's events reasserted themselves in her features.

"Matt's an engineer, not a poet," Nicole slowly began. "I love his pragmatic approach to life and his strong work ethic, but those qualities don't always lend itself to romance. So, whenever I imagined him proposing, I expected a sweet proposal but not necessarily a romantic one. What made Matt's proposal so special to me was that he tried so very hard to arrange a perfect romantic day, but the day and his proposal ended up being nothing as he had planned.

We were on our way to the Kenmore Air Harbor Seaplane Base when he received a call that due to heavy fog, our scheduled

THE WEDDING SLIPPER

flight had been cancelled. Matt had planned to surprise me with tea at the Empress Hotel in Victoria, Canada. I was so touched that he had surreptitiously arranged for tea as it was something he knew I would love, and I knew he would never seek to do on his own. Plan A thwarted, he drove to Seattle. When planning the day, he discovered that the Fairmont Olympic Hotel in downtown Seattle also served tea, but the setting was not as picturesque as Victoria Harbor, so he had initially passed on that option. Now it seemed to him to be a good Plan B. He pulled up to valet, an extravagance for him, and we made our way up to the dining room. The room was closed as it was being remodeled, but we were told the bar was open and serving food. I was getting hungry and perfectly happy to eat in the bar not knowing Matt was searching for a more romantic place to propose. With grumbling stomachs, we went down and had the valet retrieve his Jeep.

Next, Matt headed to the waterfront and pulled into the Edgewater Hotel, famous for a legendary 1964 photo of the Beatles fishing from the window of their suite. We once again valet parked and headed to the dining room which is known for both great food and a lovely view of Elliott Bay. The hostess at the counter let us know that the dining room was closed but would re-open again for dinner at five o'clock. The look on Matt's face reflected pure defeat but after a moment he rallied. He turned to me and said, Nicole, I will be right back and marched off leaving me standing there, the hostess and I looking uncomfortably at each other.

The hostess suggested I take a seat in the bar, and several minutes later Matt returned in triumph holding a room key and stated, "Turns out room service is available 24 hours."

260

J. KIMALIE

We headed up to our suite which had a fabulous view of Elliott Bay and a chilled bottle of champagne in an ice bucket promptly arrived followed shortly by a feast. He had ordered three appetizers, a grilled salmon dinner for us to share, a favorite of both mine and his, and four desserts because he could not decide what I would most like. About the time we had finished gorging ourselves, there was a knock at the door. I hopped up saying I would get it and I opened the door to another white cloth clad trolley being quickly wheeled into the room. The tray contained a red rose in a crystal vase, an assortment of chocolate truffles, and another bottle of champagne.

"What's this?" both Matt and I asked almost in unison.

"Compliments of the manager," the beaming bell hop announced, "to congratulate you on your engagement. I'll leave you to it," he grinned as he swept out of the room not waiting to be tipped.

Confused, I turned to Matt whose head was hanging down and his eyes were shut. With resignation, he walked over to me, dropped down on one knee, reached into his pocket to retrieve a ring box and said, "Since we are engaged, you should have the ring. You do have to agree though that we are engaged before I put the rock on your finger."

Nicole wiped a tear from her cheek and said, "I was overjoyed but Matt was clearly disappointed by how the day and events had unfolded which were not at all as he had planned or wanted for me. Maybe it wasn't the most romantic proposal in the world, I told Matt, but things worked out well as ultimately the venue had some compensating advantages, I assured him glancing toward the bed. Matt had decided things had worked out very well indeed by the time we left the hotel." Nicole

THE WEDDING SLIPPER 261

blushed and then hastily stated, "That last part I shared, that is just between the three of us. I have been editing out that part of the story." Ian was crossing his heart when his cell phone finally rang.

The three jumped, startled by the phone that sounded abnormally loud. Ian answered and listened without saying anything for what seemed like an excruciatingly long period of time. The features on his face unreadable as he listened intently to the caller. "OK, we'll see you at Harborview." Nicole made a sound, something between gagging and choking.

"What is it?" Jacq asked Nicole.

"Harborview is the only Level 1 trauma center in the area so it must be bad," Nicole speculated, with what little composure she had left beginning to fracture.

"Ian?" Jacq prompted, searching for answers in his somber face.

"The extent of injuries is still unknown. But both Matt and Garrett are being life flighted to Harborview," Ian finished.

Nicole prayed that she could not have heard correctly.

"You mean Matt and Mason are on their way to the hospital," Jacq clarified.

"No," Ian continued, shaking his head to indicate that Jacq's statement was not correct. The look Ian gave Jacq was filled with such compassion that her knees almost buckled. "Mason has cuts, scratches, and probably bruising but he will be fine," Ian stated flatly.

Jacq's mind was whirling as she played back what she had heard a moment ago, Matt and Garrett are being transported to the hospital. This cannot be happening she thought as her unwilling mind was trying to come to terms with what this meant. "Not again, not him", her unspoken thoughts echoed loudly in her head.

"Wait, Garrett must just be accompanying Matt to Harborview," Jacq said, her words ringing hollow even as she voiced them. Ian, put his hands on Jacq's shoulders and guided her to sit down on the couch.

"Donovan had Garrett in sight and was just about to catch up to him on the trail when the path gave way under Garrett's feet, and he careened down the slope. He hit his head on a jagged rock. He's still alive thanks to his helmet, but he has not regained consciousness," Ian recounted in a dull tone not sounding at all like himself.

Jacq felt her world collapsing in on itself. She was completely numb. She did not feel Nicole wrap her arms around her in anguished solidarity, nor did she register the hurried, hushed, call that Ian made to Emmett. And later when she would recall this tragic night, she would have no memory of walking herself to the car before the three raced to Seattle.

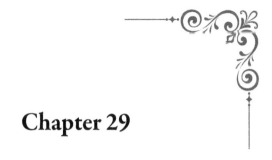

Chapter 29

Matt was in surgery and Garrett had been placed into an induced coma by the time a frazzled Nicole, Jacq, and Ian reached the hospital. The only reason they were able to ascertain that much information is that Ian claimed to be Garrett's stepbrother, while a clear biological untruth, not an emblematic one. The nurse had looked dubious that Ian was related to Garrett but took pity on the stricken group taking Ian's claim at face value and shared what she knew promising an update when she learned more.

As the disconsolate group made their way to the waiting room, a weary looking Donovan came purposefully striding in from the entrance. All at once, Ian, Nicole, and Jacq began peppering him with questions and Donovan put his hands up as if to ward off the verbal and emotional assault.

"As I was walking in, I saw that Emmett was parking his car, so he is right behind me and I don't want to repeat the story twice," a tired Donovan calmly said. "I also need some water," Donovan added matter-of-factly.

As if on cue, a stoic looking Emmett walked into the room his sharp eyes searching for familiar faces and quickly located his friends.

"How are they?" he asked, not waiting for an answer before enveloping each person one by one into a consoling hug. Ian shared what they had learned from the nurse before Emmett finished his round of hugs concluding with Ian. Both men embracing longer than usual taking strength from the other.

"Let's all head to the cafeteria," Emmett suggested looking worriedly at Donovan, "It's probably going to be a while before we hear anything else, and Donovan looks like he needs something to eat and drink."

The group settled into seats around a large, well worn, round table in one corner of the room. Donovan passed on food but downed two bottles of water in rapid succession before recounting the harrowing events. The group listened with rapt attention as Donovan described the night's disturbing details. Donovan slowly relayed his account in a smooth organized flow of information not unlike a news anchor person conveying a report.

Jacq's emotional reaction to what she was hearing prevented her from digesting the news. She was only able to focus on bits and pieces of what Donovan was sharing as if the information was coming in jerky headlines. Nitro barking wildly trying to warn Garrett. The ground disintegrating below Garrett's feet. Donovan commanding Nitro to come to him before Nitro could advance toward Garrett and share his same fate. A failed culvert. The satellite phone lost in rubble. Donovan backtracking down the path until he could get cell reception and call for help. Mason's quick actions saving Matt. The slow and meticulous rescue. Matt and Garrett strapped to spinal boards before being carried down the trail. Ambulance medics stabilizing the patients but calling for life flight support. Concerns for Garrett

THE WEDDING SLIPPER 265

of intracerebral bleeding. Matt's broken left leg and possible internal injuries. Garrett's concussion and lack of consciousness but no apparent broken bones. Mason driving Matt's car back to Matt's place to pick up his own car. Donovan dropping an unhurt but disconcerted Nitro back at Garrett's house before coming to the hospital.

After Donovan had stopped talking, Jacq slowly became aware that a jacket had been placed around her shoulders and Emmett was holding one of her hands and Ian the other. With his other hand, Ian also held tight to Nicole's trembling hand.

Nicole suddenly stood and said, "I have to be there when he comes out of surgery. I have to go back. Oh God, I have to call his parents, how am I going to tell them?"

"Why don't you let me make that call," offered Emmett. "I already have another one I need to make," Emmett added.

Nicole nodded her consent in quick, shaky, movements and then started for the door and the group of troubled friends all stood and followed her to the waiting room.

After an excruciating wait, a middle-aged doctor, still in his blue sweat-stained scrubs, came down the fluorescent lit corridor to provide an update. Matt, they learned, was still in surgery and would be for at least another hour. Following surgery, he would be in recovery for an additional hour or more before anyone could see him. A blow to his left upper abdomen had ruptured his spleen and bruised his liver. His spleen had to be removed but overall, he would likely make a satisfactory recovery. Currently an orthopedic surgeon was setting and pinning his fibula together which has been fractured in three locations.

At the conclusion of the surgeon's report, an audible expulsion of air could be heard from the group. Everyone had been holding their breath while listening to the surgeon. Nicole started to slump and Donovan, standing closest to her, wrapped his strong arm around her waist to literally keep her from sliding to the floor. "Thank God, thank God he is going to be okay," Nicole sighed, everyone sharing her relief.

"What about Garrett?" Jacq asked in a beseeching tone.

"I'm sorry, who?" the surgeon asked already turning away to attend to other emergencies.

"Garrett Olsen, he was transported in the same helicopter," Jacq clarified.

"I don't know," the surgeon replied, "he is not my patient. But I will find out who the treating physician is and request that you be updated on his condition. And now, I must get back."

The buoyancy the group felt at hearing Matt would recover, was quickly tempered by the unknown status of Garrett. Jacq's thoughts had started ricocheting from bad to worse from the moment she heard that Garrett had been placed into an induced coma. The thought of losing Garrett was unthinkable to Jacq. She couldn't let her thoughts go too far down that road because she didn't know if she could survive another loss on the heels of losing her family. She was realizing that Garrett meant more to her than she had previously been willing to admit to herself. The thought she might never speak to him again or laugh with him or share sweet moments of intimacy was too distressing to even contemplate. Why had she not realized the depth of her feelings for him this clearly before now? Garrett was a man she could build a life with and wanted to build a life with—she knew that now. All other considerations about her plans and ambitions paled in comparison.

THE WEDDING SLIPPER   267

Why hadn't she been listening to her heart instead of her head? Her mind kept telling her three months was not enough time to fall in love with someone or to know someone well enough to completely change the trajectory of her future. Past experience, however, had already unequivocally proven that it had only taken one tragic moment to completely change her life. That same fateful moment had also changed Emmett's future she acknowledged to herself in painful realization. Jacq lost her family and Emmett lost his love. So, one moment could indeed change the course of one's life for better or for worse. From the time they first met in the greenhouse, Jacq knew she was attracted to Garrett; but she could not precisely pinpoint exactly when she had fallen in love with him.

Jacq looked up into Emmett's eyes and found that he was already looking into hers. "How ya doin' sweetheart?" Emmett tenderly inquired. Emmett could see she was struggling to find her voice and so he simply took a seat next to her and put his arm around her shoulders, providing her a shoulder to lean on. She melted into him, grateful for the comfort he offered.

After a few minutes of silent contemplation, Emmett realized he needed Jacq's comforting presence as much as she needed his. Tragedy had brought them together and now another shared tragedy bound them more tightly. A bond quickly forged through intense grief of past losses and searing concern for a potential one.

Perhaps it was the comprehension of the forged bond of intimacy between them that emboldened Emmett as he turned his head and whispered into Jacq's ear at a volume no one else could hear.

268

J. KIMALIE

"I am going to say this just once, because frankly I have no business saying it at all." Hearing Emmett's earnest words crystallized Jacq's focus. "Your Aunt Rose and I wasted a lot of time we could have spent loving one another because I felt it was disloyal for me to love someone else when I was still grieving my sweet Grace. What I did not realize at the time was that I would always grieve Grace's loss in my life. But what I came to understand is that loving Rose was a tribute to Grace because it was Grace who taught me that love is not some finite thing that runs out. Love is an infinite source within us that we can draw upon and it is intended to be shared. So, what I'm going to suggest is that you don't waste time or let anything get in the way of your love for Garrett or his love for you."

At hearing this, Jacq breathed in a sharp intake of air and leaned away from Emmett so she could look into his compassionate and knowing eyes. "Yep, it is that obvious to me that you both love each other. I would hate to see anything thwart or delay your chances at happiness. But like I said, it is none of my business and I won't bring it up again." With his impromptu speech concluded, Emmett leaned in and tenderly kissed Jacq on the forehead. He then sat back in his chair leaving Jacq to contemplate his words and to wonder if Garrett did, in fact, love her as she had come to love him.

Jacq had little time to sort through her thoughts at Emmett's words before a tall, impossibly young-looking doctor in a lab coat stopped by the nurse's station and was directed to their waiting group. The neurologist introduced himself and unceremoniously launched into a dispassionate report. "Garrett suffered a concussion which is basically a brain injury. Without a doubt his helmet saved his life. The good news is that he has not

THE WEDDING SLIPPER   269

experienced seizing or intracranial bleeding. He does, however, have some brain swelling which is why he was placed in a medically induced coma. I know that may sound extreme but tens of thousands of patients who undergo surgery on any given day are given anesthesia to essentially place them in a reversible coma during the surgery. While Garrett didn't require surgery, shutting down some brain function can give the impacted part of the brain time to heal more easily. We will keep him in a coma until a reduction of his intracranial pressure reaches, more or less, normal levels. We are hoping for a best-case scenario which would be to bring him out of the coma in about 12 hours. One way or another, we will know a lot more by then. The drugs administered to put him in a coma causes reduced blood pressure. So, he will have to be closely monitored which is why he is in the critical care unit (CCU). I would characterize his current condition as serious but not critical. He's a lucky man, it could have been a lot worse," he added.

"At this point, he can have two visitors in his room at any given time. And it wouldn't hurt to have voices familiar to him quietly talk or read to him," the doctor finally concluded.

"Will he suffer any long term affects?" Donovan asked, giving voice to everyone's unspoken concern.

"It's just way too early to tell," replied the doctor. "Again, we will know a whole lot more in 12 hours."

Emmett suggested that Ian and Donovan be the first two to see Garrett so Donovan could go home and get some rest after checking on his friend. Both men turned to Jacq, and she said, "Go, you two should absolutely be the first ones to see him. I'm not going anywhere, and I'll stay with him tonight."

While Donovan and Ian were in with Garrett, Matt's parents, his brother, and a bandaged Mason arrived at the hospital. Nicole ran to them with the news that Matt would likely recover from his injuries and to share the surgeon's update. The group's relief was palpable. When Emmett and Jacq walked over to join the cautiously optimistic group, Nicole, with unapologetic tears flowing down her face, was thanking Mason for saving Matt's life. Witnessing the absolute love Nicole had for Matt, there was not a dry eye among them.

Mason was first among the group to inquire about Garrett's condition. The image of a pale and unresponsive Garrett on the ambulance gurney was still vivid in his mind. Emmett recounted what the neurologist had shared. "Now that you are all here, Jacq and I should head over to the CCU waiting room," Emmett informed them. "You should all stay here as Matt's surgeon should be coming out anytime now with an update."

With promises made to keep each other informed, Emmett and Jacq hurried to the CCU wing of the hospital.

Time seemed to trudge along in the waiting room at an agonizing pace. While it seemed like hours, Donovan and Ian rejoined them in the waiting room forty-five minutes after they had gone in to see Garrett.

"Except for all the tubes and wires they've got connected to him, it looks like he is taking a very peaceful nap," Ian commented.

"While we were in with him, a nurse confirmed it would be hours before there would be any change. So, I'm headed home to get cleaned up and some rest. On the way to my place, I'll check on Garrett's animals and ensure that they have plenty of feed

THE WEDDING SLIPPER   271

and water. I'll be back tomorrow morning," a weary Donovan promised.

Ian gave Jacq and Emmett directions to Garrett's room and then settled into a none-too comfortable chair in the corner of waiting room. Jacq needed no encouragement to see for herself how he was doing. After emotionally bracing herself, she and Emmett entered the dimly lit hospital room crowded with machines monitoring different aspects of Garrett's vital signs. They took seats across from each other on opposite sides of his hospital bed and kept vigil talking softly to his nonresponsive form.

Sometime later, Emmett rose announcing he was going to find something to drink and to check on Ian, asking Jacq if he could bring something back for her. Jacq suspected that Emmett was graciously providing her some alone time with Garrett and her own swirling thoughts. Shaking her head indicating she had all she needed, Emmett walked out and quietly shut the door behind him.

"Oh Garrett," she said, snaking her hand through the tubes and wires connected to him to grip his hand, "I don't think I can bare to lose you. I love you and I don't think I could live with myself if the last thing I ever said to you is that I'm leaving for a job." Tears sprang from her eyes, and she let them flow, welcoming the cathartic release.

The next hours passed at a glacial pace. The monotony was interrupted occasionally by nurses checking vital signs, replacing intravenous bags, and syringes of medicine being inserted into a catheter. Ian and Emmett switched off joining Jacq in the room, insisting that she stay as long as she liked.

Jacq's eyes felt gritty and her throat thick and dry. She was just about to nod off in the chair when the door abruptly opened and an anxious looking woman, quickly advanced into the room, pulling up short when she glimpsed Jacq holding Garrett's hand. Instantly, Jacq knew that this woman, now slowly advancing toward Garrett, was his mother. Garrett and his mother shared the same blue eyes and pronounced angular jaw line.

"Hello, I'm Patricia, Garrett's mother," she said, reaching out her hand to shake Jacq's.

"Nice to meet you," replied Jacq, "I'm Garrett's neighbor, Jacq," she added.

"How is he?" Patricia asked, already assessing for herself, eyeing the blood pressure and heart rate display, the electroencephalography (EEG) read out, and feeling for his pulse.

"He's been just like this all night, not agitated at all, he looks as though he is just sleeping," Jacq reported in an exhausted voice.

The phrase "all night" was not lost on Garrett's mother. Patricia looked at Jacq wondering who this woman was who had sat with Garrett all night and was holding his hand when she walked in. More importantly, what did she mean to her son? Patricia had walked past Ian and Emmett who were both asleep in the waiting room without waking them, expecting Garrett to be alone in the room or for Donovan to be there with him. Finding this beautiful redhead in his room, was a bit of a shock as Garrett had not mentioned anyone new in his life on their last telephone call.

"Since you're here, I think I'll step out to stretch my legs," Jacq said, not wanting to intrude on Patricia's time with her son.

THE WEDDING SLIPPER 273

Patricia was grateful to the woman for giving her some time alone with her only son, as she simply wasn't up for making small talk with a stranger even if she was curious about how Garrett and Jacq were connected. The drive up from Portland seemed to take forever as concern for Garrett weighed constantly on her mind.

Jacq cautiously took a seat next to Ian careful not to wake the softly snoring man or a slumbering Emmett on the other side of him. Within minutes, exhaustion overtook her the moment she shut her scratchy eyes. Even with the early morning's increase of activity and noise going on around them, the three enjoyed some precious minutes of restorative sleep.

Emmett's phone simultaneously buzzed and rang causing him to jerk up. In a cartoonish, chain reaction, Emmett's action caused Ian to stir and Jacq, whose head had ended up coming to rest on Ian's shoulder, was also jostled awake.

"No, nothing new to report," Emmett gruffly said into the phone. After a pause he added, "Sounds great, bring one for Patricia, she should be here anytime," before hanging up, his hand came up to cover a wide yawn.

"She's already here," Jacq replied, covering her own yawn, and blinking her eyes to moisten them enough to focus them. Ian just groaned and stretched his neck and back as he stood.

"Donovan's on his way over with coffee and breakfast burritos," Emmett reported.

"Why that guy isn't married is beyond me," Ian stated. "He has an uncanny way of knowing what you need before you can figure it out for yourself," he added appreciatively.

An hour later, the four friends were polishing off their breakfast, when Patricia entered the waiting room. All four jumped up, not a graceful demonstration to be sure, as each were balancing the last of their meal and cups filled to various levels with coffee. All four hoping and anxious for good news about Garrett.

Patricia shared that the neurologist had just made his morning rounds and was pleased with Garrett's progress. He had scheduled the anesthesiologist to start bringing him out of the coma at one o'clock. The process itself would take several hours.

Patricia suggested that they all head home to get some sleep and return early in the afternoon. Emmett seconded the plan stating it was good advice. Donovan, not having seen Garrett since the night before, asked if Patricia would mind him slipping into the room to see him.

"Not at all," Patricia said, "in fact, I'd like to hear directly from you as to what happened out there last night. When he called, Emmett gave me the highlights, but I'd like to hear your firsthand perspective." Before the group broke up, Emmett read off an encouraging text update from Nicole regarding Matt's condition and Emmett thumbed back a text updating Nicole on Garrett's status.

The process of bringing Garrett out of his drug induced coma later that afternoon was not a quick one. The medications given to him were slowly lessened over time. The procedure did, however, progress at a steady rate as Garrett was stabilizing quickly after each incremental dose reduction.

The group had been warned that once Garrett was conscious, he might experience reduced awareness, confusion and/or disorientation because of his injury. Each of his loved ones were guarding their own worried and concerned thoughts regarding if Garrett would fully recover. Head injuries were notoriously

THE WEDDING SLIPPER 275

tricky and hard to predict a prognosis. Additionally, Jacq was guarding her heart, desperately wanting Emmett's words to her to be true. Did Garrett love her? With all her heart she hoped so.

Garrett's mom stayed by his side as Garrett slowly regained consciousness. His friends took turns visiting him as still only two people were allowed in his room at any one time.

As Garrett fought his way to the surface of consciousness, he heard familiar voices fade in and out. His eyelids were too heavy to open but the voices seemed to be getting closer and he had the sense he was just about to understand what was being said when the sounds became allusive and unintelligible once again. He let himself drift for a time riding along with the current of the murmurings. The sound of the voices was comforting, and he wanted to float along with them. Garrett's body felt pinned down like something heavy was tied to his arms and legs. He did not like the new sensation and desperately wanted to keep drifting until he heard her voice. When finally, he did, her voice cut through the fog like a carillon bell and then he wanted, no he needed, to go to her even as he was slipping back into unconsciousness. He knew he had to reach her and once he did, Garrett intended to never let her go.

Chapter 30

While Garrett was recovering in the hospital, Jacq's past few weeks had been a blur of organized turmoil. Patricia had graciously kept everyone apprised of the slow and steady progress Garrett was making and the doctors were confident that, in time, he would make a full recovery. The accident and aftermath had everyone reflecting on how fragile life is and the importance of seizing the opportunities to do what matters most.

At the same time, Matt's accident had impressed upon Nicole how fleeting life could be and her desire to solidify her life with Matt. While Matt was still in the hospital, Nicole had insisted that they get married immediately as she had realized the wedding is just one day in a lifetime of being husband and wife. In the hospital, Matt had pulled his fiancé aside to discuss their plans knowing Nicole had her heart set on a large formal wedding. He didn't want her to give up her dream wedding out of fear of losing him and settle, instead, for a small hospital chapel ceremony. Nicole had taken Matt's face in her hands and assured him all the pomp and circumstance now seemed silly when all she really wanted was to be his wife. They finally brought Jacq into their conversation and asked if she would help pull together a wedding that they would both cherish, but in

THE WEDDING SLIPPER

277

a more compressed timeframe than what they had originally planned. Jacq assured them she could arrange an event they would both treasure.

Making good on her promise, Jacq had spent, the unseasonably warm morning planting pansies in front of the tall grasses around the perimeter of the greenhouse in preparation for the wedding. She liked the look of their violet and yellow faces turned toward the sun and believed they would make the perfect backdrop for the other decorations she had planned.

Jacq swiped her forearm across her sweaty brow, as she stood to look through the trees where a car slowly made its way up the gravel drive to the farmhouse. She wasn't expecting visitors and it was much too early for Christopher's shuttle to have made it from Seattle. Aunt Rose had always told her working with flowers was one of the more relaxing chores around the farm, so Jacq was trying her Aunt's relaxation technique as nothing else had worked to stop the twitchy feeling that had been Jacq's constant companion for the last few weeks. Planting the flowers gave her something else to concentrate on, but she felt the unease creeping up on her the minute she came close to the end of her farm beautification projects.

Jacq had been carrying around a knot in her stomach knowing she had made a colossal mistake choosing her career over Garrett. He was healing, but she hadn't spoken directly to him about her feelings as he was busy with physical therapy, and she was scrambling to pull off another wedding at the farm. Jacq didn't know if he would be open to a conversation since they had all but ended their relationship. The accident had solidified her feelings for Garrett. There was nothing like a near death experience for a person to realize how idiotic they had been not to recognize the love she held for the man that had lit up her world for the last several months.

When her parents and Aunt Rose had been killed, Jacq had chastised herself for not making more time in her schedule to spend with those she loved. Stupidly, she felt in some ways, she had made the exact same mistake with Garrett. She hadn't recognized their time had been slipping away as she kept telling herself she needed to get back home and resume her old life. She of all people should know how fleeting life was and that you should grab on to what you want with both hands and never let go. Jacq had let go of Garrett and now all she could do was dream of having him back in her life and in her arms. She realized the sick feeling that had been dogging her days was a direct result of fear that a relationship with Garrett was no longer a possibility.

When he had heard about the accident, Christopher had continually called to check up on Jacq and to ask after Garrett and Matt's recovery. He also was excited to relay an idea that had been percolating in his psyche. They could open up an event venue together. Jacq had been surprised when Christopher had asked if she would consider becoming his business partner rather than take the position as regional manager for the new hotel chain. The call had been an unexpected, but not an unwelcome surprise.

"We can do this Jacq and it will be a smashing success. With your talent at managing things, my incredibly good taste along with our creative streak, how can we lose?" Christopher had questioned her.

Jacq had argued that it was one thing to hold sophisticated events when you had the resources of an entire hotel chain behind you, but they would be starting from scratch.

THE WEDDING SLIPPER   279

"Not really," he countered, "you have a farm."

In fact, she had a farmhouse, a barn, a greenhouse, and a neighbor with a crazy one-eyed ewe named Pirate that liked to eat all the wedding greenery when she escaped from her neighbor's corral. The sheep talk made Christopher raise one eyebrow and pause for a second, but it didn't curb his enthusiasm. He was already thinking of ways to incorporate Pirate's myopic personality in marketing materials. Christopher had also surprised her with the amount of investment he was willing to make in the new business. Jacq hadn't known Christopher was sitting on a trust fund from his grandparents that would allow him to become an equal partner.

Outside of his attire, Chris didn't spend lavishly, and most people assumed the modest income he earned at the hotel defined his lifestyle. It had been nice to surprise Jacq with the news that he had the resources to go into business with her. Christopher didn't talk about his finances with anyone outside his attorney, broker, and bankers. The trust fund his grandfather had set up for him years ago had been invested wisely early in his life, and he had followed up with some calculated risks using a portion of it along the way that turned out to reward him handsomely. It's amazing what one could learn working at a chic, exclusive hotel. Many interesting conversations took place within earshot of a concierge and event planner that nobody paid much attention to unless they needed something. He had the resources to start a business and he and Jacq had a proven track record of working well together.

Slowly, phone call after phone call, they worked out the details. Jacq would sell her condo in New York and put-up Aunt Rose's farm as collateral and Christopher would come in with the additional cash. They had worked out a business plan and had Jacq's attorney draw up the contracts. Both Christopher and Jacq had independently talked to Beth to persuade her to join them, but so far, she hadn't been willing to make the move. Beth had been speechless but then, she had congratulated them in an upbeat, but stressed voice. Jacq had asked her to accompany Christopher to help with Nicole and Matt's wedding, so she could get a feel for the venue and what she and Christopher were trying to create. Beth had not given her a definitive answer, but knowing her methodical friend, Jacq realized Beth had to take some time to think things through thoroughly before taking the leap. As a result, Christopher had come out alone and was due at the farm this evening ready to put their plan into action.

Jacq put her hand to her forehead, shading her eyes, to catch a glimpse of Nicole's Subaru being parked by the barn. Nicole waved as she jumped out of the vehicle holding a thick folder of papers. She was a picture in pink. Pink jeans topped with a silk blouse the same color as her pants and, if Jacq wasn't mistaken, Nicole was wearing pink tennis shoes that looked like they were bedazzled given how they sparkled in the sun.

"I've brought all my ideas for the wedding," Nicole called as she drew closer. "I know we don't have much time, but we can select all the things we are able to pull together in a couple of weeks."

Jacq smiled and pulled her friend into a hug.

"It's good to see you," she said looking into Nicole's eyes that were devoid of stress and fear now that Matt was on the mend. "Let me show you what I've done to the greenhouse so far and then we'll go get something cold to drink while we go over your ideas."

THE WEDDING SLIPPER

Jacq took this as a sign that her and Christopher's events venue would be a success since, how better to start off their new business than with the wedding of two people whom she had come to adore.

Jacq tugged off her gardening gloves and opened the door of the greenhouse for Nicole to precede her. Nicole looked around in amazement. The space had been completely cleared of empty garden pots and potting tables. The floor was swept of debris. The windows had been meticulously cleaned so the sun created rainbow prisms on the concrete floor. All the beautiful plants had been strategically placed along the walls creating a natural green aisle interspersed with colorful orchids. A trellis of curly willow had been constructed underneath the arching dome of windows with orchids placed on platforms and columns of different heights and sizes. The whole effect looked like a tropical oasis surrounded by glass.

"It's beautiful," whispered Nicole in a reverent voice, "how did you get this all done?"

"Only with Emmett, Ian, and Donovan's help, of course. It isn't finished. Christopher has some ideas for the altar, but he wanted to check his concept with Donovan first," Jacq said, "He should be here in about an hour, if you would like to stay and share your ideas with him as well."

The two women walked to the kitchen door of the farmhouse arm in arm. As Jacq was opening the door to go inside, Nicole asked "Aren't you going to ask me about Garrett?"

Jacq hesitated and then continued toward the kitchen. Just the mention of Garrett's name made a lump form in her throat. "How is he?" Jacq said in a husky voice trying to conceal her feelings with a light tone but failing miserably.

"He's been asking about you. I don't think the texts you've been trading have satisfied his need to see you," Nicole answered.

"I saw him a few days ago, but it's been impossible to get any time alone with him. Plus, his mom has been at his side and I don't want to intrude on their family time. He needs her more than he needs me," replied Jacq.

"Are you sure about that?" questioned a clearly skeptical Nicole.

"You do know that before the accident we had decided we could not continue our relationship. Just because I realized I couldn't live without him doesn't mean he will forgive me for picking my job and old life over making a new one with him," Jacq said looking at Nicole with a tight smile.

"You need to tell him how you feel. And you need to tell him you are establishing a new life here," Nicole stated looking at Jacq with a combination of sympathy and insistence.

"He needs to concentrate on getting well. I just want him to be ok," Jacq said with a small hiccup as a single tear rolled down her cheek.

"Oh Jacq, he is going to be ok," Nicole stated firmly, "but promise me you won't walk away from him."

Jacq nodded her head and walked into Nicole's embrace. Their quiet moment was shattered by a sharp rap on the door. Both women jumped, startled by the unexpected sound.

"Hola," Ian shouted, bursting into the kitchen.

"Ian," Nicole shouted back, "you scared the hell out of us." Nicole stepped in front of Jacq to give her a chance to pull herself together. "What are you doing here?"

"I came to make your wedding day a success by delivering the chairs," Ian said in a harried voice. "You do need chairs, do you

THE WEDDING SLIPPER   283

not? Or are you expecting people to sit on the floor?" Ian asked with an unrepentant grin on his face.

"Hey Girly," Ian said walking around Nicole to grab Jacq in a bear hug. "Why the tears?"

"Jeez Ian, you aren't supposed to ask a woman why she's crying, especially when she's working hard to compose herself," an aggravated Nicole said.

"Why not?" Ian continued.

"You're a Neanderthal," Nicole declared.

"That's me. Ian the kilt wearing cave man," he confirmed as he twisted his hips causing his black and white herringbone kilt to swing back and forth around his legs.

The banter and insults between Nicole and Ian continued while Jacq stood back, pressing a tissue to her cheeks and grinned.

"Ok," Ian said, clapping his hands, "where do you want the chairs?"

"Over here," Jacq said, stepping back outside, grabbing a couple of chairs off the truck, and leading the way to the greenhouse. "Christopher should be here soon, so let's put them out of the way for now while we finish decorating," Jacq said.

"Did somebody say my name," asked Christopher walking into the greenhouse.

"Christopher!" Jacq exclaimed, as she threw her arms around her best friend. They held each other tight for a moment absorbing the comfort of seeing each other after so many months.

"I missed you Jacqueline Rose," whispered Christopher into her ear.

"And I you," Jacq whispered back.

284 — J. KIMALIE

"Let me introduce you to Ian," said Jacq, backing out of Christopher's arms. "Ian, Christopher and Christopher, Ian." The men sized each other up as they shook hands.

"Nice suit," Ian uttered. Christopher was wearing a navy European cut suit with stove pipe pants and denim blue socks that matched the color of his shirt. Cordova Italian loafers completed the outfit. He had foregone a tie given the long flight, but he still looked like he walked out of a fashion show or a high-powered corporate meeting. Jacq realized Christopher was a lot like Nicole, in that he always had an aura of sophistication and confidence that surrounded him.

"Nice....ah kilt?" Christopher stated like he was questioning what he was seeing.

"Thanks" Ian replied, "I got it at my favorite kilt store."

"You have a favorite kilt store?" Christopher inquired, still with a note of surprise in his voice. "I didn't know that was a thing."

"You have a lot to learn, my friend, a lot to learn," Ian said as he made his way out of the greenhouse whistling to himself.

Christopher watched Ian walk out then turned to Jacq with his eyebrows raised. "He's an acquired taste," Jacq said laughing as she grabbed Christopher's hand. "Come on, I'll introduce you to Nicole, she has some ideas she wants to share with us."

Christopher tightened his grip on Jacq's hand and tugged her back as she walked ahead of him. Jacq turned to him and Christopher looked into her tired eyes asking, "Jacq, are you ok?"

"I'm much better now that you're here," Jacq murmured squeezing his hand as she continued to lead him to the house.

THE WEDDING SLIPPER 285

Ian walked to the truck to unload the twenty or so chairs he was delivering for the wedding. Stacking them along the wall of the greenhouse, he heard laughter coming from the open door. It was good to hear Nicole and Jacq laughing after the few harrowing weeks of worry for Matt and Garrett. He heard Christopher laughing right along with them. Although Jacq introduced Christopher as her best friend, he didn't like the look of the "I missed you" hug the two had traded. That was a whole-body clench if he had ever seen one. Of course, he knew men and women could be friends, but he needed to talk with Garrett. Getting in the truck, he drove the few minutes to Garrett's place, ran in the house and changed into his leathers. Bolting out of the door, he almost mowed down Emmett who was standing in the middle of the path slapping dusty work gloves on his even dirtier jeans.

"Whoa, sorry, I didn't even see you there," Ian exclaimed stopping himself abruptly so as not to knock over his friend.

"What's the hurry?" asked Emmett with his hand out to steady Ian, if needed.

"I need to talk to Garrett, so I was just grabbing my bike to make the trek to Seattle," explained Ian.

"There are such things as telephones," Emmett said.

"This is one of those times when men need to talk face to face," Ian said seriously. "Hey, have you gotten a chance to meet Jacq's friend Christopher?" asked Ian.

"No, isn't he due here soon?" Emmett asked.

"From what I just witnessed in the greenhouse, those two are really close. Maybe a little too close. I don't want anybody poaching on Garrett's territory before he can get his head together and tell Jacq how he feels," stated Ian. "He's going to lose out on the best thing that has ever happened to him, if he doesn't make his move."

Looking down and shaking his head, Emmett emitted a husky chuckle and walked around Ian looking him over.

"What, don't you think that Jacq and Garrett are perfect for each other?" Ian asked as he twisted around to keep his eyes on Emmett. "What are you doing?"

Emmett looked at Ian and replied, "I'm looking for wings." At Ian's raised eyebrow, Emmett clarified, "I was wondering if you had morphed into cupid. Jacq and Garrett will be together if they both wish it. If you push them, you might not like the consequences."

"I'm doing what I've always done for Go-Go, I'm watching his back. He needs to know that Christopher is here and staying with Jacq. What he does with the information is up to him, but as you know, it's always best to go into battle with as much intel as possible. Besides," Ian said over his shoulder as he walked toward his motorcycle, "I kind of like the idea of being able to fly around and shoot people in the ass with arrows. However, I do draw the line at wearing a diaper."

"I don't know Ian, it might provide more coverage than some of your kilts. At least it would keep your private parts private."

Ian's laugh almost rivaled the sound of the revving bike engine as he catapulted down the driveway.

Chapter 31

Jacq sat at her vanity putting the finishing touches to her makeup. In two-hours Matt and Nicole would walk down the aisle and say their vows. Right now, Jacq was soaking up the semi-quiet house before Nicole arrived and it would be time to help the bride get ready for her ceremony. Across the hall, she heard Christopher hum-whistling what sounded like a commercial jingle as he prepared himself to welcome their guests. Christopher had worked like ten men to get the greenhouse ready for the wedding. He and Nicole acted like they had known each other all their lives and luckily their ideas had meshed so well, it only took a few pots of coffee and a couple of dozen homemade cookies to work out the rest of the wedding plan.

Christopher had even helped her do a few minor repairs to the farmhouse, including painting the bathrooms to give them a fresh look for guests. She and Christopher had agreed that the first order of business was to build outdoor dressing rooms and facilities so the house could stay off limits for those events that didn't include family and friends. Christopher had also made the greenhouse wheelchair accessible. Although Matt could get around on crutches, he tired easily and Nicole wanted to make sure he would have his wheelchair handy in case it was needed.

288   **J. KIMALIE**

Somehow Christopher had incorporated the ramp into the design of the greenhouse, so it looked like a part of the original construction.

Jacq made her way into the kitchen thinking she would make herself a cup of tea and relax for ten minutes. As she turned away from the sink to put the kettle on the stove, a wolf whistle sounded right behind her.

"Jacq, aren't you the vision," Christopher said grabbing her hand and twirling her into a pivot turn, "but you may want to rethink your choice of footwear." Jacq had chosen to wear a lace sheath of cobalt blue with a scalloped neckline and three-quarter length sleeves. Her only accessories were a pair of platinum chandelier earrings and a small silver and sapphire ring, Jacq had found in her Aunt Rose's jewelry drawer. To set off the earrings, she had piled her hair on top of her head in a casual style of ringlets cascading down her back. In response to Christopher's comment, Jacq looked down at her feet ensconced in her rubber floral gardening boots and smiled. "What, you don't like them?" she questioned.

"I love them, but the pink, green and rubber don't set off your earrings," Christopher replied with a smile. He continued to hold her as they swayed together to a silent song around the kitchen.

Jacq tilted her head toward a nude pair of high-heeled pumps sitting by the door. "There are a few things to do before the bride heads down the aisle, so I thought I would spare my feet for now. You better be careful you don't get your shoes dusty." They both stopped dancing for a moment and looked down at his favorite style of Italian loafers. Jacq knew he had the same pair in several colors. He had matched his loafers with a more casual tuxedo with black pants, white shirt, pink jacket, and a black bow tie with tiny pink dots. The style and colors were all Christopher – very sophisticated with a little edge.

"You are incredibly handsome," Jacq said in her best imitation of a smoky Lauren Bacall voice. She rested her head on his shoulder and for just a moment enjoyed having her dear friend by her side.

"Have you recently talked to him?"

Jacq didn't have to ask to whom Christopher was referring. "I went to visit him, but he was in physical therapy, so I left a note. We've texted briefly back and forth, but it's only been me asking how he's doing and him telling me the progress he's making. He decided he would stay in the city until he didn't have to do therapy three times a day. It's just easier that way. Ian and his mom have been supporting him through his treatments and Patricia and Ian have kept me updated on his daily progress. He will be here tonight, and I don't know if I'm thrilled or terrified," Jacq uttered looking up at Christopher.

"I think you should be thrilled, and I think you should share those thrilling feelings with Garrett," declared Christopher as the tea kettle began to whistle.

Jacq stood beside Matt's wheelchair as they welcomed the wedding guests into the greenhouse. The building was lit with rows and rows of fairy lights Christopher had wrapped around every inch of the building. The light reflecting off the glass gave the structure a crystallized glow in the growing darkness. Jacq had encouraged Matt to take some weight off his leg so that he could stand, with a little help from his crutches, during the ceremony. Jacq put her hand on Matt's shoulder to lean down and whisper, "I'm going to head into the house to see if Nicole needs anything." Matt nodded and turned to his parents who were just entering the venue.

Jacq walked the lighted path toward the house and smiled as Donovan came toward her. She reached out her hands and he took them, leaning forward to give her a peck on the cheek. "You look beautiful," Donovan murmured as he leaned back, "and you have outdone yourself yet again," he said as he glanced over her shoulder and took in the greenhouse and the colorfully dressed guests excitedly mingling among the plants.

"Thank you. I just wanted it to be special for Nicole. I think after the accident she would have gotten married anywhere as long as Matt was well enough to stand beside her," Jacq said. "I didn't want her to regret getting married in such a rush."

"She will always remember this night," Donovan stated squeezing her hands. "I need to have a few words with Matt, then we'll get ready for the ceremony. Let's catch up afterwards. I've missed you."

"I....," Jacq started to speak and make an excuse as to why she had avoided the Longhouse, but just shook her head.

"It's ok Jacq," Donovan said looking compassionately into her eyes, "there's no need to explain."

Jacq nodded swallowing a lump in her throat. He leaned forward and kissed her other cheek. "I'll see you after the wedding," he said quietly as he walked away.

Jacq walked through the house checking out the set up for the food tables. She and Christopher had moved most of the furniture out of the living room and set up buffet tables along the walls. She heard the caterers in the kitchen setting up serving

THE WEDDING SLIPPER 291

dishes and talking quietly among themselves. Her steps took her down the hall to the master bedroom where classical music was playing quietly. Jacq tapped on the door before entering the room. Nicole was standing in front of the mirror as her mom finished fastening her gown.

"I have no words," Jacq asserted as she looked at the exquisite bride. Nicole was dressed in a simple but sophisticated silk crepe wedding gown with a choker neck and cut-away bodice. The body-hugging skirt fell to the ground where her left leg peeked out of an asymmetrical split to just above the knee. Nicole had decided not to wear a veil so that the cut away back was in full view. Her hair was done in a loose bun with tendrils of hair artfully escaping down the sides of her face. Her mother had placed small silk forget me knots tucked into the bun to signify something blue. She wore long, gold chain earrings with pearls at the end that swayed as she turned around to look at Jacq. Nicole's face was glowing with so much happiness that Jacq thought it probably didn't matter what Nicole wore as nobody would notice the gown. They would only notice the huge smile on her face.

"I am so ready to get married," Nicole declared, "is it time?"

Her mother chuckled as she said, "We have about 15 minutes yet."

"I just came to see if there was anything that you needed?" Jacq asked.

"No, just tell me that Matt isn't tiring himself out greeting all the guests," Nicole said with a little worry frown appearing between her eyes.

"Matt is great. I had him sit in his wheelchair while carrying out his greeting duties, reminding him that he would probably

292   **J. KIMALIE**

want to stand during the ceremony, and have enough energy for his wedding night," Jacq stated waggling her eyebrows.

"That was a line right out of Ian's playbook," Nicole giggled.

Jacq laughed. "I'm headed back out. Are you ok?" Jacq asked again. Both women nodded. "I'll send your dad back when it's time."

As Jacq walked out of the room, she heard Christopher talking with the caterers in the kitchen, so she bypassed that room and walked back outside. It looked like everybody was finding their seats in the greenhouse. Donovan stood behind the altar that Christopher had fashioned of curly willow to match the trellis. He and Nicole had decided to leave the trellis and altar plain to set off the array of orchids that surrounded it. It was the perfect backdrop for Donovan. He was wearing, what must be his favorite look, a black suit with a Nehru jacket, only this time he was wearing a beautiful turquoise necklace made up of different sized stones set in beaten silver. She looked around for Ian as she would need him to start the wedding. Looking to the right, her eyes snagged on a familiar head of chestnut brown hair. Garrett had his back to her, leaning down to say something to his mother. He must have felt her eyes boring into his back because he straightened and turned around looking directly at her, their eyes locking. His face was pale and his expression unreadable. His cheekbones stood out in sharp relief, evidence of the weight he had lost in the hospital. A section of his hair had been shaved over his ear where stitches were visible.

Jacq wanted to walk over, but somehow couldn't get her feet to move as she saw the sadness and resignation in his eyes. She jumped as Christopher put his hand on her shoulder leaning down to whisper, "Is everything ready?"

THE WEDDING SLIPPER   293

Turning toward him, she nodded and said, "Yeah, give me five minutes to get Matt and Mason in place, then we'll be ready," Jacq said. When she looked back at Garrett he had already turned toward his mother.

Nicole had requested Ian start the ceremony with his bagpipes. Jacq hadn't known Ian played the bagpipes and was pleasantly surprised when she heard him practicing earlier that morning. He had been marching up and down beside the greenhouse in a hot pink kilt and muscle shirt like he was a solo marching band. He had declared if Christopher could wear pink to the wedding so could he. Luckily, Jacq noticed Ian had dressed in all his traditional tartan regalia for the wedding.

At that moment, Ian walked up and inquired, "Are we ready?"

"Yes," Jacq answered. "I just need to ensure Matt and Mason are in place, then I'll let the girls and Dad know it's time. Hang tight and I'll give you the sign in a minute," Jacq told Ian as she walked toward the house.

Nicole's dad was waiting inside the door. Jacq squeezed his arm as she walked past toward the master bedroom. Tapping on the door Jacq walked in to let Nicole know it was time to get married. Nicole had decided she wanted her mom to stand up with her and her brother was waiting to escort her mom down the aisle.

Jacq led Mom out of the house and on to her son's arm. She nodded at Ian who began playing Amazing Grace, the song Nicole had requested saying it was the first thing she had thought of when the doctor announced Matt was going to survive his accident. Jacq watched Nicole's brother lead their mom to her place and then he took his seat. She turned to the door of the house and beckoned Nicole and her dad down the lighted path. Nicole clutched her dad's arm on one side and held a simple spray of white calla lilies and pink tulips with three wedding slipper orchids in her other hand. Nicole's smile never dimmed as she disappeared into the greenhouse. Matt stood beside the altar slightly hunched as he leaned on his crutches. One side of his tuxedo trousers was split almost to the hip to make room for the cast and brace that was holding his leg together, but nothing took away from the look of stunned joy and pure love on his face as he watched his bride walk down the aisle.

Christopher sidled up to Jacq, took her arm and escorted her to a couple of chairs they had set up in the back for their use.

Nicole and Matt faced Donovan as the guests took their seats. Donovan waited until the last note of the haunting pipes finished before he asked the couple to clasp hands. He took their hands between both of his and said, "May you walk gently through this world and know its beauty all the days of your life." Then he looked up at the family and friends gathered and said "You all are a part of the beauty that Matt and Nicole embrace every day. I ask that you commit your time and energy to strengthen them through their days just as they commit themselves to each other." Looking down at their clasped hands, Donovan continued, "Hold tight to each other's hands and protect each other's hearts."

Donovan gestured for Nicole and Matt to face each other. There was a pause as Matt shifted his ungainly leg to the side. The couple smiled over the ungraceful way Matt moved around and a ripple of quiet laughter could be heard from the crowd. Matt and Nicole looked into each other eyes and Matt reached up to

THE WEDDING SLIPPER   295

cup Nicole's cheek. She turned her head into his hand and kissed his palm.

Matt began his vows saying, "I love you, Nicole. I promise to be your lover, companion, and friend. I am blessed because I get to walk beside you. I belong in your arms and finally, I have found a place where I fit perfectly. You are my heart...," Matt said in a voice that cracked on the last word.

Matt looked up at Donovan and Donovan looked at the crowd, helping Matt out he said, "I think there was supposed to be a little more to his vows, but we'll give Matt a break since it has been a trying time these last couple of weeks." Matt looked at Nicole and silently mouthed "I'm sorry." She just shook her head, leaned forward, and gave him a kiss on the cheek.

"Matt, you are my man. I look forward to falling in love with you over and over and over each day. You bring out the best parts of me, my darling and when given the choice, I would choose to be your wife every time. I love you and I will hold you tight and never let you go," Nicole vowed

Quietly Donovan closed the ceremony with a sacred blessing spoken in his native tongue and announced that Matt could kiss his bride. With a little more awkward shuffling around Matt's leg, Nicole and Matt scooted close enough to share a kiss. As Donovan introduced them as man and wife, Ian snuck in from the side with Matt's wheelchair. Still holding Nicole's hand Matt maneuvered himself into the seat and with Ian steering, the couple "walked" down the aisle with smiles on their faces and tears in the eyes.

Jacq and Christopher had carried their seats to the side in order to create an open space for Matt and Nicole to greet their guests in the back of the greenhouse. Since there were only about twenty guests the set up worked. As the couple traded joyful hugs and unabashed laughter with their friends and family, Jacq snuck out to make sure the caterers were ready. The guys, with Christopher directing, were even now breaking down the chairs and rolling in tables where people could sit and eat. The plan was for the guests to gather their food from the house and return to the greenhouse to eat among the abundant greenery.

As Jacq was approaching the kitchen door a quiet voice called her name. She stopped, closed her eyes, and slowly turned to see Garrett walking toward her. A nervous catch in Jacq's throat rendered her speechless.

"I know this is a bad time, but I wanted to say hello," Garrett quietly said leaning forward to give Jacq an awkward peck on the cheek. His familiar masculine scent with just a hint of cedar almost undid her.

Finding her voice, she simply said, "I'm so glad to see you up and around. I mean I knew you were doing well. Ian has filled me in on your recovery beyond your texts, but it's good to see you," realizing she was rambling her words came to an abrupt halt. They both started to say something, when Christopher walked up to announce that the tables were in place and it was time to invite the guests to the buffet. Christopher held out his well-manicured hand and introduced himself to Garrett.

"I need to talk to the caterer," Jacq apologized, hurrying away, almost running to the kitchen to hide like the coward she kept telling herself she was.

Watching Jacq walk away, Garrett sighed, his heart aching he turned to his mom and said, "I'm ready to go home."

THE WEDDING SLIPPER   297

As they slowly walked toward home, his mother slipped her hand through his arm and enquired, "Are you doing okay? Was this too much too soon?"

Garrett nodded, turning his sad eyes to his mom, and said, "Don't worry Mom I didn't overdo it, tonight's not the right time to talk to her, she's busy and Jacq already made it clear we don't have a future together."

Patricia stopped, turned toward her son, raised her eyebrows, and stated, "Oh really, I'm not so sure about that. She doesn't look like a woman ready to say good-bye."

Once all the guests were seated and enjoying their meals, Jacq had found her resolve and went to seek out Garrett. It didn't take long to discover that Garrett and his mother had quietly skipped out on the reception.

Chapter 32

Jacq rose early the morning after Nicole and Matt's wedding even though she had a difficult time falling asleep the night before. She had been keyed up following the reception pleased that a joyful Nicole had gushed over, and was extremely appreciative of all the lovely details that she and Christopher had expertly pulled together on short notice to make her wedding extraordinary.

She and Christopher did make a good team, their organizational and creative skills complimenting one another's and propelling each other to rise to any occasion. She knew that they would make a successful go of their new events business and she was excited for the business possibilities on the horizon. But what primarily kept Jacq up into the wee hours of the morning were the churning possibilities of what might be on the horizon for her and Garrett. Jacq wondered how early was too early to walk over to his house as she simply had to see him. She was both eager and, if honest with herself, a little apprehensive to catch him up on all the decisions she had made over the past couple of weeks and to let him know what he meant to her. Jacq loved him and she intended to let him know leaving no room for ambiguity or misinterpretation. She fervently dared to hope he felt the same for her.

THE WEDDING SLIPPER   299

Jacq poured herself an extra-large mug of coffee, snuck past the guestroom careful not to wake Christopher, and quietly got dressed. She knew Garrett rose early to tend to the animals and she planned to seize the chance to have a private conversation with him which had eluded her over the past couple weeks. Between his mother being by his side at the hospital and her last two weeks comprised of a whirlwind of professional and personal meetings and decisions as well as planning Nicole's wedding, she had not once been alone with Garrett. Her overwhelming need to see him had become a driving force the minute she woke.

By nine o'clock, Jacq had not seen a sign of life over at Garrett's place. She could not take it a minute longer; she had to see him and fully open her heart. Her resolve firmly in place, she quickly jotted a note to Christopher letting him know she was off to find Garrett and they were still on for dinner at six at the Longhouse. She exited the kitchen door where a gentle breeze welcomed her as she headed across the pasture.

It was Patricia, not Garrett, who answered Jacq's knock on the door. Patricia must have read the disappointed look on Jacq's face because she said, "Garrett's not here. I'm getting ready to head back home, but after we said our good-byes, he left to go clear his head. But you are welcome to come in and wait for him although I'm not sure when he'll be returning, but I do know he would really appreciate seeing you"

"Thank you for the offer, but if he returns before you leave will you just tell him I'm anxious to speak with him," Jacq replied.

"Of course," Patricia responded. "And Jacq," she hastily added, as Jacq had started turning back toward her house, "I've never thanked you for being there for Garrett at the hospital. It meant a lot to me, and I know it meant the world to him." Patricia's kind words instantly made Jacq eyes glisten with threatening tears.

Jacq managed a weak smile, nodded, and said "It was my honor." With that, Jacq turned and departed.

Jacq was thumbing a text to Garrett as she crossed the pasture when she realized where he might be. Rather than send the text, she flung open the kitchen door to find a startled Christopher standing at the sink wearing what looked to be a silk smoking jacket right out of a fifty's movie. She fleetingly wondered if he always looked so pulled together in the morning. "Good morning," Jacq said, as she kept moving to her purse already fishing out her keys. "I'm off to find Garrett, "I'll be back" she stated already heading back out the door.

The door crisply closed behind Jacq, before Christopher managed to say, "Good morning to you too. Yes, I slept quite well thank you. No, I don't need a thing. I thought I would take my run this morning and was going to invite you to accompany me, but I see that you are otherwise engaged. Ta-ta, have fun, don't worry about me!" By way of punctuating his wasted soliloquy he lifted his teacup in silent salute at the empty doorway.

As Jacq pulled into the marina, she spotted Garrett's distinctive form sitting with his long legs dangling over the dock, his relaxed torso silhouetted against the sparking blue water. Occasional gusts from the breeze sent ripples across his loose-fitting shirt highlighting his back muscles as the fabric caught against his

THE WEDDING SLIPPER 301

well-defined form. Her whole being fluttered at the sight of him partly out of desire and partly out of trepidation.

"This is it," she thought to herself, "no matter the consequences, I need to tell that man how I feel about him." Her biggest concern, at the moment, was that words could not express what she wanted to communicate. She took in a slow, deep breath, smelling a combination of a fishy, tangy odor and a clean, salty scent mingling together in the breeze. She steeled herself as she realized that the rest of her life was riding on her ability to convey to Garrett what her heart had finally fully grasped and how Garrett would receive her words.

So lost in his own thoughts, it didn't register with Garrett that someone was approaching until a shadow fell over him and Jacq was lowering herself to the rough wood dock next to him leaving about a foot between them.

"I finally get you alone," Jacq stated as they greeted each other with guarded smiles.

"How did you know I'd be here?" Garrett asked in surprise.

"I didn't really, but I took an educated guess given that you shared you sometimes come here after a difficult rescue. From what I heard, your rescue qualified as difficult."

He reached out and took Jacq's hand in his, lifting it gently, he kissed the back of her hand. At that pure, simple, gesture her hope solidified, perhaps they would have a future together after all.

"I have so much to tell you," Jacq intently began to say, but Garrett leaned over and stopped her words with a soft, chaste, kiss to the lips. "I have something to tell you as well and I need to say it while I still have the courage to get it out. No matter what you plan to tell me, it won't change what I have to say to you. So please, let me start."

The hope Jacq had for a life with Garrett seconds before dissolved as she studied Garrett's face which was solemn and foretold a grave mood. No, nooo, she thought, this cannot be happening, not now, not after realizing how much she loved him. Dread spread in her heart threatening to shatter it as she waited for injuring words that she was sure were coming. Why had she told him that she was choosing a career over a life with him?

"I don't remember a lot of what happened immediately before my accident, but I do distinctly remember the ground falling away from my feet," Garrett slowly began. "It was so surreal. The whole thing seemed to happen in slow motion and there was absolutely nothing I could do to stop the plummet. For the first time in my life, I felt completely and totally out of control. Regardless of what I wanted, regardless of my actions, regardless of help nearby, in that moment, I knew for certain I was going to fall, quite possibly to my death." Garrett paused for a moment reflecting on the past and gathering his thoughts in the present. "Some people say at those times, your life flashes before your eyes. That didn't happen to me. What flashed before my eyes was a life I could have had with you. My last thought before blacking out was of you."

Upon hearing his life altering words, Jacq's entire body went numb—hope daring to creep back into her heart. "But then," Garrett went on, "Miraculously, I didn't die."

"Where was Garrett going with this?" Jacq wondered, her heart thumping from the rollercoaster of emotions consuming her.

THE WEDDING SLIPPER   303

"I have had a lot of time over the past couple weeks to clarify what is important to me," Garrett continued. "What I've concluded is that regardless of what I thought I wanted to do with the animal shelter, regardless of what actions I will have to take in the future, regardless of my friends and family nearby, I know for certain that I don't want to live my life without you. I don't want to sacrifice a life we could share simply because I'm holding on too tightly to other important, but less important things. So, Jacqueline Rose, if you'll have me, I will follow you to New York, or Boston, or anywhere else you may end up. I just don't want to end up without you. I love you and I can't imagine you leaving when hopefully it is within my control to do something about it."

Jacq was so stunned she couldn't speak. She had dared to hope for a life with Garrett, but she had never dreamed that he would give up everything for her. The revelation touched the core of her being forever bonding her to him in that blissful moment. She shut her eyes and let out the breath she had been holding. She opened her eyes to see that Garrett had leaned toward her closing half the distance between them and was searching her face for a reaction to his declaration. Jacq quickly closed the other half of the distance between them her lips crashing into his. There was nothing chaste or gentle about their long and frenzied kiss. The kiss reflected a host of emotions, communicating what words could not through their probing, testing, lingering, urgency and a dozen other nuanced invitations and responses. When reluctantly they parted, the look they saw in each other's eyes frantically brought them together once again in a slow kiss of pure passion and promise.

A high piercing wolf whistle from a passing boat instantly jarred Jacq and Garrett back to their public surroundings. They both laughed when a tanned, tattooed, man in his early twenties aboard a fishing trawler returning to port gave them two thumbs up and knowing exaggerated head bobs. It took a beat or two before they had each regained their composure and their breathing returned to normal, the wolf whistle having perhaps saved them from a more embarrassing situation as they had been completely lost in their own impassioned world.

"Now, what is it that you have to tell me?" Garrett inquired, softly stroking the side of Jacq's smooth face, letting his fingers get tangled in her sunlit hair, shades of gold, red and auburn setting off her green sparkling eyes.

"I will gladly have you Garrett. In fact, I would like to have you in as many ways and as many times as possible," Jacq retorted, red rising up her neck and a mischievous grin spreading across her face in the familiar way that Garrett found captivating and utterly irresistible. "And" Jacq continued, her features softening and gaze becoming unequivocal, "I'm not planning to go anywhere. I have so much to tell you starting with I love you. It took almost losing you to realize that I love you desperately, completely, and unconditionally."

Chapter 33

Jacq followed Garrett's SUV back to his place. Before she could get out of her car, Garrett was at her door. He opened the door and as she climbed out, he pinned her against the cold metal of her car. Caging her between his arms, he leaned in to capture her lips. Sweeping his tongue against hers and nipping her bottom lip, he slowly pulled back, taking her hand, and tugged her toward the house.

Once inside they were both greeted by exuberant canines. "Out," Garrett commanded, and the dogs raced out the door toward the barn.

"I'm not sharing you with anyone," Garrett stated as he led her toward the bedroom.

After thoroughly celebrating their reunion, they lay lazily in each other's arms. Jacq's stomach growled and Garrett's answered. "Sounds like we could each use something to eat. Mom left me plenty of her cooking. How about a picnic in the den?" asked Garrett.

Garrett slid out of bed, pulled on his jeans, and retrieved a soft flannel shirt from his closet. He held it up for her to shrug into. The oversized shirt hung to her knees and Jacq rolled the sleeves back several times laughing as she followed him to the kitchen. After raiding the refrigerator and loading up a tray, they made themselves comfortable on the couch.

Before Jacq even took a bite, she turned toward Garrett and said, "I can't believe you were willing to walk away from this life to be with me."

Garrett smiled and said, "And I can't believe you're staying. What changed?"

"Seeing you in the hospital I knew I couldn't go to Boston. In fact, I realized nothing has ever made me happier than being with you. When I saw you lying in the hospital bed everything became clear. I didn't need you to tell me you loved me to make my decision to stay."

"Even though it was your dream job?" questioned Garrett.

"I'm creating my own dream job."

Garrett gave her a puzzled look.

Jacq went on to explain, "Christopher and I are creating a business and I'm keeping Aunt Rose's farm to turn it into an events venue. After all, I've already hosted two successful weddings."

Garrett gathered both her hands in his and said, "Can this day get any better?"

"Actually, yes it can. Christopher and I have already agreed that regardless of what happened between you and me, we would make some space available for your animal rescue."

At a loss for words, Garrett pulled her into his arms and softly whispered, "I love you."

They cuddled together, sharing from their hearts as the afternoon flew by.

"I have dinner with Christopher at the Longhouse that I need to either cancel or bring you along. Would you like to join us?" asked Jacq.

"Absolutely, I think we have cause to celebrate."

By 5:30 PM, Christopher had not heard anything else from Jacq, so he wrapped up the work he was doing on the marketing campaign and headed over to the bar. There wasn't much of a crowd gathered, but the place was busy enough and he noticed Ian behind the bar giving smiles and refills to a couple of attractive female patrons. Christopher slipped in and took a seat on the other side of the bar where a woman he hadn't seen before was busy pouring drinks and where he would have a good vantage point for people watching—one of his favorite past times.

He ordered a Dubonnet and club soda, then sat back and watched Ian lay the charm on the gals at the other end of the bar.

Feeling a tap on the shoulder, Christopher turned to find Donovan behind him.

"Hi Christopher, welcome to the Longhouse," Donovan said in his direct, friendly way. "Are you here alone tonight or meeting up with friends?"

"Jacq and I are getting together for dinner and I've been curious to see the place," Christopher replied. "It's every bit as eclectic and cool as Jacq described it."

Donovan smiled and said, "I'm glad you like it. It's a blend of my heritage from both my parents' sides."

"Aha, that makes sense now. There are some uniquely beautiful pieces on display here. "

308   **J. KIMALIE**

At that moment, Ian popped over and both the men laughed at the timing of the statement.

"Whaaa? Am I missing out on a good story?" Ian asked

"No, just admiring your shapely legs," replied Donovan, giving Christopher a conspiratorial smile.

"They are one of my best features," Ian added before executing a half twirl and going back to his adoring patrons.

Christopher and Donovan had gotten along famously while working together on Nicole and Matt's wedding and were already beginning to feel like a friendship was developing. "Ian's been friendly enough with me, but there is something there that feels like he doesn't exactly like me a lot," Christopher confided.

Donovan chuckled softly and said, "He's jealous."

"Of me? Why?" Christopher asked.

"Jealous by proxy," Donovan replied. "He is worried you are a rival for Jacq's affections with Garrett and he's Garrett's closest friend."

Christopher laughed and said, "You're kidding? He doesn't realize that he'd be closer to my type than Jacq?"

"Nope. And I didn't feel like telling him."

"You realize that I could really mess with him if I wanted to have some fun," Christopher added with a wink.

"You could," Donovan simply replied without any encouragement.

"I could, but I probably won't." Christopher mused, thinking it might be best to just carry on and let the poor man suffer a little longer.

Donovan nudged him and said, "Look who's here?"

Christopher looked up and saw Jacq and Garrett had entered the bar and his heart filled up to see Garrett's arm draped

THE WEDDING SLIPPER   309

lovingly around Jacq's shoulders and Jacq's arm around his waist. Jacq was trying to look composed, but she was beaming with joy and Garrett's expression was a mirror image. They had obviously had a fruitful conversation.

Donovan said in a low, wise voice, "I thought this would happen. Two forces that are stronger together than apart will always call to each other until they connect." And with that, he went over to clear a table for them. Christopher stood up and waved, caught Jacq's eye, and nodded toward the table Donovan was readying. Jacq gave him a look back that told him everything—her happiness was being restored.

Christopher went over to the glowing couple and welcomed them. "Hi Christopher, I hope you are fine with Garrett joining us for dinner?" Jacq asked hopefully. "You met at the wedding I think, but you both already know about each other," she added.

Garrett greeted him as well and reached out his hand to shake Christopher's and smiled warmly.

Christopher did the double clasp handshake and said, "Of course, I couldn't be happier! I say we make it a party and we invite Donovan and Ian over."

Garrett helped Jacq out of her coat and pulled out her chair. He turned to Christopher and said, "I think I owe you a big thanks."

"Moi?" Christopher asked, "How so?"

"Well, in addition to being one of her closest friends, you've become her business partner and that's enabling her to stay here in Poulsbo. I believe we still would have worked things out, but I have to admit I'm about as happy as a guy could be that we get to stay here," he said with such sincerity that Christopher felt moved by it.

"It's going to be an adjustment for me, but an exciting adventure as well. I'm looking forward to getting to know you better Garrett, and I am really happy for both of you." Christopher sat down across from the happy couple and just enjoyed the love emanating from them both. Donovan was the next to join them and after wrapping Jacq up in a big hug and delivering a side hug to Garrett, he took a seat next to Jacq, and motioned to one of the waiters to come take their orders as Ian made his way to the table.

He turned to Christopher and playfully asked him, "Can I squeeze my chair in here or do you got a problem sitting next to a guy in a skirt?"

Christopher chuckled and retorted, "No not at all. In fact, I've dated a few."

Ian, rarely at a loss for words, just stood there dumbfounded for a moment, which of course ignited another round of laughter at the table. After a moment, he grinned and said, "Finally, someone around here who appreciates a man with a fine sense of fashion." He pulled up a chair, gave Jacq a wink and began pouring the carafe of wine that had been delivered to the table. Nobody felt the need to toast the obvious. Jacq and Garrett were together, and everyone was thrilled.

Before they knew it, the place had nearly emptied of customers. Donovan finally stood up and announced that he needed to get a few things done before closing for the night. Ian said he'd go help out behind the bar to allow the wait staff to go home. Christopher put a generous amount of money on the table toward the tab, clapped Garrett on the shoulder, gave Jacq a kiss on the cheek and said good night.

THE WEDDING SLIPPER   311

Jacq and Garrett stayed at the table voicing their hopes and dreams about their future together. Garrett pulled Jacq a little closer and nuzzled her neck, planted a kiss under her ear and asked her if she wanted to come back to his place. Jacq nodded and said it sounded wonderful. They gathered their coats and started toward the door. Just as they were about to exit, Garrett touched Jacq's arm to pause her. "Give me a minute, I forgot something," he said.

Puzzled, Jacq said, "Sure, I'll wait."

Garrett took two steps over to the bar and beckoned to Ian. "Hey Ian, can you get me a bottle of Patron and a couple of limes to go?"

"Sure," Ian said. "What, did you lose another bet?" Observant as ever, Ian noticed the blush that began to crawl up Jacq's face. His eyes shifted to Garrett and noticed that he was turning a little bit red as well. Ian set the requested items on the bar and shot him a curious look.

Garrett replied, "No, but I hope to," saluted him smartly, gathered the goods in one hand, took Jacq's in the other, and used his shoulder to push the door open for them to leave. Jacq started giggling once the door had closed behind them and then Garrett joined in with her. By the time they got to the car, they were both in fits of laughter. Once they finally got themselves under control, Garrett put their supplies in his SUV. He gathered her in his arms and tilted her chin up slightly so that he could look directly into her eyes that were shining brightly from the tears her laughter had wrung.

"Let's get out of here," he said in a husky voice. "I feel like the luckiest guy in the world, and I can't wait another single moment to have the woman I love all to myself. "

Jacq smiled up at him, brushed her hand through his hair and delivered a kiss that was clearly a promise of more. "There is absolutely nowhere else on earth I'd rather be."

About the author(s)...

J. Kimalie came to be when three friends (**Kim**, **Mal**isa, and **Ju**l**ie**) decided to write their first book together during the Covid 19 pandemic in 2021. These three women have distinctively different personalities but also many things in common like their professional government and non-profit leadership backgrounds, love of reading (many genres,) and exploring the different small towns of their home in the Pacific Northwest. Their shared sense of humor and mutual devotion to friendship, family, and community is easily recognized in their prose.

Together, they have drawn upon their varied experiences, interests, and combined imaginations to jointly write their first romance novel and plan to continue the series.

Lightning Source UK Ltd.
Milton Keynes UK
UKHW010658260123
416005UK00001B/226